THE SWORD AND THE DAGGER

by

Ardath Mayhar

THE SWORD AND THE DAGGER

by

Ardath Mayhar

To Jordan Weisman, Margaret Weis, and Tracy Hickman...
sine qua non

Battlefield technical writing by: William H. Keith

This book is published by FASA Corporation
P.O.Box 6930
Chicago, IL 60680

Cover Art by: David R. Dietrick
Illustrations by: Duane Loose
                David R. Dietrick
Maps by: Dana Knutson

BATTLETECH is a Trademark of FASA Corporation.

When he stood up, Ardan almost fell. His head began its interior rocking, like a vessel on a stormy sea. But he was determined to stand, to walk. To get away while his attendant was gone.

Even as he made his legs cooperate, Ardan wondered about his situation. He was a captive. Surely the MedTechs knew what their medications could do. Why had they left him alone just when he would be regaining consciousness?

He shook his errant mind back into order. Whatever the reason, he had to get out. Find his unit again. There was so much to do...and he had no idea how the attack had gone.

Beyond the curtain was an empty hallway. At the end of it, behind a closed door, he could hear voices. He crept into the corridor and turned in the opposite direction. Doors lined the way, some open into empty chambers like the one he had left, some closed. Pushing one open, Ardan found himself staring at a bandaged shape spreadeagled on an orthopedic rack.

He moved on, trying a door from time to time. At last, he found one that led into another passageway. This was dark, as if little used. Glass-windowed doors on either side let dim light into the corridor, and he stepped to the one on his left and peered through into the room beyond.

It was a big chamber, filled with unusual and somehow disturbing equipment. Glass-fronted cubicles lined the side wall, and there was the throb of motors, as if compressors were operating beneath the floor.

The sound was echoed faintly from one of the cubicles. He turned awkwardly, trying to see through the faint frost that covered the glass.

Someone was inside. Someone...familiar...? He moved closer, pressed his hands to the glass, and set his face between them, peering hard at the dim shape. As if summoned by his attention, the light intensified around the body inside.

"Hanse!" he whimpered, scrabbling at the glass with his numbed fingers. "Hanse, what have they done to you?"

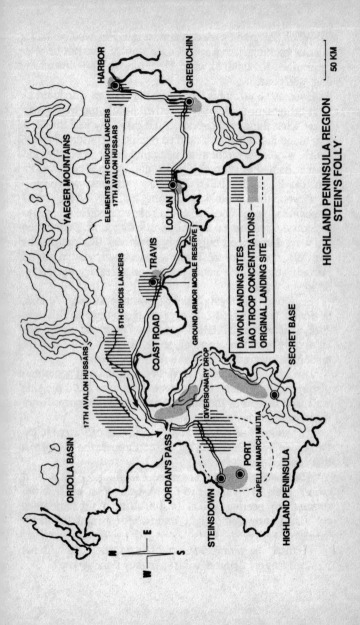

HIGHLAND PENINSULA REGION
STEIN'S FOLLY

50 KM

N
E
S
W

ORDOLA BASIN

YAEGER MOUNTAINS

HARBOR

GREBUCHIN

ELEMENTS 5TH CRUCIS LANCERS
17TH AVALON HUSSARS

LOLLAN

5TH CRUCIS LANCERS

TRAVIS

17TH AVALON HUSSARS

COAST ROAD

GROUND ARMOR MOBILE RESERVE

DAVION LANDING SITES
LIAO TROOP CONCENTRATIONS
ORIGINAL LANDING SITE

DIVERSIONARY DROP

JORDAN'S PASS

SECRET BASE

STEINSDOWN

PORT

CAPELLAN MARCH MILITA

HIGHLAND PENINSULA

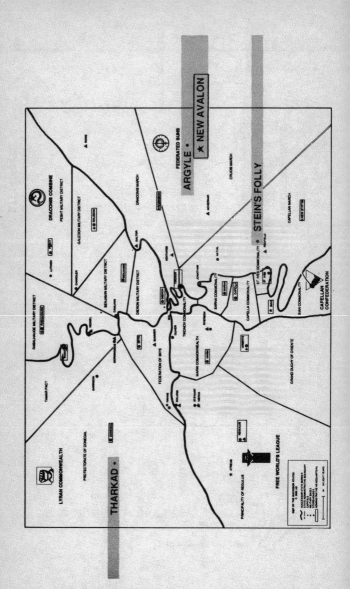

MAP OF THE SUCCESSOR STATES
3025 A.D.

SUCCESSOR STATE BORDER
STATE ADMINISTRATIVE BOUNDARY
CAPITAL WORLD
SUPPLY DEPOT & STOREHOUSES
REGIONAL HEADQUARTERS

LYRAN COMMONWEALTH

★ THARKAD

TAMAR PACT

PROTECTORATE OF DONEGAL

RASALHAGUE MILITARY DISTRICT

DRACONIS COMBINE

PESHT MILITARY DISTRICT

GALEDON MILITARY DISTRICT

BENJAMIN MILITARY DISTRICT

DIERON MILITARY DISTRICT

DRACONIS MARCH

FEDERATED SUNS

ARGYLE ●   ★ NEW AVALON

CRUCIS MARCH

STEIN'S FOLLY

CAPELLAN MARCH

FEDERATION OF SKYE

TIKONOV COMMONALITY

SARNA COMMONALITY

ST. IVES COMMONALITY ●

CAPELLA COMMONALITY

SIAN COMMONALITY

CAPELLAN CONFEDERATION

MARIK COMMONWEALTH

GRAND DUCHY OF ORIENTE

PRINCIPALITY OF REGULUS

FREE WORLD'S LEAGUE

PROLOGUE

It is the year 3025. Man now inhabits the stars, but has taken his warlike nature with him. The thousands of worlds radiating out from Sol, first sun of the human race, were once bound together in a Star League that fostered technology, expansion, and prosperity for all. With the fall of the League in 2781, a Dark Age descended, as each of the five surviving star empires began warring for dominion. To this day, more than 200 years later, none of the five Successor Lords has been able to triumph decisively to become supreme Lord over the others.

The leaders of these five great star empires are known today as the Successor Lords of Houses Davion, Kurita, Steiner, Liao, and Marik. The devastating battles they have been fighting among themselves almost continuously for over two centuries have come to be called simply the Succession Wars.

To fight their wars, the Successor Lords have armies of BattleMechs, vaguely humanoid but gigantic battle machines bristling with lasers, particle projection cannons, long- and short-range missile launchers, autocannon, and machine guns. Though these walking tanks rule the battlefields, intrigue and plots rule the courts of the Inner Sphere, as each ruler seeks to win by deceit what he cannot achieve through force.

For a time, the endless Succession Wars brought death and destruction to civilization and to nearly all the learning and high technology of the Star League era. Better days may lie ahead, however, because the Successor Lords are now seeking to reestablish universities and to recover the scientific knowledge and technology long believed lost.

Most powerful among the five Successor States is House Davion, ruler of the Federated Suns. Since the start of the Succession Wars, House Davion has managed, through skillfully conducted military campaigns and subtle diplomacy, to double the number of star systems under its control. The current Prince of the Federated Suns is Hanse Davion, who ascended the throne unexpectedly in 3013 when his older brother Ian was killed in battle.

At 42 years of age, Hanse Davion is the youngest of the current Successor Lords. Based on his accomplishments so far, the accident of fate that made him Prince Davion twelve years ago may have been one of the great turning points in the history of the Successor States. Under his leadership, the Federated Suns have reached new heights of power, with Hanse becoming known as The Fox by both enemies and friends. He is, of course, a brilliant military strategist and a skilled negotiator, but his nickname also stems from Hanse's skill in playing the deadly games of intrigue and power that are the order of the day. For example, it is believed that Davion's agents provocateurs are responsible for fomenting unrest among the Free Worlds League, which has tied up House Marik's best military units trying to suppress the rebellions.

The Lyran Commonwealth, formed in 2341, is ruled by Katrina Steiner, Archon of the Commonwealth and Duchess of Tharkad. A woman of middle age, Katrina is a strong and determined leader who once trained as a MechWarrior, and who has since proven herself a canny strategist both militarily and politically. Realizing that Hanse Davion would make a potent ally, she negotiated ceaselessly to bring about a peace treaty with the Federated Suns. Steiner and Davion have also signed a secret treaty betrothing Hanse Davion in marriage to Melissa, Katrina's daughter and the Archon-Designate.

At this point in history, the border world of Stein's Folly, belonging to the Federated Suns, has been overrun by the forces of the Capellan Confederation, ruled by Chancellor Maximilian Liao. This is just the latest in a series of moves and countermoves toward worlds belonging to the other that has brought Davion and Liao into open conflict.

Though the Capellan Confederation is the weakest of the five Successor States, Maximilian Liao is nevertheless a shrewd and crafty leader who is currently engineering a plot to unseat Hanse Davion and undermine the power of the Federated Suns. Liao's allies against Davion are House Kurita and House Marik. Though neither of these is actively involved in the current plot, both would benefit by anything that weakens the Federated Suns. Takashi Kurita, descendant of a long line of ruthless forbears, rules the highly military Draconis Combine with an iron hand. Janos Marik is leader of the Free Worlds League, which is slowly coming apart at the seams because of internal strife.

Even Michael Hasek-Davion, Duke of New Syrtis, might take an interest in the plot against his brother-in-law Hanse. Though he is the appointed ruler of the Capellan March, the ambitious Michael dreams of one day becoming the undisputed head of the Federated Suns. Prince Davion has no heir, and so the Duke would ascend the throne if anything were to happen to him. Hanse Davion publicly expresses only the greatest confidence in his relative, but Michael believes some of the Prince's recent military moves against the Draconis Combine were aimed at reducing his own influence and power. Not only did Hasek-Davion resist requests to reinforce the Davion offensive against Kurita, but it is rumored that agents of Maximilian Liao have paid several visits to the palace at New Syrtis.

All these interests are focused on Stein's Folly, an unimportant world located near the Davion/Liao border in the Capellan March sector of Davion space.

1

With the fall of Redfield, the Davion commanders knew that it wouldn't be long before Liao came gunning for the nearby world of Stein's Folly. They were expecting it, the troops were expecting it, and even the battle computers were predicting a 73 percent chance of an attack within ten days. But the clever Duke of Sian managed to take them by surprise after all.

First came a lightning strike by a squad of Liao Death Commandos who planted explosives at the huge radar communications station at the system's zenith jump point. By crippling the microwave relay dish aimed at Stein's Folly 1 AU away, no warning of the attack could get through to the Davion forces onworld. At the same time, an unmarked Liao freighter popped in from less than 8,000 klicks away. Even before unfurling its sail or engaging its station-keeping thrusters, the ship disgorged a quartet of *Union* Class DropShips, which headed straight for the two Davion *Invader* Class JumpShips parked at the station, jamming the JumpShips' communication signals as they went.

The JumpShip crewmen repeatedly ordered the Drop-Ships to change course, but the four vessels just kept on coming. Then they began frantically radioing the jump station for further instructions, but the only reply they got was electronic noise. How could those Davion crewmen have known that Liao saboteurs had just transformed the jump station's communications gear into wreckage and debris and that a furious firefight was raging in the comm center at that very moment?

Meanwhile, the DropShips had begun spearing the *Invader*s with high-energy lasers, crippling them. By the time the JumpShip crews had gotten to the weapons lockers, or had even realized that they were under attack, space-armored invaders had already boarded the ships and were turning the passageways into slaughter pens.

13

Only now did the first of the Liao warships materialize at the jump point. As grapples swung back and restraining bolts exploded in silent rushes of vapor in the vacuum of space, the warships freed the huge *Overlord* Class Dropships they carried. Next came specially rigged and fitted freighters that disgorged hosts of AeroSpace Fighters strapped with fuel tanks more massive than themselves.

Even before the last Davion crewman lay dead amid the victory shouts that rang through the corridors of the Jump-Ships, the invaders were on their way to Stein's Folly, their drive flares creating an awesome display of light and power.

Phase One of the Liao assault had lasted sixteen minutes, ten seconds from the moment the first plastique charge exploded at the jump station, but the groundside defenders were still not even aware that they were under attack.

* * * *

Steindown lay deep within Stein's Folly's night hemisphere when the emergency call came through from DESTra, the Deep Space Tracking station in an elongated polar orbit about the planet. Colonel Winters was asleep when the orderly entered his chambers.

"Snuh-huh?" Winters tried to focus on the young face looking down into his own old and bleary-eyed one. "Whazit, Lieutenant?"

"DESTra reports a DropShip fleet inbound, Colonel, pushing at three Gs. They do not respond to our signals. Combat Intelligence believes they are hostiles, sir."

Winters closed his eyes again. "Relay it to Fleet Captain Vandenburg."

"Colonel...*please!* The jump station does not respond! Not one ship at the jump point responds! Colonel, wake up! Please!"

"What time is..." He came wide awake, eyes staring. *"How many Gs?"*

14

"Three Gs, Colonel. And they're already well past turnover and decelerating. ComInt estimates they'll be here within four hours."

"My...God..." Winters shook himself, rolled from his bed. The lieutenant helped steady him as he stood. "Go man ...go! Scramble the defenses! Sound Red Alert! Good lord, man, don't just stand there! If they catch us asleep on the ground...!"

But the mournful keening of the base siren was already sounding across Steindown. The lieutenant of the watch had shown rare initiative in sounding a full Red Alert without an order from his commanding officer. That might have been grounds for a courtmartial, but any military court would probably excuse the extraordinary circumstances of the offense. Besides, within five hours, whether or not the lieutenant might face courtmartial was no longer in question. He would not survive the Liao invasion of Stein's Folly.

* * * *

Uchita Tucker shrugged her shoulders against the cockpit harness that held her secure against the seat of her TR-7 *Thrush* AeroSpace Fighter. She hurt, and every muscle in her body shrieked for release. Her squadron was still decelerating at three Gs, and after ten hours of sitting wedged into her narrow cockpit with the equivalent of two people seated in her lap, the stress of high-G boost was wearing her down. Normally, fighters ferried from jump point to world in the bowels of *Union* or *Overlord* Class DropShips, but the *Overlord*s that trailed her squadron this time carried the assault force reserves. The fighters of Dagger Squadron had begun the passage with extra tanks of reaction mass strapped above and below their squat, disk-shaped bodies. Those tanks, empty now and discarded, preceded the squadron toward Stein's Folly at nearly 1000 kps, the speed they'd retained when jettisoned. The fighters had slowed now to a few hundred kilometers per second.

15

The drive flares of the six *Thrush* fighters continued to slow them by thirty meters per second, leaving Uchita with the feeling that her lithe body's usual 57 kilos had massed to over 170 kilos. She was very tired.

Unconsciously flexing her right hand, Uchita knew she had one advantage over her squadron mates. Both of her legs and her right arm were bionic grafts, the result of a bad crashlanding in another *Thrush* that was now scrap and memories. All that had happened on a world far from the mottled green sphere whose image was now appearing in her aft camera viewscreen, beyond the dazzle of the drive flare. Her left arm was numb with strain and each breath was painful, but the mechanical parts of her body still functioned effortlessly, painlessly.

If only I can keep my mind clear and functioning, too, she thought.

Less than three hours remained until they reached atmosphere—even less than that until they tangled with the local Davion space defenses. When it was time for combat and adrenalin was pouring through her system, Uchita would be fully alert and at a fighting pitch, despite the strain of the past ten hours. That's how it always was. She checked her instruments again and peered past her drive flare at Stein's Folly. The surface was a patchwork of green land and deeper green seas, except where the local sun reflected gold and orange from cloud tops and water.

Some would think that sight pretty, she thought. The smile that touched her lips was bitter, and there was winter's ice in her eyes. But not me. Not the 'Mech-woman …the Automaton of Destruction…Old Iron Pants…

She closed her eyes, her jaw muscles tensing. It might be that Uchita had won the respect of the other pilots in her squadron, but she had never won their friendship nor enjoyed the special camaraderie of the wardroom. She had long since stopped caring about the people around her, though, to the point where she'd been disciplined several times for disregarding battle tactics and squadron coordination. She had a reputation as a loner, a combat ace who cared more for upping her tally of twelve kills than for her comrades to port or to starboard.

The bastards. She would show them. She would show them all. She didn't care what they thought...and if she was half-machine, she was a machine with purpose—a killing machine.

The names they called her still hurt, but that was deep down where she could keep the pain and never let it show.

* * * *

The flight of Davion *Sparrowhawks* cleared the cloud-tops, contrails streaking aft from their wing and tailtips in the thin, icy stratosphere of the Folly. The rising sun tinted the cloud layer orange-gold and edged the fighters in red.

Lieutenant Adam Valasquez greeted the sun with a shout and laughter. "Yo! Red Flight! This is Red Flight Leader! Are y'all with me?"

A chorus of voices sounded in his earphones, and his combat screen showed green lights for each of the six ships in his command. This was the day he'd been waiting for, ever since he'd heard that the Liao bastards had taken Redfield. He'd known then that he would get to lead the Hellraisers against the best pilots the Capellan Confederation could throw at them...and a beautiful day it was for it, too.

The SPR *Sparrowhawk* was an ideal first-response space defense fighter. With its high rate of thrust, the craft could clear the planet and meet the enemy well out in space while heavier fighters were still being readied on the ground. Valasquez harbored no illusions about the place his Red Squadron would hold this day. They would take the whole first brunt of the Liao fighter attack on themselves, hoping to blunt that attack, to turn it aside, to so delay the enemy's approach that heavier line fighters could reach the enemy formation before it had a chance to reform.

Such challenges required a special temperament, a special cast of mind. Many of Valasquez's friends thought

17

he was crazy. The rest were certain of it. Valasquez himself would be the last to deny the charge. It was part of an image he cherished and went out of his way to foster.

"Let's haul it, Hellraisers!" he shouted over the com circuit. "We got some tail to kick!"

There was a volley of rebel yells and cheers as he shoved his stick to full throttle forward. Savage acceleration kicked him back into his seat, and the SPR-H5 clawed into the darkling sky. Then, one by one, the other ships of Red Squadron spewed white flame as they leapt skyward after their leader.

* * * *

Pilot Uchita Tucker was the first to spot the oncoming flight of Davion spacecraft.

"Dagger Leader, this is Dagger Two. Bogies at one-eight-zero, straight in line with objective. Range seventy-five thousand, closing." She kept her voice glacially level, coldly precise.

"Dagger Squadron, Dagger Leader. Look alive, boys and girls. The long ride's over, and the fun is about to start. Arm your weapons." There was a snap and a hiss as Dagger Leader shifted from the general combat frequency to a private ship-to-ship channel. "Tucker, this is Captain Chen. A warning: stay tight and close, no hotdogging, no lone-wolf berserker tactics, got it? You stay with the flight, and hold tight to my wing. If you sideslip or lead me by more than ten meters from my port wingman position, I will personally burn you down—got me?"

Uchita's left hand—the flesh-and-blood one—was trembling, her breath searing in her chest. The familiar blood-lust burned behind her eyes, dulling the pain of her body's long captivity. Her right hand closed around the joystick between her knees.

"Got it...Captain."

Her left hand killed her ship's thrust. To Uchita's eyes, the other five *Thrush* fighters of Dagger Squadron appeared

18

to be accelerating past her, away from the planet and into deep space at rapidly increasing speed. This was only an illusion, though, created by the fact that her ship was no longer decelerating at thirty meters per second squared and was now hurtling planetward more quickly than her still-slowing fellows. Machine-precise fingerings of her attitude jets flipped the tail-first *Thrush* end for end, then steadied the ship while Stein's Folly filled her forward canopy with green and orange splendor.

"Tucker!" Chen's voice screeched over the private circuit. She palmed the comm switch, cutting the voice off in mid-threat. Let him burn her down...if he could catch her. She was going to kill Davions.

Her heads-up display sprang into sharp illumination in front of her eyes. Red pinpoints of light projected the positions of the approaching Davion fighters, as steadily dwindling decimal numbers recited the closing range.

Kill them, she told herself. Kill them all!

2

Ghostly fingers of radar had first detected the approaching Liao ships, which the *Sparrowhawk*'s tracking computer painted as a ragged circle of five white pinpoints of light on Lieutenant Adam Valasquez's heads-up display. There were other enemy ships further out, he knew—at least three more six-ship squadrons and a small fleet of massive *Overlord* Class DropShips—but these five were the leaders, the ones charged with opening the way for the landings certain to follow. Their jettisoned fuel tanks had made a blazing display of meteoric fireworks in the chill, twilight skies above Steindown's north pole; he'd seen the images relayed from DESTra's cameras. That they'd been willing to burn that much reaction mass to hump the void between the jump point and Stein's Folly at a crushing three Gs could only mean they were coming to stay, hoping to catch the ground defenses unprepared. Those *Overlords* farther out carried thirty-six BattleMechs apiece. If they got through...

But the *Overlords* were someone else's responsibility. Heavy assault fighters still being readied at Steindown's port would be the ones to vector against the *Overlords* in hopes of burning them down before they could release their deadly cargoes. These five leaders were the targets for Valasquez's squadron. They had to be burned so that they couldn't soften the Davion ground defenses or provide air cover for the BattleMech drop. After they were out of the way, well...

Valasquez rubbed his gloves against his thighs in a futile effort to wipe away the sweat trickling across the palms of his hands. He'd never had a chance at an *Overlord*. They were big...terrifyingly big, and heavily armed and armored, but...

20

"Red Flight, this is Red Leader. Steady up, now. We've got 'em right where we want 'em. Just keep cool and stay tight. On my command...three...two...one...*punch it!*"

The squadron of *Sparrowhawks* cut in their overthrust as one, vectoring for the oncoming Liao ships. There had definitely been six enemy craft—the usual complement of a battle squadron—but now Valasquez read only five. He almost widened his scan, but decided against it for fear of losing the fix on the targets he had. That missing ship...a malfunction, perhaps? A drive failure could leave an aircraft helplessly plunging on into space at the velocity it retained when the drive died. The sixth ship might already have plunged into the skies of the Folly's pole and burned hours ago, following the trajectory of the empty fuel tanks. He spared a thought for the pilot, a passing shudder for the man's terrible death.

At 3.5 Gs, the Davion *Sparrowhawks* closed on their targets.

* * * *

Uchita had not burned. Three times she had made high-G burns to correct her vector, slowing her ship and clearing the radar-swept line between Dagger Squadron and the outbound Davions.

She was still not in visual range, but her computer had painted wire-frame plan and elevation view diagrams of her targets in green lines on her number two computer screen, while her main screen displayed the enemy squadron's arrowhead formation. The Davion fighters were easily recognizable without computer identification—six stubby *Sparrowhawks*, the twin lances of their paired Martell medium lasers extending forward like the antennae of some grey, squat insects. Range figures flickered across her heads-up display. Her own trio of Kajuka Type 2 lasers had a maximum effective range of over 50,000 kilometers, but she was determined to hold her attack until the very last

21

possible second. She was at 12,000 kilometers now and closing at 300 klicks per second.

She selected one of the six targets, and locked it into her targeting computer. Behind the black reflective mask of her flight helmet visor, her lips wer drawn back in a wild rictus that she thought was a smile. *Kill them!*

* * * *

Space combat tended to be a drawn-out affair of maneuver and countermaneuver, punctuated by brief periods of fire-shrieking fury and fear. Lasers, PPCs, and long-ranged missiles can deliver damage across respectable ranges, but target acquisition and targeting technologies were no longer able to cope with the ranges and velocities involved. Extensive weapon firing caused ships already heated by maneuver to overheat faster than the heat pumps could handle. Expert pilots had learned to wait until they were within a few thousand kilometers to open fire, trading the slim chance of multiple, long-ranged hits for the certainty of hits at close range during rapid passes.

Red Flight and Dagger Squadron interpenetrated, their respective velocities on opposite vectors adding to a passing velocity of over 500 kps. At such speeds, human reactions dragged too slowly to select targets or to plot vectors. Under computer control, four *Sparrowhawks* concentrated their fire on one *Thrush*. Armor on the broad, oval disk of the fighter's wing flared white where invisible beams of coherent light scored successive hits, wreathing the *Thrush* in a mist of rapidly condensing droplets of molten alloy. Return fire scored hull armor and left molten slashes across fuselage and wing.

Valasquez flipped his fighter end for end and slammed his thrust control forward. Savage deceleration bucked and sang through his stubby ship, but he continued to fire at the Liao ships now receding against the green and orange disk of the Folly's sun. Another hit!

He'd had only a fractional instant's glimpse of his enemy before they'd passed out of visual range, but that view had confirmed his computer's ID of five, tight-grouped TR-7s. A combat readout flickered across one of his computer screens. At least two of the Liao ships were hurt enough to degrade their performance. He identified those two to his squadron as optimum targets, then cut in a short burst of overthrust that hammered him against his seat. For an agonizing moment, Valasquez thought the Liao TR-7s were going to ignore Red Squadron and race them for the atmosphere of Stein's Folly, but the traceries on his HUD proved otherwise. All five ships were decelerating as savagely as he was, using their maneuvering thrusters to swing them around and bring them into line for another pass. He noted that four had paired off in wingman formation, but that the fifth was alone.

Valasquez gave a long, hooting rebel yell as he lined up all four of his little ship's lasers on the lead *Thrush*, and triggered a rapid burst of invisible bolts of light that stitched across the target's nose and wing.

* * * *

Uchita's battlelust had grown as her instruments described to her the opening rounds of the battle. There was no indication that she had been detected. She watched one of the *Sparrowhawk* fighters open fire on Captain Chen's *Thrush*. Gently she eased her stick forward, letting her fingers caress the target acquisition controls under her unfeeling right hand. Her vector had already been set. As her target accelerated, she dropped into line behind him, so close she could see his drive flare as a brilliant, diamond-sharp beacon star through the soft illumination of her HUD.

Fire! Fire!

* * * *

23

Alarms screeched in Valasquez's helmet speakers as his instrument display lit up with red trouble lights. He was hit!

"Red Leader, this is Red Five. Y'got one on your tail!"

"I see him, Red Five! I've got some damage here..." Damage control reports flashed across a screen. Uh oh...his starboard control surfaces were really fouled. It was a good thing he wouldn't need those until he hit atmosphere again. He'd worry about that later. His threat indicator flashed purple.

"The bogie's closing, Red Leader! Break left! Break left!"

His hand played across thruster controls. The maneuverable little *Sparrowhawk* flipped end-over and decelerated sharply as he swung onto a new vector. Warnings shrieked at him, and he cut them off. A combat spacecraft's most serious problem was heat build-up—heat from engines, from laser fire, from enemy hits. Each maneuver he made was making the temperature problem worse, but there was no way to shed waste heat now.

Where was the bogie? There! He fired, a snap shot without a lock, but he was certain he'd scored at least one hit. Red Five was closing on the bogie now, angling for a shot. A momentary brilliance flaring about the target showed Red Five had hit. Good!

Then there were more Liao fighters, two of them in tight wing formation. "Red Five, watch yourself, starboard quarter high!" His own heat overload warning lights were flashing balefully in time to a raucous buzz in his helmet phones, but he slapped the override again and triggered invisible fire from all four lasers.

"Red Leader, this is Five!" Dugan's voice was high-pitched, the youngster's battlepitch distorting his words. "The bogie's flipped again! Watch your..." At that moment, Red Five exploded in white light, the silent burst punctuated by the shriek of static in Valasquez's helmet phones.

The laser fire shredded his tail stabilizer and pocked craters in the armor over his engines. He fired his thrusters to flip an undamaged flank of his *Sparrowhawk* into the attacker's line of fire. Sluggish! She wasn't reacting fast enough! Metal vapor exploded into space.

He tracked a target, firing paired medium and light lasers with grim determination. His target began tumbling, its disk shape shredded and hacked by repeated hits, its thrusters silenced. Valasquez's course and speed were close enough to that of the target that he was able to fire volley after volley into the wreckage. Finally, he was rewarded by a flash that consumed the crippled *Thrush* in a dazzling gout of light. A kill! But his computer marked that kill as the Liao flight's leader, not the mystery ship that had attacked him from behind.

He switched to wide scan, searching. Where was that other one? Whoever he was, that pilot was damn good. Valasquez had already watched the guy perform maneuvers that should have blasted him into unconsciousness. Was it a man piloting that ship, or some incredibly efficient fighting machine? He fired again—damn! Miss! The battle was becoming a one-on-one duel with this unknown Liao pilot. Hit! Hit again! Then a rapid-fire sequence of laser hits scored his port wing, punching through delicate control surfaces and blasting his port Exostar light laser into tattered, twisted wreckage. Warnings keened. Override! Target! Fire! Another hit!

"Red Leader! Red Leader! This is Red Three! Watch your vector, Red Leader!"

Vector? Valasquez checked, blinked, checked again. The battle had carried him toward Stein's Folly. So intent had he been on the grim killing efficiency of the Liao pilot that he'd ignored the dazzling, swollen, cloud-girded sphere of the planet behind him.

"Copy, Red Three." He did some fast calculations, chose a new vector, kicked in his drive...but nothing happened. For a moment, he kept cold panic at bay by resetting his controls and punching the throttle controls again. Still nothing. The intolerable heat overload had shut down his drive. Malfunction lights winked and flickered at him. His ship jolted as another trio of laser bursts stitched into his wounded *Sparrowhawk*'s hull.

He palmed thruster controls. Where was the bogie? There! Following him down! He fired his twin Martells. His surviving Exostar was winking a malfunction light at him. *Thrush* and *Sparrowhawk* traded fire as the pair of them drifted into the thin upper reaches of the Folly's atmosphere. Desperately, Valasquez used his surviving thrusters to boot his *Sparrowhawk* over into a nose-high, nose-forward approach. Landing his shot-up bird was going to be tricky. Atmosphere dragged at him, making his ship buck and shudder as he fought to control a sudden, irresistible starboard yaw with savage twists of his control stick. The control surfaces weren't responding, weren't...

Oh, God, no...the control surfaces! He craned his head around, saw smoke and tattered debris whipping aft from the laser-pocked ruin of his port wing. A violent thump marked the departure of what was left of his tail fin. Then the damaged port wing tore free, and the *Sparrowhawk* began tumbling, engulfed in an orange fireball, trailing debris.

Valasquez didn't start screaming until smoke boiled up into the cockpit, and the legs of his pressure suit began melting in the heat.

* * * *

Burn, Davion, burn! Uchita watched the fiery meteor streak across the cloudtops below her with a curiously cold and shuddering emotion that might, remotely, be termed satisfaction. Her own ship's engines were gone, wrecked in that final exchange of fire with the enemy *Sparrowhawk*. Her craft's thrusters had functioned long enough for her to flatten her trajectory and skip off the Folly's atmosphere like a stone from the surface of a lake. She was receding into space now, her *Thrush* a battered wreck—power out, engines dead, her cockpit open to vacuum. A strange, numb sensation from the attachments of her mechanical left leg had proven, on examination, to be nothing less than complete amputation. Her hull armor had failed at a critical point, and her left leg was missing below the knee. The heat from that millisecond pulse seemed to have partly melted the fabric of her spacesuit's leg, sealing it against what remained of her plastic knee and thigh, maintaining pressure in her suit. She took grim satisfaction in knowing that that hit would have killed any other pilot. She was the Automaton of Destruction—indestructible.

At least, indestructible if she were rescued. She followed the course of the battle on her screen. Including her kill—her thirteenth, she realized—three of the attacking *Sparrowhawks* had been destroyed, the others damaged and scattered. Two Liao fighters had been put out of the fight, her own and Captain Chen's.

The DropShips were already maneuvering toward the atmosphere, as their fighter reserves emerged from cavernous cargo bays and descended to engage rising squadrons of Davion defenders in the atmosphere. The Davions would be at a disadvantage now. Dagger Squadron's thrust had blunted the leading edge of their defenses. The way was open for the *Overlords* to drop their readied 'Mechs behind a screen of sheltering fighters.

Her own life, she realized, hung on the outcome of that invasion. Her life support would last for another day, time enough for the invasion to establish a foothold on Stein's Folly—or be repulsed. If the invasion failed, no one would have time for her, locked in her crippled ship, falling stern-first into deep space at well above the planet's ten kilometers per second escape velocity. If it succeeded, she would be rescued by DropShips homing on her automatic radio distress beacon. Her squadron-mates might not like her, but she had proven her worth to them time after time. She would rejoin Dagger Squadron again, would kill again.

Thirteen kills!

With a cool, almost remote sense of mild anticipation, Uchita Tucker watched the invasion ships deploy on her screens.

* * * *

Colonel Pavel Ridzik stood with arms folded across his barrel chest and smiled with grim satisfaction through his red beard. The sky above Steindown was heavily smudged with oily smoke from a dozen burning fuel tanks, warehouses, and shattered BattleMechs. Skeletal shards of blast-ruined buildings poked at the sky from rubble piles still smoldering. The landing field itself was heavily cratered, and shadowed by the vast bulk of the pair of *Overlord* Class DropShips that had settled their landing jacks deeply into the fragmented ferrocrete. Hatches gaped open beneath the upraised arm-and-katana sword emblems of the Capellan Confederation emblazoned on the curves of those black hulls. BattleMechs—Liao BattleMechs—were still being offloaded from both transports.

In the sharp breeze above the spaceport, the House of Liao flag, inverted green triangle with the raised arm-and-katana against a red field, snapped and cracked. The ground struggle for the port had lasted just fifteen minutes from the time the first Liao *Phoenix Hawk* had touched down on flaming jets to the moment the *Overlords* had grounded and begun disgorging their reserves. The defenders had thrown down their weapons the moment the *Overlords* had grounded, had surrendered or fled into the surrounding countryside. A few had made it.

The ground under Ridzik's boots trembled to the tread of a formation of heavy 'Mechs moving off the field. A pair of sixty-ton OSR-2C *Ostrocs*, the massive, armless, bullet form of a *Catapult*, and the eighty-five-ton thunder of a BLR-1G *BattleMaster*, Fire Lance of a Company of House Liao's St. Ives Armored Cavalry, raised dust and thunder as they made their way across the shredded ruin of the facility's security fence and into the grassland beyond. Another *BattleMaster*, an *Archer*, and a pair of TBT *Trebuchets* followed the line infantry 'Mechs, the horse-and-rider emblem of McCarron's Cavalry freshly painted against their green-camouflaged right legs.

28

Ridzik turned and strode back toward the Administrator's Residence, the low, modern villa that he had made his headquarters at the edge of the field. After the seesaw battle in space, the ground battle had been almost anticlimactic, because the defending 'Mechs had been scattered at key garrison points across the planet.

House Liao intelligence operatives had long ago pinpointed the most important concentrations of Davion 'Mechs on the planet. The invasion fleet had concentrated on the four most important of those, overwhelming them in a firestorm of missiles and beams before the others could come to their aid.

Only twenty-four 'Mechs had been stationed at Steindown itself, and of those, only fifteen had been operational when the first space-dropped Liao 'Mechs and Death Commando infiltrators had descended around the port. One of the defenders still stood behind the villa, a fifty-ton *Enforcer*, intact except for its head. Trickles of flame and roiling smoke rose from the jagged crater between the 'Mech's shoulders. Its leg actuators had locked, leaving it standing erect like some monstrous ten-meter-tall piece of junkyard sculpture.

The defenders had not had a chance. Sprawled in the shadow of the *Enforcer* were two sodden forms lying like ragdolls in pools of still-liquid blood—the fat colonel who had commanded this garrison and a young lieutenant from his staff, both cut down by fire from Liao Death Commandos dropped ahead of the main assault.

A captain approached Ridzik, making the fist-to-breast salute of House Liao. His brown uniform was fire-smudged and muddy, the green trim nearly indistinguishable from the rest. Instead of the customary ceremonial katana, a 12 mm Hawking automatic pistol hung in a holster at his side. The man's helmet was missing, too, and his head was encircled by a bandage shockingly white against his dirty blond hair.

"Captain Dyubichev." Ridzik stopped and turned, returning the salute with a nod. "Situation report?"

"Yessir. Both the port and Steindown itself are secure, with light casualties. Forces at Lollan and Grebuchin report continued heavy combat, but all other DZs are secure as well. The entire peninsula is ours. A number of 'Mechs escaped into the swamps and hills north of the peninsula, and there are some isolated outposts still holding out, but..." The young face struggled a moment, then broke into a smile. "We beat 'em, Colonel!"

"That we did, Captain, that we did. How many 'Mechs did we take here?"

"Nine in the repair bay. Eight more were crippled and abandoned in the fighting, but we'll have them repaired and in the field in a few days. Three were destroyed, and four escaped into the swamp to the north. We also captured a large number of Techs and Tech assistants, and quite a few civilians who were living on the base." He jerked a thumb back across his shoulder. "They're under guard at the hangar."

"Treat them well, Dimitri," Ridzik said. "Reunite them with their families, get them food, medical attention, whatever they need. We'll want them to join us. Can't go wasting prime Techs now, can we?"

"No, sir."

"As for the rest, take them outside the base, question them, and..."

"Of course, Colonel. No survivors." The captain saluted again and turned back toward the base.

Colonel Ridzik returned to his temporary headquarters, composing the report to his lord, Maximilian Liao. He scarcely noticed the two bodies as he stepped across them and mounted the steps to the villa.

3

Ardan Sortek paced the terrace like a caged cat, his steps clicking sharply against the artificial stone. At the moment, he hated the terrace, the palace, and its surrounding gardens filled with alien plants brought from a dozen worlds. He hated the artificiality of the place, of his friend Hanse. And even of himself.

He paused beside the low wall bordering the terrace. His friend Hanse, Prince of Davion...he sighed unconsciously. The two had been companions ever since Ardan's boyhood, when he had tagged almost worshipfully at his older friend's heels.

Later, when he was old enough to take the MechWarrior training that would eventually fit him for the Royal Brigade, Ardan believed that his life had reached a peak, that never again could he feel quite so happy. Especially joyful were those times when Hanse had overseen his training personally. After their grueling workouts in their 'Mechs, the two would relax together, drinking cold ale beside the lake bordering the drillfield.

They had both been so young and idealistic. Though Hanse was ten years older, he had not yet been burdened with the weight of rulership, and felt free to concoct wide-ranging plans for the improvement of the worlds administered by House Davion.

The two had taken thought for the good of everyone from MechWarrior to serving wench, with the agrarian population and the merchant class properly cared for in between. Ardan, because of his origins in a house of lower nobility, could make suggestions that would never have occurred to the younger son of the Davion dynasty.

He remembered all this as his steps echoed across the terrace. Would Hanse never come?

He felt sick, now. Betrayed. When Ian Davion had died in battle and Hanse become Prince of Davion, Ardan had

31

believed that his friend would manage to put into effect some of the reforms that were so badly needed among the Federated Suns. But it hadn't worked out that way. At every turn, he had watched Hanse make decisions that showed him far more influenced by politics and power than by concern for those he ruled.

Footsteps behind him brought Ardan around. He stopped, stiffened...then moved deliberately toward the ruddy-haired man approaching.

"Ardan! My friend! I am so glad we have time to talk. I was distressed at your request for transfer. Is there no way to persuade you to remain here with the Brigade?"

Sortek took the offered hand. Grasping its hard, broad strength, he felt a surge of the old affection. Whatever Hanse might have become, he was still the big almost-brother Ardan had known for so long.

Then he remembered...and loosed his grip. Stepped back. Shook his head slightly.

"No. Things haven't gone...as I expected them to, Highness. I find myself dissatisfied with everything. The Court. Myself. Even...even those I work with."

Hanse grinned. "The lovely Candent Septarian has been rubbing you the wrong way?" he asked, his tone suspiciously innocent.

"Sep? Who said anything about...No, it's just that these days, just about everything and everyone seems to irritate me. Things I thought were true have turned out not to be. People I trusted seem different. Unlike themselves. I thought it would pass with the years, but it hasn't."

The older man's grin evaporated, and his brow furrowed.

"Listen, Dan," he began, "I know what we used to say when we were younger. Before my brother was killed and I was still ignorant of the realities of rulership and power. We said a lot of things, you and I. And you have to admit that I *have* put many of our dreams into effect."

"Things that make the Federated Suns stronger, the troops better fed, the people less likely to be restless!" Ardan said, interrupting.

32

"Those are also what make everyone happier and more comfortable." Hanse sounded relaxed, but the furrow was still between his brows.

"But you are working with people we can't trust...doing things that I can't approve!" Ardan insisted.

"There is a grimy underside to politics," Hanse admitted. "That's how the thing works, though I didn't realize it until I had to deal with it firsthand. You've never stood in my shoes, Dan. You just can't know how hard it is to keep everything working together. It's like being a juggler trying to keep fifteen balls in the air...but using only one hand!"

Ardan shrugged and turned to look out over the garden. Hanse came up beside him and set a hand on his shoulder.

"See the gath-trees in the garden," he said softly. "They could never grow there without the special soil about their roots and the treated water in their irrigation systems. And the illgrass from Kentares must be fertilized with animal blood or it would die. Politics, too, is a strange weed. It has odd and sometimes ugly needs and habits. But it has not changed much over the thousands of years of human history." Hanse frowned as if trying to find just the right words.

"Even the best ruler, over the generations, has not been able to force virtue between its teeth. I cannot wave a wand and make men honest in their dealings with each other. And if I could, I probably wouldn't, anyway. I don't always know what is right."

Ardan turned to stare into his friend's face. "I have seen things...that I cannot accept. I have seen you change. I have seen myself begin to change. War is my profession, Hanse. I am not suited to politics, even at secondhand. I know I would be far happier simply not knowing about many of the things happening here at Court."

Hanse opened his mouth to speak, but Ardan spoke first. "I am wasted here. New Avalon is secure, but our borders are again under attack. Redfield and Stein's Folly have fallen to Liao forces, and our enemies seem intent on penetrating more deeply into our sphere. Your brother-in-law Michael seems unable to stop them without assistance. You have plans, I know, for a counterinvasion of Stein's Folly. That's where I can do the most good…transferred to active duty."

The Prince sighed. He, too, turned to gaze across the gardens.

"Do you remember how it was, Dan? In battle? The terror and the blood and the noise? The devastation of the countryside as the 'Mechs battled it out, crushing forests and cropland and houses beneath their armored heels? You hated it, I know. We are too much alike for me to doubt that, though I was busy with other things by the time you were trained sufficiently to go to war. Do you really want to return to all that?" Hanse turned and took the younger man's shoulders between his big hands.

"Think of what you will leave behind!" he said. Though Sep's name was not spoken, Ardan knew it was to her that Hanse was referring.

"What other use is there for a MechWarrior?" Ardan asked quietly. "I cannot stay here any longer—and I've known it for two years now. Blood and death are no worse than deviousness and dishonor."

Hanse drew a shocked breath. Never before had his friend spoken so bluntly to him. Even though there was closeness between them, Ardan was also a subject who had till now always observed the proprieties.

Though he had reddened, temper rising, Hanse controlled himself. "You are naive, Ardan. You think that the straightforward techniques of war can be applied to diplomatic dealings among powers. That's where you're wrong, though." Hanse turned to look out over the expanse of garden and beyond to the distant wall of forest that bordered the great royal house.

"I grant your request," he said finally. "You will go with the strike force to Stein's Folly. I wish you well." Hanse took a step backward, almost spoke again, but seemed to reconsider. Then he turned toward the doorway beyond the terrace. The soft sound of his cushioned boot-soles on the stone was far more menacing than the sharp click of Ardan's heels as he retreated in the opposite direction.

The young man slowed a bit as he passed through the gates, with a nod to the 'Mech on guard there. Though he had been moving toward this point for two years, it had taken all his courage to face his friend and ruler so frankly. And now that he had what he wanted, Ardan felt suddenly without direction.

His life was about to change drastically. Even though he drilled regularly with the Royal Brigade to keep his skills at their peak, life at Court had softened him. He had not smelled ozone mixed with blood for a very long while. Going to battle also meant going away from Sep, but he quickly forced his thoughts away from that.

She was a MechWarrior, too. They had never spoken to one another of their feelings, and Ardan had no intention of changing that. But something inside him felt empty at the thought of facing battle with anyone else at his flank. Sep was good, and she was dependable.

He was going to have to bid her goodbye, along with the rest of his company. Because of his relationship with Prince Davion, many had been too jealous to seek Ardan's friendship, but there were three with whom he did share a closeness. It was not going to be easy, saying goodbye.

He strode away toward the drillfield and barracks. The Royal Brigade was housed in a shielded building capable of withstanding a full-scale assault by most weapons. Stored beneath the complex in double-shielded armory/workshops were the Brigade's 'Mechs.

Ardan thought, too, of the Techs who worked so faithfully to keep his *Victor* in topnotch order. He'd miss Lal and Nym almost as much as his fellow officers. But he had to make the break, and as quickly as possible. By keeping his ear to the ground in recent days, Ardan had figured out that Hanse was sending troops to retake Stein's Folly within the week.

It would normally take almost two months to make the eight jumps between New Avalon and the Folly, but via the Command Circuit, they could make the trip in a matter of hours. Nevertheless, the last jump would be a doozy...right into the firepower of the Liao forces.

He stopped for the I.D. scanner, then passed into the barracks, which was quiet at this hour. With drill and combat training over for the day, the others in his command were cleaning up, relaxing, or playing quiet games of strategy while waiting for the evening meal.

Ardan knew that he would find Sep and Jarlik in the common room, where every afternoon they spent an hour at the computers, matching wits, polishing their strategic reactions, testing reflexes. He would wait to see them later in the mess hall. As for Denek and Fram, they would probably be in the quarters they shared. Quarrelling lazily, no doubt. Drinking ale. Teasing.

Ardan smiled. To listen to them, anyone would think those two were the worst of enemies instead of the best of friends. He tapped at their door and heard a chuckle beyond it.

"Come on in!" Fram yelled. "Friend or enemy, we need somebody to keep us from scragging each other!"

Ardan pushed open the door and stepped inside. "Well, you're going to have to find someone else to keep you from each other's throats. I'm off to the Folly."

Two sets of boots hit the floor from their precarious positions propped on the table. Two pair of eyes stared at him, startled, from two brown faces.

"No lie?" asked Denek. He pushed a chair toward Ardan. "Here, sit and tell us. Action? Holy Roarer! While we sit here and cool our heels and drill, you're going to be back in a real war! Sheee! Now is that fair?" He turned to Fram for confirmation.

"Not fair at all," agreed the slighter warrior. "But just what you'd expect from someone with the Prince's confidence. Now we'll all have to be worrying about Ardan, as well as keeping our 'Mechs slick and our reactions smooth."

"Have you told Sep and Jarlik?" Denek rose to pace back and forth in the scanty space. "They're going to be almighty upset."

"No. I'll see them in a bit. Probably over chow," Ardan said. "I still need to get used to the idea myself, now that His Highness has given his consent. I guess I really didn't expect him to let me go." Suddenly weary from so many mixed emotions, Ardan leaned back against the neatly made bunk.

"You going because of some of the things we keep hearing?" Fram asked. "About secret treaties and such?"

"I can't answer that," said Ardan.

Before anything more could be said, a chime sounded, echoing through the corridors of the vast barracks.

"Dinner's served, gentlemen," said Ardan, rising from the bunk. "Shall we go?" At the door, he stepped aside to let Fram and Denek pass first. Now that the time had come, he found himself dreading his last encounter with Sep.

4

It had been a long day already. Sep had put her huge *Warhammer* through its paces for six hours without stopping, keeping Fram and Jarlik, in their lighter but more maneuverable *Valkyries* on the hop. Though they had almost gotten through her guard a couple of times, she had managed to hold them to a three-way draw.

Given their abilities, Sep was rather proud of that. She would like to try the same sort of practice with Ardan, but in his present mood, she knew better than to ask. He was so touchy these days.

Unwinding at the computers afterward, testing her wits against Jarlik's, Sep had again managed to come out appreciably ahead. This was becoming a regular thing, and Jarlik grumbled that she must have reprogrammed the system to give herself the edge. He was joking, of course. She understood the big fellow too well to take offense, though others sometimes bristled under his heavy-handed humor.

Sitting in the common room, the two MechWarriors had talked of the growing rumor of a Davion counterattack against Maximilian Liao, who had seized both Redfield and Stein's Folly near the Federated Suns border. The loss of those worlds had set the mighty House Davion on its ear, and everyone in the armed forces was on edge. Something would have to give soon, Sep knew.

"Hanse must act," Jarlik had said. "He can't afford to hold back...There are too many powers watching his reaction. If he shows signs of weakness, we'll have others besides Maximilian Liao at our throats. Even Steiner isn't above a little polite planet-snatching, given the chance."

"Not to mention the nasties out in the Periphery, just waiting to dart in and grab whatever they can catch," Sep put in. "I wonder if that's the reason Hanse's Institute of Science is working so hard at a new security system?"

38

"New security? I'd have thought our old system would stand up to anything."

"Well, it might, but last week I was drafted into a team assigned to try breaching all the systems in the palace. A couple of times, we *almost* succeeded. The NAIS observer kept nodding and making notes and muttering into a comp. Maybe she found out what she needed to know."

Now, after freshening up in her quarters, Sep was thinking about that conversation while making her way to the mess hall. Something was in the wind. Every Mech-Warrior on New Avalon was antsy, edgy. Even Ardan, who was usually so reserved, had snapped at his men more than once.

She entered the big hall and looked to the corner where she, Ardan, Jarlik, Denek, and Fram usually supped together. The others were already in place, full trays in front of them.

Jarlik raised a hand and beckoned to her, then pointed to a laden tray at an empty spot beside him. Bless the man! He'd picked up her supper as well as his, saving her a lot of standing in line. Sep grinned, knowing Jarlik would take his toll. She never ate a whole trayful, and he would get to clean up anything she left.

She slid onto the bench beside Jarlik and smiled across the table at Ardan. When he didn't return the smile, she looked around at the group, realizing that they all were unusually grim.

"All right, what's up?" Sep asked, looking straight at Ardan.

He dropped his gaze, fiddled with his fork, then raised his eyes to hers.

"I've been transferred," he said, voice low and gruff. "I asked for it. Things have been…getting to me lately. It was time for a change."

Sep felt a hot lump rise in her throat, but she swallowed it back down with grim determination. She quickly took a taste of soup, which burnt her tongue badly enough to excuse the tears that rose to her eyes.

"Whoof!" she panted. "Hot!" She breathed deeply, cooling her mouth and throat. In those few moments, she had gotten her emotions under control again. "It's what you've wanted for a long time," she said. "I hate to see you go, but I know how it is. Some people can stand Court service, and others find it unbearable. After four years here, I admit it's been a nice rest. But a day will come when I'll want to get back into the thick of things, too."

"Yes, but it's good to be part of the Brigade, which is the service everyone hopes for, if they're good enough," Denek interjected. "I'd hate to leave it...now. Though I suppose the time *might* come when I get bored with mock battles, too." He looked thoughtfully into the mixture of vegetables and meat on his plate.

"I'm not bored," said Ardan, his tone dry. "I'm—No, better not to talk about it. Let's just say that the time has come for me to move on to something else. I wasn't cut out for life at Court. Or in government. Or around politics. Leave it at that."

Sep took a bite of something tasteless, chewed it carefully, swallowed, took a sip of wine. She wished desperately that that there were something light and funny to say. The atmosphere at their table had become thick enough to cut with a vibroblade.

Besides, she knew what was eating Ardan, having seen his increasing dissatisfaction with policies Hanse was putting into effect among the worlds ruled by the Federated Suns. She had never really understood what it was that so distressed him, though. Treaties that kept a system out of war were good, no matter what it took to get them ratified.

Sep took another bite of food, but it could have been desert-rat or chewyweed, for all the flavor she found in it. To save her, she couldn't think of anything to say except things sure to irritate Ardan even further. The new security systems, for one thing. Ardan thought a ruler should be completely and openly available to his people. That might be a wonderful theory, but she wondered how many of those who'd tried it in millennia past had ended up dead in the midst of all that access. At least four that she could recall from school history tapes popped into her head.

No, it was best not to mention security. Nor the war. Nor Hanse's probable intentions with regard to House Steiner.

Fram saved the situation. "You know, the strangest thing happened today. My coolant vest just conked out. While I was cooking away in there, my throat mike began malfunctioning, and my earphones began picking up beeps from the biofeedback sytem."

Ardan chuckled. Jarlik grinned, and Denek choked on a bite of food. Sep smiled, too, thinking how often similar things had happened to her.

"Anyway, there I was listening to my blood pressure, stewing in my own sweat, and trying to talk to my left toe, and I happen to look up to see Tigerwoman, here, about to take off my legs. Don't tell me comfort isn't necessary to a MechWarrior! You get distracted, and you're dead. If that had been a real battle situation, I'd have been a goner, for certain."

Pushing back his now-empty tray, Ardan grinned. It made Sep glad to see that it was not the false and strained version he'd shown earlier.

"I'll remember that when I get out to the Folly," he said. "After all, those Capellan 'Mech-jockeys will be playing for keeps. Somehow, here on New Avalon, it's hard to forget that the 'Mech you're sparring with is piloted by someone you'd protect with your own life in a real battle. It does make a big difference." He drained his glass and stood up.

"Anyone want to take a walk to settle dinner?" he asked with elaborate casualness.

Sep felt her heart thud solidly against her ribs. She stretched and stood.

"Might as well." She took her tray and followed Ardan to the racks where the soiled utensils were stacked for later cleaning.

Turning to look at their other three chums, she asked, "Anybody else?" Her expression, however, promised instant annihilation to anyone who volunteered to come along.

Three heads shook solemnly. "Too full of food," said Fram. Denek sighed and rubbed his belly. Jarlik dabbed his lips with a napkin and shrugged.

"Fine," said Ardan. "Come on, Sep. We'll walk out to the lake and back. Just the right distance to get the kinks out."

Walking out of the mess hall beside him, she wondered if he would say anything...then she knew he wouldn't. No more than could she. They were friends, first of all. Soldiers second. Anything else was best left unsaid.

They headed for the lake, which was inside the military compound that included the palace grounds as well as the building where the Council sat when in session. In the context of their times and their history, it was best to keep everything as protected as possible.

They moved in silence until out of earshot of the other men and women strolling in the twilight. Then Sep turned to look at Ardan.

"I think you're wronging your friend Hanse," she said. "He does what he must. You know what a good man he is...one of the best rulers in any of the systems. We just don't have all the information to understand everything he does, Dan."

"He has compromised his ethics," he said bitterly.

Though Sep wanted to reach out and shake him, she continued reasonably. "Look, it's a different thing for a ruler. He has to work with matters we never even think about." She tried to think of a way to bring the issue into focus for him.

"You are a sword, Ardan. Straightforward. Sometimes lethal, sometimes painful, but always honestly what you are, impossible to conceal, sharp and ready for action, no matter what comes. Do you understand that?"

"Of course." He sounded puzzled.

42

"Hanse is a dagger. A dagger in a sheath beneath the sleeve of an elaborate garment made to impress as well as to conceal. All smoothness and beauty on the outside, lulling to anyone who might try to challenge his position and power. And you know that some *have* tried."

Ardan nodded grudgingly.

"He has to have defenses that don't show. He must possess power that others can't see, hidden in the sleeve of his charismatic character. There is nothing evil about a dagger, Ardan."

"Perhaps not. But there can be evil in the way it is used."

"Also in the uses of a sword, my friend. A sword drawn in evil cause is no more virtuous than a dagger used likewise." She stopped, faced him, and placed one hand on his arm. "Can you seriously believe that Hanse is evil?"

Ardan leaned against the straight bole of a tree and gazed across the water. After a moment, he bent to pick up a pebble and skipped it across the smooth expanse.

"No, not really. But misguided...that I can say. Seriously so."

Sep sighed. A real hardhead was her friend Ardan. But at least she had given him something to think about. She skipped a pebble of her own.

"After you have gone," she said softly, "if there should ever be need, call for me. I will come, no matter where it might be. I have a feeling, Ardan. Something is in the wind. Something strange. Take care."

He nodded without speaking. They stood together and watched the light fade from the sky, leaving the lake a black mirror studded with stars.

5

To his surprise, Ardan slept deeply after saying goodbye to his friends, though he knew the next day would be filled with stress. There would be strategy sessions with the commanders of the strike force being sent from New Avalon, and decisions to be made about which 'Mech units to transfer from Dragon's Field, Hamlin, and Ral to support the invasion of the occupied world, Stein's Folly.

He would see Sep and Jarlik and the others again, but they would have no time for talk...or for sentiment. Probably a good thing, too. The more he realized how deeply he valued his comrades, the harder it became to leave them behind.

Just after early workout, Ardan received a summons to the Palace. He had dreaded seeing Hanse again, although knowing it was necessary. The counterinvasion of Stein's Folly was not going to be easy, and the planners would have to try to prepare for every eventuality.

Ardan found Hanse already in the war room with Ran Felsner, who had been, until very recently, commander of the Royal Guard. A formidable warrior and strategist, Felsner seemed a good choice for this sticky assignment.

Before his appointment to the command of Davion's Royal Brigade, Ardan had served under Felsner as a battalion commander in the 17th Avalon Hussars. Indeed, they both had good reason to remember the last time they had fought together, four years before in the battle for Tripoli, a Davion/Kurita border world. It was then that the two had become friends as well as comrades. Ardan had led his unit in a daring raid that turned the tide of battle in Davion's favor. Having thus distinguished himself as a tactical commander, Ardan was promoted to his current position with the Brigade. Ran, in turn, had been promoted to Brigadier as a result of the campaign's success.

Ardan greeted him, made the ritual obeisance to the Prince, and nodded to Lees Hamman, who would, no doubt, be second-in-command of the attack group. Hanse motioned Ardan to approach the table over which they pored.

It was one of the rare 3-D holotables that allowed one to plot planetary orbits, approaches of ships, space debris... anything that was programmable into the computers. You could also adapt it to reflect the details of an ongoing battle, if you were able to keep the programs abreast with reports from all parts of the field.

A useful item, indeed, and one that could be of great help to Davion. Progress reports from the field would be made through ComStar each day, though Ardan knew they would probably have to send a ship out to a station at some nearby Davion-held world until Stein's Folly could be retaken.

Ardan leaned beside Felsner, gazing into the depths of the table. Points of light representing JumpShips made erratic skips between the orange lights that were the worlds lying between New Avalon and Stein's Folly. Ardan pinpointed Argyle, site of Hanse's Summer Palace. He had joined the Prince there on many a long holiday, both before and after his friend's accession to the throne. The other worlds blinking on the dark pseudospace background had to be Vincent, New Cleveland, Emerson...yes...He had visited those, too.

Hanse touched a button, and a portion of the tabletop expanded to give a close-up view of the most distant range.

"We will use Dragon's Field as a staging area, because it is nearest our objective. The whole planet is surrounded by a cloud blanket that should shield much of our activity from any enemy probes or spyships. We can ready our assault force in fair safety, before committing them to the Drop-Ships for transport." He looked about the group. "Any questions?"

Ardan cleared his throat. "Being a latecomer to the mission, I'd like to know a couple of things. First, what size force will be going all the way from New Avalon? And

45

second, is there any word so far on the size and capacities of the occupying army on Stein's Folly?"

Hanse looked at Lees, who glanced at the readout on his side of the table. "A relatively small group will make the entire trip from here to Stein's Folly—one company, in fact. We, our 'Mechs, our Techs, and our weapons and supplies will go straight through on the Command Circuit."

"One company? To fight a war?" Ardan was puzzled.

"Never fear, Ardan," said Hanse. "The 5th Crucis Lancers is already on Dragon's Field, and Felsner will command them. You'll command the 17th Avalon Hussars, which are on their way now...And my brother-in-law Michael has graciously agreed to loan us one regiment of his Capellan March Militia, which Lees will command." Ticking off items with his fingers, he went on, "To the 'Mech forces, we've added three regiments of armored vehicles, two regiments of infantry, and two regiments of AeroSpace Fighters. By the time we have everything in order for your departure, they'll be very close to their objective. We've been planning this for weeks."

Felsner cleared his throat, interrupting his leader. "Is there anything else we need to think through before beginning to get things on the move, Your Highness?"

Hanse looked about at the others. His expression was inscrutable, but Ardan sensed that he was sad deep within and less confident than he seemed.

"There will be a messenger in from the staging world tonight. Tomorrow, we will hear his report. At that time, we will decide any other matters that may come up. But for now, I think it's time to put things in motion."

He turned to Ardan. "Tomorrow we will also get the latest word on the size of the force occupying the Folly. So far, our estimates are that Liao has stationed at least three to five regiments to hold Stein's Folly and Redfield. He has other problems elsewhere, however, and has withdrawn some of the original assault force to cope with those. We're watching closely, though, and by tomorrow should know as much as we can about what we're up against."

46

Felsner, Hamman, and Ardan saluted and turned to go, but Hanse caught Ardan's elbow as he passed. "Wait a moment, Dan. I'd like a word with you."

Ardan stopped obediently, though feeling a surge of resentment. It had already been too difficult. A repetition of that last scene with his old friend would be simply too much.

Hanse, however, was staring absently into the holotable. "I hate to see you go," he said, "but you are a MechWarrior, and it's fitting. What I hate worse is to see you leave in bitterness and anger." He lifted his head to look into Ardan's eyes. "You can't live with the thought of those agents provocateurs, can you?

"No." The answer was too blunt, but Ardan saw no way to soften it. "No, I cannot. War is terrible enough when it's necessary. When we are nominally at peace with a power, it seems wicked to stir up trouble for that House."

"Then think about this," murmured Hanse. "If House Marik were not embroiled among their own worlds—admittedly in problems of my making—they might well be at our flank, while we try to retake our own worlds. I know you too well to believe that this will change your attitude, but do consider it from time to time....When you *have* the time." He sighed and gestured, dismissing the younger man.

Ardan had indeed considered those very points, and certainly didn't need them pushed into his face. But he had been brought up with a code of honor that seemed to be far more demanding than even that of the illustrious House of Davion. Perhaps it was because his own family, while noble, had never been one of great power. Honor, rather than power or glory, had become the watchword of his ancestors.

Ardan felt a sudden restlessness, knowing that he must now dismiss his Techs. Normally, both Lal, his main Tech, and Nym, his standby, would go with him. But they had families on New Avalon, and Ardan was unwilling to whisk the two away to a war in which they had little personal stake. No, he would find new Techs on Dragon's

47

Field. There would be many 'orphaned' men there, Techs whose 'Mechs and MechWarriors had been destroyed in the desperate battle for Stein's Folly.

The scanners passed him into the workshop/storage area beneath his barracks. The familiar clang of metal on metal and the odor of welding and heat-processed sealants immediately assaulted his senses. There was never a quiet moment in the workshops where the active 'Mechs were repaired and maintained, and the damaged or worn ones reassembled into usable combinations.

The stall where his own *Victor* was stored came into view. Nym was polishing a weld, while Lal applied a coat of rust-preventive paint to the sole of one of the machine's immense feet. The sun-and-sword emblem of House Davion had just been redone, and the paint gleamed bright and fresh.

"Greetings," Ardan called over the din being made by a nearby metal worker.

Nym looked up and smiled. He and Lal would have gone on working, but Ardan signalled them to join him outside the work area.

"Anything wrong, Colonel?" asked the Tech, looking worried. He was the kind of man who prided himself on his work, constantly anxious that something might be less than perfect.

"Not with you or Lal," said Ardan. "I couldn't ask for a better pair of Techs. But I'm going offworld, and I refuse to take either of you away from your families. And especially because I know that your mother is sick, Lal. And Nym's young one is due to arrive at any time. Sella would come after me with a neural whip if I took you away now."

Nym looked upset. "It is my duty. My honor. I must go where my work takes me. Sella knows that."

"Well, this time your work will be with Candent Septarian. I asked her yesterday, and she needs you both. Her Tech and his standby both were injured when her *Warhammer* fell from its braces while the control bundles in its knee joints were being repaired. By the time they're functional again, I may even be back here."

48

Ardan took a deep breath. "You need to ready the 'Mech for transport. Check everything, of course. And I need a last exercise. Is the Gauntlet set up and ready to run?"

Nym nodded. "Will it be the *Victor*, as usual?"

"What else?" said Ardan. I've never understood why Sep likes that bunglesome *Warhammer* so well. Me, I'll take maneuverability."

"Probably because the *Warhammer* can simply step on anything it can't blast out of the way," mumbled Lal.

Ardan left, laughing. That was true. At seventy tons, the *Warhammer* could mangle a forest or a city without realizing it had stepped on anything. His *Victor*, on the other hand, was ten tons heavier, but could still rise up on its maneuvering jets. Ardan felt that his 'Mech's ability to move was a priceless asset on the field.

The Gauntlet was an exercise ground laid out in a large meadow beyond the lake and the forest. Set between high parallel walls of stone and metal, it extended just short of a kilometer in length and resembled a natural canyon, with every sort of straightaway, angle, curve, and bend.

Every centimeter of those forty-five-meter high walls was embedded with special effects that could simulate rocket launchers, lasers, autocannon, and any other nasty surprise a 'Mech might encounter in combat. When a MechWarrior wanted to work out there, a Tech was assigned to arm and control those weapons effects. They could only be disarmed by that Tech or by a direct hit on a sensitive plate of a slightly different color than the surrounding stone of the walls.

In a big building adjoining the Gauntlet rested the prototype 'Mechs. These were uncoded machines that could be programmed to behave like any known 'Mech that a pilot might want to operate in practice. Today, it would be a *Victor* for Ardan, its computer-controlled reactions simulating every effect of weapons hits, heat buildup, damage, and so on.

In the dressing chamber, Ardan stripped off his uniform and donned the cooling vest and neck and shoulder pads. To his arms and legs, he attached the biofeedback patches that provided temperature control and monitored heat in his sensor helmet. Finally, he fitted the neurohelmet over his head, setting it in place over his neck and shoulder pads. The helmet was the key to piloting a 'Mech, feeding information on the pilot's sense of balance into the 'Mech's computer to keep it erect and balanced even during jumping, kicking, or dive-and-roll combat. In return, the computer fed impulses back to the pilot through his helmet to keep him from being disoriented while locked up inside the head of a giant, maneuvering machine.

To 'unlock' a neurohelmet, the pilot transmitted a special, brief series of motions or entered some word or number command into the onboard computer. This code was secret and different for each individual pilot and his 'Mech, and prevented anyone else from simply climbing in and taking over the machine. Failure to transmit the proper sequence could result in damage to the helmet or the wearer.

After pushing the signal button to warn the Gauntlet personnel that he was ready to make his run, Ardan climbed into the *Victor* and plugged his helmet into the cables connecting it to the 'Mech. He almost went through his coding sequence before catching himself. To operate the prototype 'Mechs of the Gauntlet, MechWarriors simply used 'open systems' that made the 'Mechs ready for immediate use.

As the big doors ground open, Ardan flexed the muscles of the 'Mech, lifted a ponderous foot, raised and lowered his arms. Good. The myomer muscles were working perfectly.

Now he could see the walls of the Gauntlet begin to glow, and his own body answered with a surge of adrenalin. The 'Mech's heat intensified it, as he strode out into the sunlight.

Even after so many years, Ardan still found it strange to be transformed from a human on foot to a deadly, ponderous giant. The 'Mech's height gave him a superb view of all his surroundings. What he was looking at, however, were the tiny glints of light that seemed to wink malevolently in the walls ahead of him. Those were the lasers and other simulator weapons readying themselves for a battle.

Ardan grinned. He needed a good fight. Now he could work off the uneasy fury he had felt these past months without hurting anything—or anyone—he cared for.

6

The towering walls of the Gauntlet were three times the height of the *Victor*. As Ardan approached them, cautiously and with every muscle tensed for a sudden spring to left or right, a laser spat at him with its red light. This was followed almost instantly by a stream of small rockets from a projectile weapon coming from his other side.

Blessing the *Vic*'s jets, Ardan jumped high, letting the laser detonate the first of the rockets. The rest pocked the farther wall of the corridor as they exploded. He came down whirling, his own lasers raking the walls, taking out a row of weaponry set into the stone.

Testing every step, he moved forward again, using his sensors to seek out hidden mines. Many a 'Mech had been disabled after stepping on a concealed vibrabomb, but there was no knowing at exactly what weight/pressure the things might be set to explode. Ardan managed to stroll through the Gauntlet without triggering a single one, and he smiled, thinking how Sep would have bounded her way through, triggering a chain of explosions.

Just then, a laser beam seared the air, and he leaped and whirled, just barely dodging it. Every nerve alert, all his senses caught up in the death-game, Ardan moved through the perilous corridor in a series of spurts, jumps, quick turns, and ricochets. As he neared the end of it, a barrage of laser fire and rockets converged on the spot where he had just landed. He dived head-first, moved and sustained by his jets, then bounced, shoulder-first, off the rock of the wall.

Twisting desperately, he straightened to land on his feet. He was sweating so hard now that only the pads of his helmet kept the perspiration from blinding him. His heart was pounding, too.

Ardan was feeling better than he had in weeks.

At another sudden spurt of laser light, he wheeled, sidestepping the blast. Firing his own upper laser, he took out the enemy weapon. There was only one way he could think of to pass this last stretch, and that was to take it in one leap. Accurately. Without faltering. Should his own sense of balance be disturbed, he would also lose his ability to stabilize the huge machine.

All the while, he was drawing a deep breath, as if his own puny human lungs could assist the eighty-ton monster he manipulated. Then he launched himself into the air again, forcing the 'Mech's immensity toward the light at the end of the corridor.

When he came down, it was nine meters too soon, still within the deadly walls of the Gauntlet. The vibrations set his teeth on edge, made his heart hammer even harder, but he willed himself steady. Gritting his teeth, Ardan rolled the *Victor*'s body to its feet. It staggered, leaned against a wall. Heat seared even into his insulated compartment as he jerked the 'Mech upright. Again he jumped forward…this time onto the clean dust beyond the Gauntlet.

He was soaked in sweat now, panting, battered, and aching. But he felt a satisfied exhaustion. Turning the huge machine back toward the building, he moved along the outside of the walled corridor.

When Ardan reached the big doors, four small figures were waiting there. "Good run!" yelled Jarlik, as Ardan piloted the 'Mech inside and opened his hatch.

As he had hoped, this last run through the Gauntlet had eased the tension making him irritable for weeks. Grinning down at his four comrades, Ardan made his way down.

"They've added a few things since last month," he said. "Watch that other end—the laser will kill you!"

"You made it pretty well," said Sep, her eyes twinkling. "It looked like you worked that 'Mech to its limits."

"Feel as if I've been boiled in oil, though," grumbled Ardan. "Let me take a shower and get into my uniform. Then I'll take you all out for a last round of ale…on me."

Denek leaned against the wall, eyes wide, hands clasped to his chest. "You hear that? You HEAR that, my friends?

53

Ardan the tightwad has volunteered to buy the beer! Can you believe it?"

Fram nodded solemnly. "Just goes to show what it takes to get some people to shell out. Being assigned out to where he'll probably get his buns blown to Kingdom come, then running the Gauntlet and almost getting shaken out of his boots. Some people are *tough*, let me tell you!"

In their merriment, Jarlik and Sep leaned against one another and whooped. It wasn't really that funny, of course, but all of them must have been feeling relieved that things were back to normal again.

They spent a festive evening together, all thought of Ardan's impending departure kept well below the surface. He had hoped to leave quickly, avoiding long goodbyes, but now he was glad for the chance to enjoy this last evening with his friends.

Sep kept looking at him strangely, however. In the few brief intervals when they could say a private word to one another, Ardan tried to get her to tell him what was bothering her, but she only shook her head.

"Later," she murmured.

It was, indeed, very much later when the four set out for the barracks together. Though not exactly inebriated, they were all rather elevated. It wasn't difficult for Ardan to contrive to lag behind, catching Sep's elbow to keep her with him.

"Now will you tell me what's bothering you? You kept looking at me sideways all evening. Tomorrow I move out of barracks into the ready-area, and we won't have another chance to talk. I want to know." He put his hands on his hips and glared at her, swaying a bit.

Sep turned to lean against a nearby wall of the barracks. "I just don't like it," she said. "As your second-in-command, I'll be taking over your unit. That makes sense. But you shouldn't be leaving. I don't think you have thought long enough about this step you're taking."

Though the ale had relaxed him, Ardan felt himself bristle with irritation. "I *have* thought about it!" he snapped.

"For two years! Would you have me mull it over for two more?"

"Yes, if that's what it takes to make you see the light. Ardan, you aren't a politician. Thank the Holy Roarer for that! But politicians are necessary. Have you thought any more about what I said to you the other day?"

"Sep, I understood perfectly well what you said. I just didn't agree with it." He found himself becoming angry. Why did she insist on bringing this up again, just when he had been so full of the pleasure of the evening?

"You can't see Hanse as he is, simply because he's your friend. You want him to be perfect. But are you perfect? Am I? Then why should he have to be? Hanse is a good ruler, who's doing a good job of keeping the Federated Suns together." She glared at him.

"Can you imagine what would happen if Maximilian Liao achieved his goals—took out Davion and assimilated the Federated Suns into his Capellan Confederation? Now *there's* a schemer...a user...a manipulator. And worse. You've seen worlds he's conquered before we retook them. Whatever he touches, Liao squeezes until it's dry."

Because he couldn't deny what Sep was saying, it made Ardan even angrier. He *had* seen those devastated planets, their people starved and degraded, left homeless, cropless, powerless.

"I'm trying to keep Hanse from becoming just *like* Liao," he insisted. "Power corrupts, woman. Don't you know that?"

"Hanse was born to power. His family has wielded it for generations without becoming corrupted. Why do you trust him so little?"

Sep had to yell those last words after him, for Ardan had turned on his heel, and was walking away quickly toward his quarters. Her voice rang in his ears, even after he had closed the door behind him and was standing inside, staring at the wall. He even felt a little ill.

"That's just the drink," he said aloud, and went to splash his face with cold water. It didn't help, though. The more he thought about Sep's words, the angrier he became.

Returning to his room, a touch to the light-button brightened the dim glow in the room to normal intensity. Only now did Ardan notice that on his bed, along with the small pack of personal items readied for his trip, was another bundle. It appeared to have been hastily wrapped, but was tied with a big scarlet bow. Lifting off the note attached, he read: "From C.S., J., D., and F. We hope this will be useful."

He tore off the tissue impatiently. Rolled in a light environment suit, he found a new knife, together with the sheath that would strap it to his calf. The knife was beautiful, its edge razor-keen, its haft leather-wrapped. The sheath was also a fine piece of work, soft and form-fitting, so as not to bind on the leg.

There was something else, too, a canister made to fit into the cockpit compartment where a MechWarrior kept personal and survival equipment. In it was a new set of collapsible field and camping gear.

Ardan stared down at the gifts. His friends knew that he would be issued fresh gear when he got to his destination. But this was the best obtainable, far better than government-issue. The knife would keep its edge for years, and would neither oxidize nor break. The other equipment was of the finest quality and would probably wear far longer than he would.

Though his old knife had been with him in so many battles, he had been lucky enough never to need it. No 'Mech he had piloted had ever been destroyed to the point where Ardan was forced to abandon it. But the time came to every warrior—if he lived long enough—when he had to take to the battlefield on his own, unshielded by his gigantic machine.

Ardan packed quickly, almost mechanically. Having done it so often, before so many battles, habit took over, leaving his mind free. His thoughts drifted in a mild haze.

56

Not drunken—he hadn't consumed that much—but somehow disconnected from the familiar concerns that had so preoccupied and upset him recently.

His mind moved backward in time to the last war, the last battle in which he had been engaged. It had been no major conflict. The Draconis Combine had edged into Lyran territory. Under an existing treaty, House Davion had sent troops to aid Katrina Steiner in holding the group of worlds under attack. Ardan had been in command of a 'Mech unit assigned to root out an emplacement of enemy troops.

In memory, he felt beneath him the lumbering motion of his 'Mech. He heard the thunder of his own weapons, the impact of laser beams and explosives against the armor of his *Victor*. A dedicated group, his men had plunged into the fray with gusto, intoxicated with battle.

The thud of his 'Mech's huge feet against the ground had not impinged upon him at the time. The effects of his weapons on the surrounding territory hadn't been noted. Only the effects that took out or disabled enemy troops and 'Mechs had caught his attention.

Not until his unit had stomped the Kurita forces flat and the battle was over had Ardan paused to look about him. That had been the most terrible moment in all his years as a professional warrior. It was the first time he had allowed himself to really see what toll the battle had taken on the land across which it raged. Where a forest had stood, shading a broad lake, he now saw a field of stubble. Even worse, the greenish-yellow waters of the lake were stained black and red, where both machines and men had died horribly. The surrounding croplands were trampled into dust and straw. Dead animals lay swelling in the sun...along with dead men, both his own and the enemy's.

Where a stone house surrounded by orchards had stood, only a few stones remained, and the fruit trees might never have existed. In the lane before the broken walls, there had been a child, crying...Though he shrank from the memory, Ardan could not forget how the child's entrails hung from a gaping wound in its belly. The shrieks of the toddler had

57

carried even into the shielded space of his 'Mech. Even as he had moved to unlock his entry-port and go to the little boy's aid, laser fire had spurted, blasting the child into the dust.

Ardan would never forget that blackened bit of flesh, lying in the crumbled stone and dirt. And that was exactly where he was headed once more.

He turned blindly and set the neat pack beside the door, knowing he would never again go blithely into battle, filled only with dreams of glory and adventure, as he had once. No...behind his alert warrior's eyes, his busy mind, he would always see that blasted child, that ruined valley.

Was he, then, so much better than Hanse? Hanse might be subtle and devious to get his way. But Ardan knew himself to be a destroyer.

7

Maximilian Liao stood at the wide window, gazing across the tropical garden shielded by the walls of his palace on Sian. Water mingled with trailing plants, exotic blossoms, and unusual birds to create an enthralling scene. Liao, however, barely noticed it.

He was thinking hard, mentally organizing the sequence of events he was now committed to carrying out. Hearing a step behind him, he turned to see Colonel Pavel Ridzik enter the room. A gruff and grizzled veteran of more than thirty years of 'Mech wars, Ridzik had served as de facto supreme commander ever since Liao's rise to power.

"Well, Pavel, what word from the front?"

"It is no longer a battlefront, my Lord," the red-bearded Ridzik replied. "We hold Stein's Folly. Not securely, but it is now pacified, except for a few scattered mopping-up operations."

"And our...other arrangements?"

"In hand. We will, I believe, stand a very good chance of catching Davion off-balance. If we can carry out the plan effectively, you will be several steps nearer your goal. How does it sound to you...First Lord of the Star League?" Even when he smiled, Ridzik looked menacing.

"If we can gain an ally in the enemy camp, we may shorten the process by a good deal. How are you coming with that?" asked Liao. "Have you sent agents out among the worlds controlled by Davion's brother-in-law, yet? Someone, somewhere, should be willing to sell out, in exchange for money and influence."

"That is also in hand. We have made some connections. Potentially valuable ones. But it takes time, and time is now at a premium."

"Yes." Liao's expression was stern, hard. "Now we are involved with the most exquisite timing. We must estimate

59

precisely the arrival of the Davion contingent. There is no doubt, I suppose, that he will counterattack?"

"None whatever. He has to, or else lose all credibility. And that is the one thing that has made him so solidly in control of the Federated Suns. He cannot afford to compromise it."

Ridzik moved to the side wall of the big chamber and drew down a map. "Our spies inform us that Davion's troops are moving into position. A brigade has jumped from Ral to Hamlin and even now is awaiting recharge for its jump to Dragon's Field. Another large detachment of 'Mech units and infantry has already landed at Dragon's Field. They await the arrival of the rest of the force, as well as the headquarters group."

He tapped his long, bony finger on the map. "We have excellent intelligence capacity, which is what allowed us to take Stein's Folly and Redfield. The element of surprise is always valuable, and we used it well. Once Redfield had fallen, there was no way for Michael Hasek-Davion to hold onto Stein's Folly."

The Colonel paused and turned to look at his ruler. "After all, Michael is a weak man, with great ambitions. Certainly not one to be trusted with defense of a vulnerable border."

Liao frowned. "Will Hanse Davion accompany his commanders?" he asked. "That might be...convenient."

"His Councillors will never allow it. He may well come to one of the adjacent worlds, in order to be within easier logistical distance of the conflict. But no, he will not approach Stein's Folly or Dragon's Field. Not if his ministers have any judgment at all."

"A pity. It would be fine to remove all our obstacles in one sweeping motion. But let us do what we can with what we have."

Ridzik tapped the map again. "McCarron's Cavalry is in place, and detachments of the occupation units have now joined them, ready to strike. When Davion's main body arrives at Stein's Folly, there will be a terrible surprise waiting."

Liao laughed humorlessly. "Terrible for them. With one stroke, we will wipe out the cream of Davion's forces, along with the best of his commanders. But there will still remain the man himself. Along with his webwork of treacherous treaties and unwritten understandings with other spheres of influence."

"We are trying to find some leverage," Ridzik said. "Intelligence informs me that they are making every effort to find someone suitable for use as a hostage. Davion's family, unfortunately, is too well guarded."

"No lovers?" Liao's tone was sharp.

"Oh, lovers, yes. But none who could be used to alter his policies. He chooses well, that one. His women are all loyal, not only to him but to what he stands for. They would die before letting themselves be used to damage the Federated Suns."

Liao chuckled. "Admirable. If true. What of male lovers? Sometimes that can be a less...sentimental... relationship."

Ridzik sighed. "Only one close friend. Not a lover— from what we can discover—but a friend from youth. One Ardan Sortek."

"Sortek...I know his father. A hardheaded old fool, indeed. Full of talk about honor. No, he would not be a lover...but he might well be a lever. A childhood friend can be dearer than a mere partner in fleshly concerns." Liao looked thoughtful.

"Sortek is on New Avalon," Ridzik continued, "in the Royal Brigade. A unit-commander. Hanse will never let him out of his sight, I fear. But we might keep our spies alert for anything that changes concerning him."

"It pays never to ignore any opportunity, no matter how seemingly remote." Liao said. "See to it. And send me the breakdowns on the units we have deployed. I want to be able to chart everything as the reports come in. You may go."

When Ridzik had bowed his way from the room, the Chancellor of the Capellan Federation stood for a long while at the map. He seemed to be measuring distances from world to world, from Sian to New Avalon. He traced the lines demarcating the borders of the five Successor Houses. To be Supreme Lord of them all....He sighed.

When the requested information came, he bent over the wide table serving as his desk, soon lost in the intricacies of supply and manpower. Only the arrival of an Adept from Comstar brought him out of his concentration.

"A message from Stein's Folly, Highness," the girl whispered. She was very young, and so shy that she hardly dared raise her voice to audible levels.

"Well? Well? Out with it!" Liao snapped. His patience, never notable, seemed to have worn thin within the past months, while his plans ripened.

"Command on the planet reports guerrilla activity. Severe damage to headquarters, resulting in forty casualties, among them Commander Rav Xiang. Request immediate assignment of new commander or brevet-promotion of subcommander Sten Ciu."

Liao jerked upright in his swivel chair. "What?" His sallow skin was suddenly flushed, his pale eyes blazing. "What else?" His tone was deadly.

The girl seemed on the verge of fainting as she continued. "Detachments remaining on Stein's Folly on search-and-destroy missions have reported no success in locating the source of the guerrilla activity. The swamps and the dense forests are natural hiding places for small groups of hostiles."

"The 'Mechs—what about the 'Mechs? They should be able to stalk right through such terrain!"

"Six 'Mechs lost to quicksand, together with their pilots. The other two were lost, but their MechWarriors escaped. There seems to be no way to retrieve the lost equipment, as concentration of enough men and machinery to extricate them attracts hit-and-run attacks."

Liao was now a dangerous color. "Get Ridzik!" he breathed.

The Adept bowed and scurried from the room, relief showing in every movement. In a moment, the Colonel tramped into the chamber and stood staring down at his seated ruler.

"Sir?" he asked.

"Only minor mopping-up! That *is* what you said, isn't it?" Liao demanded.

"It is. That is the information given to me on the state of affairs. It seems that our commander was in error." The soldier hadn't turned a hair before Liao's obvious wrath.

"Well, his error was a fatal one. He is now dead. You will go and take his place, and will take charge personally of springing the trap on Davion."

Ridzik looked pained. "With this most important maneuver in the process of completion, would it be wise for me to drop everything here?"

Liao seemed to swell, his small figure straightening in the chair. "You will do as I say. And you will not question my orders. There is more to this than a simple group of holdouts. I am certain of it. Find the leader. Bring him to me. We will have the truth out of him and know with certainty whether anything more than loyalty to a lost cause is at work there." He glared up at Ridzik.

"I can arrange the surprise attack quite well, as you know, Colonel. You take too much responsibility upon yourself these days. A change of scene will be good for your...health." He was almost purring.

Ridzik, who had been unmoved by Liao's anger, now seemed visibly shaken by the man's present mood. The Chancellor was most dangerous when he seemed calm and concerned with his subordinates' health.

"We have weeks yet to complete our strategy and to make ready. Our people are in place a single jump from their goal. We have not the logistical problem Davion faces. Eight jumps from New Avalon to Stein's Folly—a time-consuming matter for his commanders. The rest of his people can do nothing but wait for recharges of their JumpShips as they leap from world to world, toward their goal."

He smiled.

Ridzik shuddered.

"You will go to Stein's Folly by way of my personal jump sequence. I want to know what is going on there... How a handful of holdouts can disrupt command quarters and kill one of my best people. You will be back at Sian by the time you are needed, Ridzik."

The Colonel saluted formally. "Sir!" he said quietly. He knew when to obey his volatile Duke without question. This was one of those times.

As the Colonel left the chamber, Liao stared hard at his retreating back. Even Ridzik...even Ridzik could not be entrusted with too much power, too much knowledge of the intricate machinations of the Prefect of Sian.

He looked down at his own hands, clenched into fists on the table. He prided himself on the fact that the left one seldom knew what the right one was doing.

It was the secret of his success.

8

It had been a difficult period for Ardan as he worked with his Techs, readying the *Victor* for transport. He had supervised the loading of the bulky mechanisms into the DropShip, along with the necessary parts, supplies, and weapons for the troops accompanying the command on its swift journey to the port at Dragon's Field.

He dreaded the trip. Jump always affected his inner ear, making him nervous and irritable even when there were long layovers for recharging. To go through on the Command Circuit was something he dreaded even more, because the jumps occurred without the usual layovers in between. His trips with Hanse to the Summer Palace had always left him drained.

As the time for departure drew near, he kept putting off his farewell to his family. Adriaan Sortek was made of rock, his son sometimes thought, but his mother, Vela, tended to dissolve into tears whenever her son went into battle.

Three days before his date of departure, Ardan finally made the short trip to their modest villa. Though dreading the scene that must follow, he knew that duty demanded this farewell. If he should not return, his parents would suffer if they had not seen him one last time.

He found Adriaan stripped to the waist, supervising the loading of grain from the fields behind the villa. The old soldier had not taken kindly to retirement. Inactivity would kill him more quickly than a laser, he had always maintained. So the elder Sortek had gone into farming with the same fervor he had applied to his military career.

As a result, his fields produced twice as much grain, his vineyards twice as many grapes, his trees twice as much fruit as those of any of his dilettante neighbors. For most of the local gentry, the farms in the countryside around the

65

city were dedicated more to the amusement of the wealthy than the production of food.

Only his long service and the friendship of his son with the ruler had allowed Adriaan to situate himself and his family in such a wealthy neighborhood. However, he oversaw every step of the work, from the preparation of the fields in the planting season to the gathering at harvest time.

Covered with dust and sweat, he stepped down from a grain-bin as Ardan approached on foot through the orchard.

"Well," said the older man. "You are going back to active duty, I hear."

Ardan swallowed hard. "The Brigade isn't exactly inactive," he murmured.

His father slapped him on the shoulder. "You know what I mean. Drilling without killing just doesn't accomplish all that much when it comes to keeping your skills intact. You have to draw blood to be a soldier."

Ardan had a swift interior vision of the child in the dust, but he swallowed again, and used sheer will to turn his thoughts away from that image.

"Well, I'll be back into it soon enough; we leave day after tomorrow. Hanse has all the timing worked out. I wouldn't say this to anyone else but you, but we should arrive on Dragon's Field a few hours after the last of the detachments from Ral and Hamlin. We will all jump together then, and when our DropShips land, we'll hit Stein's Folly from a number of directions, all at once. He has some air support arranged, too, which should help distract the Liao forces from our advance." His father nodded approval, and might have asked a question or two if Vela Sortek had not come out to meet them as they strolled toward the low, comfortable-looking house. Ardan waved at his mother.

"Dan! Come, let me hug you! My soul, you have grown up to be a fine-looking man. I simply cannot think why you don't find a nice girl and provide us with some grandchildren!"

He laughed affectionately at this familiar refrain, and bent to hug her tightly. Vela was still sturdy and square, her smock smelling of fresh-baked bread, sachet, and the soil of her kitchen-garden. She was a fanatic about cooking only freshly harvested vegetables. Her servants were used to her close supervision, and, unlike those of more detached mistresses, bore with her instructions patiently.

"I have a specially good meal planned for this evening, but if I'd known you were coming, I'd have invited Listessa," she said.

When Ardan looked almost as bored as he always felt when in the company of their nearest neighbor's loquacious daughter, Vela Sortek sighed with resignation. She pinched his sleeve between two fingers and shook the cloth impatiently.

"I simply do not know how you expect the race to continue when you youngsters go off on your noisy machines and leave all the girls who aren't warriors to their own devices. Where you think grandchildren are going to come from, I do not know!" She looked up at him, her round cheeks flushed beneath their tan.

"What about Felsa? She married, right enough. Her child, if and when she has one, will be just as much a grandchild as mine would be." He grinned secretly, knowing his mother watched his sister's waistline with as much attention as he paid to an approaching enemy 'Mech. So far, though, Felsa had remained as slim and lissome as ever.

His father grunted. "Six months," he said. "In just six months, your mother will get off your back. She'll have her precious grandchild and, if the Divine is merciful, we'll hear no more about it." He sounded gruff and careless but when Ardan looked around at Adriaan, the ex-soldier was beaming helplessly.

They went together into the house, where they were soon joined for supper by Felsa and her man. When the meal was done and cleared away, Ardan and his sister reminisced about old times when she had trained as a MechWarrior with her older brother.

67

Felsa had been injured when her 'Mech's shielding failed during a fire-test, and for a long while, it looked as though she might have been blinded. When Felsa's vision did return, her mother had demanded that she leave the training.

She had not really minded, no longer being physically fit for the grueling training, much less for combat. She had soon married her Mak, whose neighboring parents had also favored the match.

Brother and sister still could talk shop, however. Felsa was eternally interested in new battle techniques being devised. "How are the 'Mechs holding up?" she asked, as they sat in the soft twilight of the terrace.

"Fairly well," Ardan said with a shrug. "Battles don't help, of course, but the Techs keep scrounging parts, combining 'Mechs that have had severe damage. We do need to redevelop the necessary technologies," he replied.

"Hanse Davion must be attempting that very thing," Adriaan said. "I hear that NAIS is working hard to relearn the old techniques and to develop fresh ones suitable for our needs."

He reached to take his wife's hand. "It occurs to me that this latest attack by the Capellans may have been motivated by the fear that we would succeed in all that. After all, their weaponry and systems, like everyone else's, are wearing out and being lost from year to year."

Ardan nodded in the growing dark. "That's a possibility, but there are probably many reasons. One of which is the fact that Hanse has persisted in meddling in the affairs of other Houses."

Adriaan moved irritably. He and his son had had many arguments over this very issue. The old soldier knew what happened when weak rulers didn't know how and when to apply pressure. He had tried to make Ardan see the realities, but their two heads were equally hard.

"Time will teach you, I fear," he said. "Time and the battles to come." Adriaan sighed then, and shrugged. "It's true that the young cannot wear the heads of the old."

Ardan rose from his comfortable chair. One of New Avalon's moons was rising, filling the fields and gardens with tenuous light.

"I must go. Another hard day tomorrow when we get a battery of medical checkups and shots. I likely won't be able to come again before liftoff."

He heard his mother make a soft, despairing sound. He turned and kissed her cheek. "You take care of this old man. Make him be careful...just a little. I'd like to see the old coot again."

Felsa rose to give him a parting hug. "You take care, yourself," she said. "And when you come back, you will probably be an uncle. That should give you some incentive!"

He laughed. "It will, I'm sure. Goodbye Felsa...Mak. Goodbye all!" Ardan called, as he turned and went down the steps of the terrace to the path. This footway led along a stream into the city. An hour's walk would see him back in the ready-barracks. He needed the time alone.

Walking away, he knew that his mother was probably weeping softly now, his father stroking her hand helplessly. Felsa would be watching him go, holding tightly to Mak's hand and being grateful that her man was a farmer, not a soldier.

But he was glad. Glad to be leaving the ease of this secure world. He had grown soft, lazy. It was time for him to get back into harness. His father, as much as he hated to admit it, was right.

Drilling without killing didn't do the job. In combat with men who were armored and weaponed as he was, Ardan was in his element, his adrenals charged to their fullest extent, his mind racing like a computer, commanding his huge brute of a mechanism to do impossible things...three at a time.

In the distance, from the shadowy bulk of a house beside the stream, there came the cry of a child.

Ardan stopped. He stared down into the star-speckled water. Ripples made the points of light dance across the stream before breaking among the reeds at the edges.

There was another side to battle, one he had not admitted to himself before that terrible day that hung in his memory like a ghost or a demon. He shook himself, however, and hurried on, knowing he must force his mind to remain focused on the necessary aspects of war.

Not just one child would suffer if the Liao forces took over the worlds of the Federated Suns. All the children of all the people would starve, would be enslaved from the cradle upward. He knew the policies of Maximilian Liao as well as anyone.

The wily Chancellor of the Capellan Confederation had only one purpose for people—to use them. If they did not serve his needs, he discarded them like so many lifeless pawns in a game. And by that time, many were, indeed, without life.

For a moment, Ardan was intensely grateful that he had not given his mother the grandchild she craved. He felt a momentary pang, thinking of Felsa's expected infant. What would come to it, in its lifetime, if the advance of Liao were not stopped now?

Of course, he knew that it would not be totally stopped. No more than had Hanse's depredations into Capellan space. There seemed no end to the back-and-forth exercise.

Politics. It all boiled down to politics, the control of men and machines by other men and machines. He hated the word now, was growing to hate it more every day of his life.

He sometimes felt as if his brain would foam up like the batter for the bread his mother had the cook make so often, running over the edges of his skull, rising and expanding and exploding. But he shook himself again.

What was the matter with him?

The cry of the child came after him through the soft, warm night. He saw, behind his eyes, that other child…and began to run up the path toward the barracks.

9

The jumps were as nasty as Ardan recalled them. He was dizzy and disoriented as the DropShip travelled from Jump-Ship to JumpShip, docking onto a fresh vessel without the long wait for recharging necessary for less-favored groups. Though a JumpShip normally needed a week to recharge before it could make its next jump, the Command Circuit used a relay system of ready-charged ships waiting at each jump point between worlds. Because it was so expensive to maintain, the Command Circuit was reserved for only the most high-priority uses.

There was no need to consult with Felsner or Hamman. All possible advance planning had been done. Details checked, rechecked, chewed to rags by the officers and by Hanse. Only the totally unforeseen could disrupt their counteroffensive, he decided.

Their arrival on Dragon's Field was a relief. Here was a busy port where the Davion DropShips would await the final sortie taking their attack force to attempt the reconquest of Stein's Folly.

Disembarking from the DropShip, Ardan was relieved to leave behind the disorientation he experienced from jump. He envied his fellows, few of whom seemed to suffer a similar distress. He steered his way around Techs arguing over the disposition of their own particular charges, Lance members disputing who had lost at the last game of chance, and officers quarreling over who was in charge of what.

It was a staging area like so many others he had seen. As a prelude to battle, he found them almost comical. A detached observer would, he thought, have written music and depicted such a scene as a comic opera. The revival of the old art would suit perfectly this conglomeration of the ridiculous and the serious.

Ardan went into the first mess hall he came to. "I don't jump well," he told the harried cook. "Do you have some soup? Or anything else that might settle my stomach?"

The man sighed, wiped sweat onto his forearm. "I've fed eight thousand men since sun-up, Colonel," he said wearily. "You just cannot believe what it's like. Not one... not...one...single...one...liked the food I gave him. And it's the best the Duke can provide. I've never cooked better. Ungrateful ..." his voice trailed off. Ardan noticed that the man's eyes were a bit glazed.

"I guarantee that if you have anything at all that is rather bland and smooth and won't upset a queasy stomach, I will appreciate it heartily and thank you from my soul," he said.

The cook sighed and turned to a huge boiler. "This should do it. Soup's always good for such problems. Here ..." He dolloped a ladleful into a thick bowl. Turning to set it on the counter beside Ardan, he scooped up a handful of crisp strips of bread. "There. Hope it helps."

Ardan smiled his thanks and took the bowl to a table in the corner, where he sat with his back to the wall. Somehow, before a battle, that was most comfortable for him. As he ate, slowly and with care, he felt his knotted insides relax.

He knew very soon why the newcomers had disliked their food. Both the soup and the bread were flavored with a rather strong, unfamiliar spice. It took some getting used to, but he found himself liking the taste. Probably a condiment rare and wonderful to the people of Dragon's Field, which they hoped would help make the planetfall pleasant for the warriors about to go into battle.

"Very fine soup!" he called to the cook. The man smiled, looking surprised.

"What is the seasoning? I find it interesting."

"Shad-seed. Our best. I'm happy you like it." He turned to serve three more men who had arrived as they spoke.

Ardan soaked his bread strips in the last of the soup and spooned them into his mouth slowly. He would make it

72

now. When they took off for Stein's Folly, he would be too charged-up to worry about his stomach. When he was in battle-mode, nothing physical, other than something life-threatening, could make itself felt.

"Mind if we join you?" He looked up to see Felsner and Hamman standing with laden trays beside his table.

"Please do. Here, let me move over." Ardan scooted himself and his empty bowl around a bit farther, letting the other two also sit with their backs to the walls. He knew they would want to.

"It looks fairly good at this point," Hamman said, setting an electronic notepad on the table and swinging one leg after the other across the narrow bench. "What do you think?"

Ardan frowned. "I can't see anything wrong. But something keeps bothering me about it all."

Ran Felsner grinned. "Your stomach always bothers you after a jump."

"True enough, but now that I have that under control"—he gestured at the bowl—"something *still* worries me."

Hamman and Felsner exchanged glances. "Well...what?" Hamman asked.

Ardan studied the backs of his hands for a long moment before speaking. "Look...just how flexible is our battle plan?" His eyes locked with Felsner's. "I mean, how easily could we change the plan, even now?"

"Just what did you have in mind?" Hamman asked. "I mean, it's a bit late in the day for..."

Ardan reached across the table and took Hamman's E-pad. He touched keys, clearing a berthing manifest from the screen and bringing up the sketch function. Hamman plucked a stylus from a sleeve pocket and handed it to Ardan without a word. Ardan sketched rapidly across the surface of the pad's screen, leaving a tracery of green lines on black.

"Here...this is part of North continent on Stein's Folly. Steindown is here, on the Highland Peninsula...right?" The other men nodded. "Now, Steindown was the first settlement on Stein's Folly—probably because it was the

73

only dry land the poor guy found first time he touched down." The others chuckled as Ardan kept sketching. "The peninsula is rugged and mountainous on its east coast and comes down to a narrow little isthmus just...here. This strip is—oh, maybe—fifty klicks at its widest. Folly's Neck, it's called. North of the peninsula is this big basin. The Ordolo River meanders south from the Yaeger Mountains, and this whole, vast bowl between these mountains here, and these over here, all the way north to the equator is one enormous, God-forsaken swamp—jungle, bogs, marsh, and a chain of minor seas they call "Lost Lakes"—probably because the mapmakers can never decide where to put 'em. During the wet season, most of the lakes run together, and it's hard to keep track of shorelines.

"Along here are other settlements. As the colony grew, way back when, you can see how settlements must have sprung up along the coast...here, at Lollan, Travis, Grebuchin, and over here at Harbor. There are other spaceports on the Folly, of course, but the one just south of Steindown is the main one. That's where the freighter DropShips call, mostly, and where most offworld trading takes place."

"You seem to know a hell of a lot about this swamp, Ardan," Hamman said.

"Like I said, I've been worrying, and that made me find out what I could." He shrugged. "It increases the efficiency of my worrying. O.K....like I said, Steindown is the trading center, offworld center, planet capital, call it what you want. The city has a population of, maybe, five hundred thousand."

"So? We'll be fighting Liao troops, not local troops."

"The point is, where do half a million people get their food from?"

"Eh?" Both men looked again at the sketch, as though searching for the answer.

"Steindown has a fair-sized fishing industry of its own, but the peninsula, except for Steindown and the plains to the east, is steep and rocky, very poor for farming. Up here

74

is the Ordolo Basin and the swamps. No...these communities out along the coastline, Lollan and Travis especially, are farming centers. See? The land is open here—rolling prairie and grassland, with rich, black soil washed down from the mountains. The Coast Road runs along here, from Harbor to Grebuchin, Grebuchin to Lollan, Lollan to Travis. Then it cuts through a pass in the mountains—right here, called Jordan's Pass—then south across Folly's Neck and down the peninsula's west coast, to Steindown. Nearly all of the capital's food comes to them by the road net, from the farms and plantations along the mainland coast off to the east."

Ran Felsner nodded slowly. "I think I follow you."

"I hope so, because things get fuzzy now. So...fleet orders call for the usual approach: secure the jump points, engage the enemy space defenses, gain space superiority. They'll send up their fighters, and we'll knock them down."

"That'll take some knocking," Hamman said, rubbing his chin. "From what ComInt says, our fighters took a pounding when the Liao strike force first moved in."

"Agreed. But if we don't win the space approaches, the whole campaign is lost anyway, right?" The other two gave assent with chorused grunts. "Next come the landings. Tactical doctrine would call for heavy air-space strikes against major ground installations, especially the spaceports, followed by 'Mech landings in force." He changed colors on the pad and circled the coast cities in red. "Here—here—here—'Mech landings right along the coast. But the main landings"—his stylus swooped a triple circle around Steindown—"have to be made here. Smack dab in and around the city and the port."

"Well, yes," Felsner said slowly. "That'll be where Liao has most of his forces, at the capital. We'll have to engage them."

"Why?"

"Eh?"

"Why...when we control their food supply? Look... Travis and Lollan both have spaceports. We secure those for

75

our supply pipelines. We grab these other cities and garrison them...and put our main force down here." The stylus circled the isthmus called Folly's Neck. "I'm willing to bet that this pass could be held by a company or two, and a battalion could hold the isthmus clear down the spine of the east coastal mountains here and hem Steindown in. We pour in lots of air cover to keep their air-space fighters grounded, and to make sure they don't use boats or hovercraft to supply themselves by sea." He dropped the stylus with a small clatter on the table. "No city holds enough food reserves to last more than three...maybe four days. After that, things get grim."

"It'll be hard on the civilians," Hamman said.

Ardan nodded. "War always is, Lees. So would having us drop right on top of them to fight it out with the Capellan 'Mechs in the streets. As it is"—he shrugged, sadly—"maybe they'll pitch in and help when the food runs out. Throw open the gates, so to speak. The Liao garrison will have to know that it won't be able to hold out long when half a million of their new subjects suddenly get hungry—and mean."

The three men studied the electronic pad's screen a moment. Felsner nodded. "Y'know, there's another thing about all this. I've been worried, too, ever since the first planning session for this show. That peninsula gives me the willies, y'know? Like it's got T-R-A-P written all over it."

"You mean the Liao forces could be planning to do the same thing to us that we've been talking about doing to them?" Ardan asked. "Let us take Steindown, while they hold the isthmus and mountains?" The same thought had been grumbling at Ardan since he'd started rethinking the Davion strategy.

"Uh huh. I couldn't put it into words until you sketched out your plan there...but Maximilian Liao *has* to know Hanse Davion's going to try to take back the Folly! What's the point in his taking it away from us in the first place... unless he's got something special in mind for us when we

76

return? Something that would tie down a huge chunk of the Federated Suns' ships and 'Mechs and men? Maybe something that would trap them on that peninsula where Liao's 'Mechs could slowly close in and crush them..."

Ardan studied his map a moment more. He picked up the stylus again, cleared the red circle from the Folly's Neck, and began marking the isthmus with neat, precise points of light. "We'll need to go over this again on a real map, but look here. If the Capellan forces *are* already here, they'd hold this ridge from here...to here, right?"

The others nodded. "They'd have to," Felsner said. "High ground, good cover. And if we land anywhere on the plains around Steindown, they have us ringed in."

"So they would. Watch. First we put a diversionary force down here..." He tapped the rugged plain between Steindown and the mountains. "If it's not a trap, they move into position in the mountains and watch Steindown. If it is a trap..."

"And it is," Felsner interrupted. His face was showing excitement now. "It is, for all the stars in space!"

"If it is a trap, the enemy will be along these heights, and they'll be watching the show on the plains below them," Ardan went on, excited, too. "Now, look here." The stylus tapped the southeastern edge of the Ordolo Basin. "Our *main* force sets down here...and here. The bad guys hold Jordan's Pass, but we hold the road on both sides and we can come south along both flanks of this ridge, one on this side, one on that side. If we move fast, we control the pass, this section of the ridge, and the road. A push down the road, and we link up with our diversionary force. The Liao forces in the mountains will be stuck here, with the sea at their backs, and us closing in from the front and their flank! If it turns out that they have heavy forces in the mountains and in Steindown, we withdraw north through the pass and seal off the whole damned peninsula. Our air patrols crack down, and we wait 'em out. If we're lucky, they'll get desperate and storm our position along the pass."

77

Ardan looked up from his notations on the pad. "That would settle things quite nicely, I think."

"The trappers are trapped!" Hamman said. "By God, Ardan, we'd have them cold!"

Ardan nodded. A vast weight had lifted as he'd discussed his doubts with these men, and now a definite plan was forming in his mind. "I think so. I really do think so. Now the question is, can we change the strike force operational orders now, at the last minute?"

Ran Felsner was still studying the map. "It'll be no trouble to change the drop pattern. We can brief the battalion commanders, and post new objectives and rendezvous points easily enough. Admiral Bertholi won't like reassigning the DZs, but I can handle him. Victor DeVries, my Operations Chief, will give me a hard time. My biggest concern is dropping at the edge of that jungle, though. That ground could be mighty soft."

"It is," Ardan said, "in the wet season. But it's well into the dry season now. Based on the tapes I scanned, I'd say the area is more savannah and grassland than jungle. It gets lots of rain during the local winter, but in summer it's bone dry."

"I've known planetological tapes to be wrong," Hamman said.

"So? You want to drop in first and check it out yourself?"

"Ha! Not likely. Just so long as it's not an actual swamp, we'll be O.K. Even DropShips could set down along the road. We'll leave that to the section tactical leaders."

Felsner nodded. "It'll be worth it for another reason, too."

"What's that?" Hamman asked.

"Well, there's bound to be one hell of a tangle, with units not getting their DZs confirmed. Hell, just finding a specific drop zone will be next to impossible because they won't have something easy to orient on from the air, like the city. And maybe some of them land in a swamp and don't come out, or hit a ridgetop hard and smear their 'Mechs across the face of a mountain. But it'll be worth it."

"I don't follow you," Hamman said.

"You're thinking of a leak," Ardan said.

Felsner nodded again. "Such things have been known to happen. Even with slow intersystem communications, even with everything secured and guarded and security-cleared half to death, leaks happen."

"Liao wasn't born yesterday," Hamman said. "Like you said, this has all the earmarks of a trap. He could have planned it all this way, or..."

"Or," Felsner continued, "he's set things up this way because of information he's been picking up from...from within our own camp."

Ardan shook his head. He didn't like thinking about these possible wheels within wheels within wheels. "He could have set this up without help from his spies," he said. "I've studied Maximilian Liao for so long, it feels like I know the guy personally. I only met him once, one time when Hanse took me with the Guard to a big conference in the Lyran Commonwealth."

He paused, looking from Ran to Lees, and back again. "You know, Liao would execute any officer who changed a battle plan he'd approved—have him shot on the spot—even if the new plan worked better than the original. I don't think the man could even imagine a group of officers rewriting an entire battle plan without first getting permission from the top."

Felsner took a thoughtful bite of his neglected food, chewed slowly, swallowed. "That's what appeals to me about this. We *have* to do the unexpected. If we don't, we're going to find ourselves up to our chins in Capellan BattleMechs. They *know* we're coming. We *have* to come, and they'll be ready and waiting. But if we set down where they *don't* expect us, well...it just might give us the edge we need."

"Well, you gentlemen had better eat up," Ardan said. He tapped the E-pad's sceen. "We have to do some talking with the battalion strike commanders, don't we?"

Hamman looked thoughtful. "We've got to get a message back to the Prince, too. At this point, even if the message were intercepted, the news wouldn't get to Stein's Folly ahead of us. And then there's also Michael..."

"Michael?"

"Michael Hasek-Davion," Hamman said. "Hanse's brother-in-law."

"Oh...right." Ardan knew the Duke of New Syrtis, of course. He was ruler of the sector, and so military operations had to be cleared through him even when he had no direct jurisdiction over them. As a matter of courtesy, they would have to inform him of the changes in the operation. The man had always struck Ardan as being pretentious and officious, but formal court etiquette and proper military discipline both required that they advise the Duke of the new plan.

It took them the better part of the afternoon to discuss the proposed changes in the drop zones with their own commands. Fleet Admiral Bertholi, charged with delivering the strike force to Stein's Folly, voiced the most stubborn protests, because he would have to pass on the extensive changes and recalculations in the approach vectors and navigational sightings to every DropShip in his command. Strangely, the one man they *had* to convince, Ran Felsner's Chief of Operations, General Victor DeVries, accepted the proposed change the moment they presented it.

"You're right," the grizzled Davion veteran said. "I was beginning to have the same doubts myself. When four pros all trip over the same instinct, maybe it's time to pay attention, eh?"

Through DeVries' official channels, then, they assembled and transmitted the plan revisions throughout the strike force. Bertholi protested until Felsner threatened to have him replaced on the spot, then pitched in and began going over the necessary navigational changes with his approach team himself.

The new plan took shape in the bowels of the HQ combat computers and in the far more important computers in the minds of the command staff. To Lees Hamman and the Capellan March Militia would fall the task of diverting the enemy's forces into believing a major landing was developing on the plains above Steindown. Ran Felsner and his 5th Crucis Lancers would come down along the road north and east of the critical gap called Jordan's Pass, while Ardan's 17th Avalon Hussars would land further west, along the fringe of the Ordolo Basin and west of the ridge. Detached battalions from the 5th Lancers and 17th Hussars would secure the coastal towns and spaceports as far east as Harbor, while the ground armor and heavy vehicles would be offloaded at the spaceport north of Travis as soon as it was secured, to operate as a mobile reserve.

There would be other Liao strongpoints, of course. Thelan and Maris were a pair of large tropical islands (or small island continents, depending on one's point of view) lying south of the Highland Peninsula, and both had several large cities. At the antipodes was Talliferro, a small continent that had a large mining settlement and commercial spaceport. All of these would have to be secured sooner or later, but with planetary invasions, first came first. The heaviest concentration of Liao firepower would be on the Highland Peninsula, and it was there that the crucial battle would take place.

Meanwhile, Ardan, Felsner, and Hamman were received with cool courtesy at the Hasek-Davion headquarters in an imposing mansion on a wooded hill above the spaceport. They passed through an ascending hierarchy of receptionists, functionaries, under-chiefs, chiefs, and executive chiefs of staff until at last they were ushered into the Green Room, where Michael Hasek-Davion burrowed his way through a sheaf of hardcopy printouts and official-looking documents. Ardan found himself wondering if they had been heaped there merely to impress them with the Duke's importance to this sector, as there could be no other reason for that inefficient paper mountain.

The Duke peered over his papers, frowning. "My people tell me your need for an audience was urgent," he said, without preamble. "What is it? I'm a busy man."

"Your Grace." Felsner gave the proper bow of one schooled by long experience at court. "It is indeed surprising to see someone of your rank place himself in the midst of such...confusion. I know well the amenities of New Syrtis. This outpost has few. Your Grace presents a refreshing departure from standard procedure."

Ardan grinned inside but kept his face a carefully neutral mask. He'd never known that Ran had such talents with the sweet oil of flattery.

The Duke's frown transformed into a smile, and he nodded graciously. "My duty calls me to many uncomfortable spots, it's true. But, when one's duty is the good of his people..." He spread his hands helplessly. "Well, what can I do for you, gentlemen?" Listening to him, Ardan realized that the Duke's own courtiers must be such sycophants that he no longer could distinguish the fake from the true.

"A formality only, Your Grace. We are bound to report to you, as the nearest representative of the Prince of the House of Davion and as the sector military commander, a change of plan in the counterinvasion of Stein's Folly. We..."

"What-what-what?" Hasek-Davion's sputter might have been the clicking of an empty autocannon. "Change? Change? What change?"

"We have reason to believe that our original plan, which called for a direct assault on Steindown, may be a trap. Our new plan calls for a landing along the Coast Road and at the fringe of the Ordolo Basin north of the Highland Peninsula. That will place us in the best possible position to..."

"Gentlemen." The Duke's momentary affability had vanished. His eyes were cold. "I do not believe that my brother-in-law makes a habit of having his plans ques-

82

tioned—changed!—by his subordinates! I happen to know how much thought went into these plans. I know. I was there! Every factor was considered—the terrain, the probable strength and disposition of the Liao forces, psychological factors, everything! What makes you three think you can rewrite all that planning"—his fingers snapped like a pistol shot—"just like that?"

"Your Grace," Felsner said calmly. "I regret that we have displeased you, but I must inform you that we have already made the decision—and implemented it. My orders from the Prince are quite specific in this. I am to keep Your Grace apprised of developments, to seek your council...but the interpretation and implementation of Prince Davion's plans are left to my discretion."

"Interpretation, yes. You puppy, this isn't interpretation. It's wholesale murder!"

"Your Grace?"

"You said that the Ordolo Swamp is your intended drop zone?"

"At the fringe of the swamp, yes, Your Grace. There are grasslands there, and..."

"That whole area is a quagmire, fool! Your 'Mechs will set down and keep going down—lost in the ooze, without a trace! A regiment could be swallowed up in there, just stepping out onto what they thought was solid ground! Or don't you realize just how heavy a BattleMech is?"

"Your Grace, I assure you..."

"You're doing nothing of the sort! Do you realize that your failure on Stein's Folly will reflect back on *me*, the supreme commander of this sector? I cannot approve such hairbrained idiocy." Michael seemed to struggle with himself. His face softened, but his eyes remained cold and hard. "Gentlemen. Such a change—and now, of all times!—is an open invitation to disaster. You are all military men! You must understand this! Think of the confusion! Think of the chaos if even one of your regiments flounders in the quicksand and mud of the Ordolo Swamps! That whole area is a death trap. Believe me, we considered all these things in the first stages of our own planning!

"It's true that I cannot command you on this. Why the Prince gave direct command to someone other than the supreme military commander of this sector is not for me to say...but I strongly—strongly!—recommend that you ad-here to the original plan! Prince Davion's plan had such brilliance! A lightning approach! A dashing strike from the sky at the Liao strongholds! A savage thrust to secure the planet's capital and principal port, followed by a wide-ranging sweep to secure the entire planet, leaving no pockets of resistance. No floundering in the swamps, no half-measures. That, gentlemen, is the mark of strategic military brilliance!"

"Your Grace..." Felsner paused. "Your Grace, certainly, we must consider what you have said most carefully..."

The Duke stood behind his desk, leaning on it heavily, his cold eyes level with Felsner's own. "Good. And consider this carefully, too. You have proven yourself a worthy, able officer. An error of this magnitude would most certainly have unfortunate repercussions on a most promising career. You would be...finished...done for. I...I speak as a friend, sir, and as an advisor."

Ran bowed again. "Your Grace is kind. We understand your position and appreciate your frankness. Believe me, Your Grace, we will carefully reconsider our position before commiting ourselves irrevocably."

"See that you do, sir. Good day."

Ardan was momentarily startled by Ran's sudden change of tactics. He had sounded so sincere that it wasn't until they were walking from the chamber and Ardan caught a wink from the Strike Force Commander that he realized that Felsner's last words had been an act.

"You old smoothie," he murmured, pitching his voice low so that only Ran could hear.

For answer, Felsner rolled his eyes toward the ornate and gold-trimmed ceiling. It was a relief to get into the fresh night air of Dragon's Field once more.

10

No soldier looks forward to a strike against a major city, because street-to-street combat can turn a skillfully defended urban area into a death trap. Nevertheless, when word trickled down the Davion line of command that the strike force would not be dropped into Steindown and the spaceport as originally planned, the troopers and Mech-Warriors greeted the news with complaints and grumbling instead of relief.

Soldiers are a superstitious lot, and have been ever since the first savage threw the first rock. They have an automatic tendency to suspect that the enigmatic and godlike decisions coming down from the remote High Command might somehow alter fate, putting a man *here*, directly in the path of an incoming round, instead of *there*, where he could have survived. After all, it was not usually the higher-ups who had to put their butts on the line. Even the veteran NCOs, who might have breathed a small sigh of relief that they would not be dropping directly into a hot strongpoint, could only shake their heads and curse the blind fumblings of Higher Authority. Why couldn't those brass-heavy paper pushers leave well enough alone, without stirring everything and everybody up?

But the changes were made. Admiral Bertholi reported that new navigational fixes had been recorded for three distinct peaks in the ridge around Jordan's Pass, and the drop zones could now be positively identified and homed on. Unit commanders down to individual lance commanders and platoon leaders reported that troop assignments had been re-set, new 'Mech assembly points positioned and confirmed, and primary targets reassigned. Contingency planning and logistical support evaluations were continuing, but these chores could be carried out aboard the DropShips. Within twenty hours of the visit by Ardan, Lees Hamman, and Ran Felsner to Duke Michael's field headquarters, the first DropShips carrying Felsner's 5th Crucis Lancers had already boosted from Dragon's Field and were hours outbound on their way to the system's nadir jump point.

Ran himself had remained behind to parry any possible official or bureaucratic delays Hasek-Davion might create because he was displeased. The Capellan March Militia were still ostensibly under the Duke's command even though they had been temporarily reassigned to Lees Hamman by Prince Davion himself. Though powerless to stop the invasion, the Duke of New Syrtis could find myriad ways to hamper the assembly and loading of his own troops. An order to loyal unit commanders simply to slow down the boarding process or to lose the clearance orders for a vital shipment of munitions could delay the unit's departure for days, even weeks.

Felsner's solution was equally simple, though risky. He made sure that Michael would not interfere with the new plan for the counterinvasion by solemnly informing the Duke that after all and after careful consideration, the Davion commanders had decided to stick with the old plan.

Ardan considered this strategy dangerous as well as dishonest, knowing that Hasek-Davion would be furious and humiliated when he finally learned that they had lied to him. Having an influential and powerful nobleman like the Duke of New Syrtis for an enemy was not going to be amusing. It was these wheels within wheels within wheels, rather than the prospect of battle, that was keeping Ardan awake at night.

But he was too busy to worry for long. Once his own unit was scheduled for loading, he found himself in a running, three-sided battle with the Dragon's Field Technical Officer and the Chief of Procurement.

A JM6 *JagerMech* in Company C, 1st Batallion of the 17th Avalon Hussars, died right on the landing field in the shadow of the *Union* DropShip it was preparing to board. An old, old fault in a leg servounit finally shorted an actuator circuit board too often patched instead of replaced.

The leg locked, freezing the 'Mech in place and blocking access to the DropShip's number one hold.

Though replacing a circuit board is not particularly difficult, the repair meant removing the *JagerMech*'s leg at the knee, a procedure that required a field repair gantry or a full maintenance facility, at least. The 17th's field gantries were already broken down and stored, and Procurement refused to provide a new circuit board unless the crippled 'Mech could be brought to the maintenance center some two hundred meters across the field. A request for a deployed field gantry was refused: why should that gear be broken out when maintenance blocks were open just across the field?

Unfortunately, the base Field Technical Services Division could spare no transports for the three hours' work needed to lower the 'Mech onto a flatbed crawler and carry it across to Maintenance. Proper authorization to redetail a transport and crew had to come from the base commandant, and he was at an official briefing with His Grace the Duke and would not be available until that evening—or possibly tomorrow. So sorry, they said, but we are really very busy and could you call back later? Or you might check with the Logistical Staff at Pallos, eighty klicks from here. They might have a transport, and if you could get authorization...

Meanwhile, the other three 'Mechs of the *JagerMech*'s lance were scheduled to board through the blocked hatch, and the entire loading schedule was falling behind. After two hours of fruitless tail-chasing, Ardan arrived at the only possible solution. He had the two heaviest of the waiting 'Mechs drag the crippled, sixty-five-ton JM6 across the field to the maintenance center and leave it there, laid carefully and squarely across the accessway leading to the building's underground VIP garage.

If the major in charge of the Technical Services Division wanted to get home for supper that evening, the 'Mech would have to be repaired that afternoon, transport or no transport.

It was, and loading proceeded almost on schedule.

As boost time approached, the scene became even more chaotic and hectic. The port facilities of Dragon's Field were a hive of activity focused on the squat shapes of the DropShips—*Union*s and *Overlord*s, mostly—resting in their blast pits surrounded by the lacelike traceries of loading gantries and crane supports. Somehow, hundreds of tons of food, water, munitions, and spare parts had to be directed from storehouses around the planet to the proper ship at the proper time.

The physics of mass and mass distribution were unforgiving of the schedules and problems of ship supply officers. If each ton of supplies was not positioned precisely, the ship would not respond as expected when the captain later tried to cut in a control jet to vector clear of incoming missiles or to maneuver through a turbulent atmosphere. Worse, if those tons of supplies were not stored in the proper order, ground troops queuing up to draw ammo might be told that their supplies lay somewhere on the far side of 400 tons of dried meat and a case of *JagerMech* leg actuator circuits.

Finally, after three days of grueling work, the last 'Mech was somehow winched into its transport niche and locked down, the last liter of reaction mass had been pumped into tanks and the hollow, partitioned spaces between bulkheads and decks, and the last squad of infantry had filed aboard and found the narrow, padded ledges that would be their homes for the next several days. Lees had departed the day before with the Capellan March Militia. With the threat of official delay from the Duke's office removed, Ran boosted to rejoin his unit hours later.

Ardan was left to send the final messages required by protocol and formal etiquette—one to Michael Hasek-Davion stating that the original battle plan had, after all and after much careful consideration, been changed; and another that went by diplomatic paths to Hanse Davion himself, explaining the change and describing the friction generated between the strike force command staff and the Duke of

New Syrtis. Ardan had composed this last with some measure of relief. Let Hanse deal with his brother-in-law, he thought. From now on, I'll just have to worry about Liao BattleMechs!

Messages transmitted, Ardan stepped aboard the *Union* Class DropShip *Exeter* and stared for a last time across the nearly deserted plain that was Dragon's Field's largest port facility. Most of the ships had already boosted, and the only humans visible were isolated groups clustered here and there trying to assess the blast damage caused by the departing DropShips. Trash and debris—paper by the ton, discarded equipment cases and cargo crates, the scattered refuse of ten thousand men, the skeletal frameworks of partly dismantled cranes and gantries—littered the field, creating a haunting image of loneliness and desolation.

Dragon's Field was the inner world of an M0 dwarf. The laws of Kearny-Fuchida drive dictated that the star's two jump points would be seven-tenths of an astronomical unit out, the zenith point above the star's north pole, the nadir point above its south pole. At a constant 1 G boost, with time out for a mid-course flip, the trip from world to jump point would take thirty hours.

With an effort, Ardan shook the lingering depression from his thoughts, turned, and boarded the *Exeter*. Twenty minutes later, the DropShip rose into the sky atop a flaring pillar of fusion-heated plasma.

11

The *Exeter'*s pilot made his final approach to the gathered fleet with care. The station plasma streams that balanced the JumpShips against the incessant tug of the red star 105 million kilometers below would kill if they swept across the unshielded hull of a DropShip at close range, and the *Exeter'*s own bursts of high-speed plasma from her maneuvering thrusters would shred the delicate black fabric of a jump sail if her course came too close to one. The DropShip's target was the elongated form of the *StarLord* Class starship *Sword of Davion*, needle-sleek when seen from afar, a bewildering complexity of angles, bulges, turrets, antennae, guy struts, and braces when seen up close. Brackets aft of the JumpShip's cargo holds provided mounts for five *Union* Class DropShips. A sixth bracket ring and open grapples invited the *Exeter* into a berth alongside the others. There was a tense moment of delicate maneuver, the firing and capture of a magnetic cable across the tens of meters that separated DropShip from starship. The electrical charge accumulated in the *Exeter'*s hull by her own plasma streams was drained away into the JumpShip's after transformers, and then the *Exeter* was drawn slowly into the reach of the *Sword of Davion'*s grapples.

There was no need to offload cargo or personnel. Each captured DropShip became crew quarters and cargo module for that part of the starship's payload. Individuals could visit other DropShips or travel to the recreation lounge forward in the starship's nose by passing through hatches and passageways that traversed the ship's length of several hundred meters. Most of the passengers preferred to wait with friends and familiar faces, gaming on the cramped deck spaces between bunks stacked six-high, clustering together in informal bull sessions where experienced veterans described Life As It Was to green recruits, or lying alone in their bunks, reading or worrying.

Conditions were claustrophically crowded and miserably low-G. The starship's stationkeeping thrusters mimicked a fractional G of gravity—far too little to keep the stomachs of spacesickness-prone troops settled. Each section maintained hourly rotating watches called, variously, cleaning details, cookie catchers, or Vomit Brigades. The details were necessary; perpetrators of these low-G nightmare incidents could rarely reach a heaving bag in time, and were invariably in no shape to clean up after themselves.

Ardan, as regimental commander, had the luxury of a tiny cubicle all to himself, complete with bunk, table, chair, desk, closet, and washroom facilities, which—when the facilities were all folded away into deck or bulkhead or overhead—was small enough that he could pace its length in three steps. Low G did not have the same effect on him as jump, and so he spent his time fretting instead of feeling sick.

The plan change had been his idea to begin with. He had set in motion the chain of thoughts and words and events that had transformed Prince Davion's plan of a lightning swoop into the Folly's capital into a war of maneuver and countermaneuver, of slash and grinding attrition in the mountains and swamps beyond. Suppose he were wrong? Suppose Michael Hasek-Davion were right, and the 'Mechs of the 17th became mired in unexpectedly soft ground around the Ordolo DZ? Suppose…Suppose…

Outside the bulkheads of his ship, the last of the strike force's fleet elements assembled and came to full charge. As each ship recorded maximum hypercharge in its banked and shielded accumulators, the crew began the delicate and time-consuming work of furling the jump sail and preparing for the hyperspace transition. This was the busiest time of all for the starship crews, but it was time that hung heaviest on the troops and warriors aboard the DropShips. They could only continue their routine of eating (those who still could), gambling, sleeping, work details, and worry.

And then the time for suppositions was over. The last of the fleet's jump sails was collapsed and furled, tightly

91

rolled into the narrow mast that jutted from each ship's stern like a monstrous sting. Aboard the flagship *Avalon*, Ran Felsner gave his assent, and Admiral Bertholi gave his command.

In a moment, space opened around the fleet and the ships vanished into it. The next moment, the same fold of space opened twelve light years away, and the Davion strike force rematerialized. The star below them was a Class K6, larger, brighter, and more orange than the sun of Dragon's Field, and just under 1 AU distant. Radar swept the area in all directions, pinpointing a bright, hard return from a large object some 80,000 kilometers away.

That would be the jump station, and the presumed hiding place of any Liao fighters on hand to deal with intrusions such as this one. Davion AeroSpace Fighters were deployed. The JumpShips themselves fired up their stationkeepers but did not unfurl their sails. Those huge, fabric disks were easy targets. Though the ships could not jump again until they had recharged their accumulators, no captain dared open his sails until the threat of enemy fighters was past.

Aboard the ship, the troops still waited. There was little gaming now and no bull sessions. Eyes searched the gray-painted bulkheads endlessly, as though they might see past them and into the surrounding vacuum. They could hear nothing, of course, and so were dependent on word passed down to them from the control room. Each man wondered if the ship's captain would actually let them know if they were about to be hit—and what possible good it would do to know.

Ardan was on the *Exeter*'s bridge, which was linked to the bridge of the *Sword of Davion* by an open vidlink. The *Exeter*'s captain, Harvey Danelle, was shaking his head as he examined the banks of monitors, then turned from the screen to face Ardan. "I think that scares me more than an assault wave of enemy ships incoming at 5 Gs."

"What?"

"Nothing."

"Nothing?"

"That's right, sir. No-damn-thing. Our fighters turned up a blank at the jump station. There's nothing there...and nobody." He checked his monitor screens again. "The patrols are returning. It looks as though Liao has left the jump point to us."

Ardan worried at this piece of information for a time. It was possible that the entire Liao space strike force was concentrated at the opposite jump point—but foolishly unlikely. Radar and IR sweeps of the entire system had so far produced equally negative results. So, it looked as though Maximilian Liao's defense of Stein's Folly would be concentrated near the planet itself.

The word finally came from the *Avalon*. Throughout the fleet, DropShip brackets opened, and grapples dropped silently clear. The DropShips began drifting away from their JumpShips like seeds scattered from slender pods. Once clear of the JumpShips, and refueled now from the stores of reaction mass aboard each larger vessel, the Drop-Ships calculated vectors and accelerations and began the long boost toward the Folly. Behind them, metal foil parasols two kilometers wide began unfurling against the stars, as the strike force fleet began the process of recharging for the next jump.

From jump point to star was .9 AU. From star to planet was .37 AUs. Simple geometery gave a distance between jump point and world of a hair under 1 AU, or over 67 hours of travel at a constant 1 G.

Ardan had been over the figures in his head many times already.

Each person in the fleet, Ardan included, now bore the expectant and frustrated attitude of one waiting for the proverbial other shoe to drop. Standard doctrine called for a defending force to meet an invading fleet as far off from the planet as possible, to inflict as much damage on the incoming fleet before the DropShips had a chance to release their precious 'Mechs or to land and disembark them.

The first attack wave came forty-two hours into the passage, long after the DropShips had flipped end for end and begun their deceleration. Davion *Corsair* and *Stuka* fighters launched from their DropShips and accelerated at high-G toward the assault formations that were spreading across the fleet's screens.

Hours passed, an impossible agony of time in which to remain charged with the expectation of immediate fury and death. Beyond the drive flares of the DropShips, ComInt scans registered distant targets and stabbing lances of energy. Screens on the *Exeter's* bridge told a story of exultant life and fiery death in tiny clots of moving, colored lights.

The *Exeter's* captain grunted. Ardan looked up from the plot screen at him. "You're not happy, Harve."

"You're right. It's too easy."

"We've lost three."

"Damn it, Ardan, their whole air-space reserves should've been there...should've been waiting for us at the jump point! I think we're being suckered in."

Ardan nodded. It would make sense if the Liao ground commander were preparing a surprise—such as luring the Davion invaders into dropping on Steindown and boxing them in from the hills. The problem was, what if there were other, less obvious traps in the offing?

Ardan watched another amber light—a Liao *Thrush*—flash white and die, and dreaded failure.

Deceleration complete, the fleet entered low orbit over Stein's Folly. In the entire passage, only three enemy fighters had broken through the Davion *Stuka*s and *Corsair*s and made high-speed runs through the DropShip fleet. One DropShip, the aging *Union* Class *Alphecca*, suffered minor damage to her fire control systems, but with no casualties among the MechWarriors of A Company, 2nd Battalion, 5th Crucis Lancers, sweating out the attack aboard her.

Davion forces commanded the space approaches by the time the DropShips entered orbit. Battlegroups of *Stuka*s refueled aboard their base DropShips, rearmed with bombs and air-to-ground missiles, then plunged into the gold-tipped clouds of the Folly's atmosphere. Reports continued to be relayed from the *Stuka* flights to the fleet: enemy 'Mechs observed in Stein's Folly and at the Highland port; Liao heavy 'Mechs observed and bombed on the coast road west of Travis; no fighters observed on any of the spaceport fields; ground anti-air defensive fire seemed light...

The *Exeter*'s captain appeared on the steel latticework deck of the 'Mech bay, where Ardan was making a final systems check of the towering, eighty-ton *Victor* in its outboard launch niche. The 'Mech itself was almost lost in the forest of tubing, cables, wire, and ablative plate that cocooned the machine.

"I came down to wish you luck, Ardan" Danelle said.

"Thank you, Harve. Any change?"

The older man shook his head. "Maybe...just maybe, we've got them cold."

"Uh-unh. Not Maximilian Liao. He's got something up his sleeve." Ardan smiled, a tug against one corner of his mouth. "A dagger, perhaps."

The *Exeter*'s captain looked at him closely. "Are you all right?"

"Oh, sure. Nervous. Scared to death...How should I feel?"

"Before being booted into space in one of those junk piles? Nervous and scared witless, I should think."

"Harve...what if I've guessed wrong?"

"Then you live with it...or die with it, whatever comes. Your course is set now. Fretting won't change it...except maybe to work the odds against you when you need to be at your best."

Ardan looked up at the *Victor*. A grey-coveralled technician waved to him from the cockpit, signalling that the instrumentation checked out and the 'Mech was ready for launch.

"Twenty minutes to drop," the Captain said. "You'd better snug in."

"Right. And...thanks. Thanks for everything."

95

"All part of your better Davion Travel Service," Danelle said, but he wasn't smiling.

Harvey Danelle stared up at Ardan as he climbed a slender ladder to the *Victor's* hatch and squeezed himself in. Young Sortek's moodiness concerned him. He'd seen too many 'MechWarriors overcome by depression or black or thoughtful moods—and more often than not, those were the ones who failed to return. Silently, he said a kind of prayer for Ardan's safety.

The landing plan called for an atmospheric drop rather than a drop from space. With the Drop Zone so perilously close to sea, jungle, and rugged mountain, absolute precision was necessary. One by one, the main drives of each DropShip flared, killing velocity, dropping the ships into the upper fringes of the Folly's atmosphere.

Sealed into his cockpit, listening to the babble of voices coming across his comchannels, Ardan could feel the gradually increasing thrum of air against outer hull, the occasional lurch and bump of high-altitude turbulence, or the jar of a maneuvering thruster burn. He fought down his seething emotions, and attended to the nearly automatic tasks of preparing for drop. He had already stripped off all clothing except for his boots and shorts—his *Victor's* cockpit was going to be a sauna in very short order—and donned a light cooling vest, taking care with the connections between the shoulder pumps and the coolant reserve in the small of his back. A Kelvin Triple-0 Lancer 3 mm laser pistol went into a holster, and he tightened the web belt it hung from around his waist. The new combat knife was strapped by its scabbard to his calf just above his low-cut boot top. The canister of survival gear went into a flat pouch hanging from the belt.

The *Victor's* neural helmet was already tuned to his brain patterns, of course. He brought the helmet down from its storage mount suspended above the back of his seat, eased it across his shoulders, and clamped it shut. Gradually, the *Victor* woke up. Feedback through the helmet gave Ardan a sense of the machine's balance and position through the nerves of his inner ear. He felt...power.

Fear melted, and his uncertainty with it. Rumor had it that MechWarriors controlled their massive charges by thought alone, as if the 'Mech became their body through some sorcery in the neuralink. Human technology had never been capable of that, of course, though there were speculations that such control might one day be possible. Donning a BattleMech neural helmet was far less taking on a new body than it was taking on a new outlook on the world. A man's viewpoint changed somewhat, from eight meters up, with eighty tons of juggernaut combat machine responding to the touch of his fingers.

His eyes flicked to the chronometer set above his faceplate. Four minutes to drop. The ride became rougher, more violent. He could feel sudden shifts of *up* and *down* through his neuralink as Captain Danelle maneuvered his ship.

"There they are!" The voice was Danelle's, sharp through his helmet commlink. "Bogies, dozens of them, coming up out of the clouds!"

Ardan could not see them and had to rely on the running commentary from the *Exeter's* bridge. Sweat beaded across his forehead and upper lip, and it wasn't even hot yet.

"We've spotted 112 of the bastards so far," Danelle continued. "They must have been bunkered underground, masked or camouflaged from our scouts. They rose from a dozen points all across North Continent...strange, though. I think they vectored wrong. They're rising to meet us, but they're having to burn a lot of mass to shift from their original course." There was a pause. "Combat Intelligence believes they were vectored on a course to intercept us if we were on an approach path toward Steindown. We're well north of that course, and they're having to scramble to adjust."

That was the trap, Ardan thought, exultant. They were waiting for us at Steindown! I was right!

"Our fighter cover is engaging them. Ha! Got that one! Oops...that one broke through, but the old *Deneb* burned him down. Look at him burn! Here come our reserves..."

There was a long pause, then Ardan heard, "We're coming up on the drop site. Nav fix is positive. DZ in sight! Twelve seconds, people." Another pause, an eternity. Every MechWarrior reserved a special dread for death striking in the last seconds before a drop, while men and machines were still cradled helplessly aboard their DropShips. Then Danelle yelled, "Good luck! Give 'em hell!"

12

The world exploded in Ardan's ears, as the *Exeter* launched him from its 'Mech bay. In a blast of metal chaff and fragments of ablative plating, the *Victor* began its plunge planetward.

Ardan fired a burst from his thrusters, stopping a vicious tumble before it could properly begin and orienting himself into a spread-eagle, face-down position. He was now a ten-meter tall, eighty-ton skydiver, accelerating to terminal velocity. After instructing his computer to disregard the metallic debris all around him, he clicked on his proximity radar and got his bearings.

The fighter battle that Danelle had been describing still raged among the clouds quite far off. Ardan was alone, except for the radar images of the other 'Mechs in his unit being fired out of the hurtling DropShip as it receded toward the southeast. The ship's course helped to orient him. There was the Highland Peninsula, bloated, huge, and ragged under scattered clouds, stretching down to a cobalt, island-dotted sea. Streaks of fire marked other DropShips on their run low over the Peninsula. Those would be Lees and the Capellan March Militia, making their diversion—and the Liao ships rising from Steindown to meet them. Clouds obscured the isthmus as well as the vast expanse of the Ordolo Basin, which was almost under Ardan's feet now. Mountains extended toward him from the east. As nearly as he could tell, he was dead on course.

He had ejected at 16,000 meters and been in freefall for seconds that dragged like hours. His altimeter flickered the dwindling meters as he kept his hands solidly planted on the controls that would trigger his rockets. His 'Mech had no parachute. Fire his jets too early, and he would run short of fuel for jumps in combat. Wait too long, and his comrades would scrape what was left of his *Victor* off the flank of those mountains. God, but they looked close!

At 1,000 meters, he plunged into the clouds. Fog whipped past the *Victor's* forward screens, completely disorienting him. The plummeting 'Mech was bucking some now, too, as it encountered the turbulence of a growing storm within the cloud. *I thought this was supposed to be the dry season,* thought Ardan, and felt anew that twinge of fear. *Suppose...?*

He burst through the belly of the upper cloud layer. Green patched with ragged white spread out in twilight beneath him. Eight hundred meters. He was level with the highest of the mountain peaks. He fired his jets, dialing up their thrust gradually. If thrust came too suddenly, the connectors to the 'Mech's backpack assembly could shred like paper. The effect on Ardan would be similar to a crashlanding into those mountains at terminal velocity. His descent slowed—to eighty meters per second...forty... ten...Treetops groped at his feet. His jets were firing steadily now, gulping fuel at a ravenous pace, but slowing his headlong plunge and lowering him toward the surface of a broad, flat field. A quick glance showed him the vapor plume of three other 'Mechs close by. Good. They'd not scattered much.

At fifty meters, he examined his chosen landing spot again. It looked like an irregular field covered with bright green vegetation, bordered by a tangle of swamp growth. He wasn't certain, but this site might be farther north and west into the Ordolo Basin than he'd planned. His designated DZ was further east on a barren slope along the flank of the mountain ridge. Still, judging by the lay of the ridge, he wasn't more than a kilometer or two off. Ardan began his final landing sequence.

Odd. From thirty meters, the ground looked peculiarly flat, with no depressions or irregularities at all. And the color...Panic struck him like a blow. He was committed now to a landing, but he had a horrible premonition that the deceptively solid-looking surface below him was, in fact, the surface of a marsh or pond covered by weeds or algae scum. If he hit that at ten meters per second in his feet-first landing mode, the eighty-ton *Victor* would plunge straight to the bottom of the marsh, driving itself so deeply into the mud that he would never be able to free himself, and would never, ever be found.

He twisted his attitude controls wildly forward, sensing the pitch of his 'Mech through his helmet. The 'Mech splayed out, arms out, belly down, once again in the skydiver's position he'd assumed after first ejecting from the DropShip.

The world stopped for that last, hurtling instant. If he'd guessed wrong, if that invitingly-solid swatch of land was, in fact, solid, his spread-eagled 'Mech would slam face on into the ground at ten meters per second. The *Victor* would be wrecked, and he would almost certainly be killed.

The field swooshed up to meet him, and he fell into it with a roar like exploding artillery. The impact wracked Ardan against his shoulder restraints and left him gasping for breath in his helmet. His 'Mech had driven through the surface of the swamp and face-down into the mud, of course, but his spread-eagle position had kept him from driving too fast, too deep. BattleMechs do not float. Nevertheless, he was not swallowed by the ooze. Driven by the full power of his 'Mech's leg and arm actuators, he moved, first one arm, then one leg, the other arm, the other leg. He could see nothing but sticky blackness through the *Victor's* forward screens, now spread out disconcertingly under where he hung suspended from his pilot's seat, but instrument lights showed that his backpack was awash above the viscous mud.

His headphones caught a burst of rapid speech, garbled but from a transmission close by. Good! His antennae was clear, too.

"This is Gold Leader, down and in need of assistance." Speaking slowly and distinctly into the slender microphone suspended in front of his mouth as he scanned the assigned combat frequencies, Ardan forced the words into some semblance of control. God, there had to be someone down close by. He'd seen other 'Mechs near, just before he'd hit.

Right now, he almost didn't care whether it was Davion or House Liao forces that found him. For the moment, everything seemed to take a back seat to simple survival.

"Gold Leader calling, down and in need of assistance. Does anybody copy?"

"Gold Leader, this is Green Three." The reply washed over Ardan like ocean breakers, leaving him weak with relief. "I copy," said Green Three."I have you in sight. Stand by for a cable."

Following carefully explicit directions from his rescuer, Ardan closed the *Victor's* left hand around a tow cable that the other 'Mech fired across the back of his machine. In moments, Green Three had braced the heavy cable around a low, spreading swamp tree more massive than any 'Mech, and Ardan was using the cable to work his way, meter by painful meter, toward solid ground.

It took almost half an hour to get free. Not only was the cable slick with mud and algae slime, but Ardan had the use of only his left hand because the Victor's right arm mounted a Pontiac 100 autocannon instead of manipulators. At least a dozen times during that slow, wet crawl, Ardan wondered what he would have done had he been in, say, a *Marauder* or Sep's *Warhammer*. Without hands, he would have been helpless, and every movement would have carried his machine deeper into the ooze.

At last, feeling solid ground under his feet, he brought the *Victor* up to its knees. His rescuer, a hulking *Crusader-D*, helped him to his feet. "You're a sight, sir," the *Crusader's* pilot told him, "but I'm awfully glad to see you! I think I'm lost!"

"You're not half as glad as I am, pilot," Ardan said, his voice unsteady, his hands trembling slightly on the *Victor's* controls. "Who are you with?" He'd already picked out the emblem of the 17th Avalon Hussars on the *Crusader's* right leg.

"Code group Red Dog. Seventeenth Hussars, sir. Company A, First Battalion."

"Company A...that's Morrison's Marauders, right?"

102

"Right, sir!" He could hear the surprise in the boy's voice. Senior officers rarely knew the details of the units in their command, but Ardan was different. He'd spent long hours studying the stat sheets of all of his tactical commanders, down to company level.

The *Crusader* gestured toward the east. "I think we were supposed to come down someplace closer to that ridge over there, but I've been having trouble finding solid ground heading in that direction."

"What's your name, trooper?"

"MechWarrior Donald Fitzgerald, sir. Number three in Fire Lance O'Hanrahan."

"Well, Donald. What say we find ourselves some Marauders. Morrison's Marauders, that is...not the other kind."

"YesSIR!"

The two 'Mechs moved toward the southeast, through swamp and open forest. The terrain was not the impassable tangle of bogs Ardan had been dreading, nor was it as dry as the planetological tapes had suggested it should be during the local dry season. He finally decided that the pool where he'd nearly lost himself was one of a large number of small, irregular, and ill-defined lakes and ponds that sprinkled the entire upland stretch of the Ordolo Basin. The name "Lost Lakes" came to him, and Ardan realized he'd found at least one of them. Seeing a small cascade of rainwater shower from the broad leaves of a tree as he brushed past, he remembered that even during the dry season, it rains periodically in a jungle. The lakes would be larger and deeper now, the ground softer, so soon after a tropical rainstorm.

The mud sucked at the feet of his *Victor* with every step Ardan took. If this was dry weather, he decided to definitely take a pass on visiting the Ordolo Basin during the rainy season.

13

As travel grew easier, Ardan's radio also began to pick up a constant stream of chatter from a number of different units. It sounded as if a battle had erupted just to the east. "Green Two, Green Two!" one voice called with sharp urgency. "Break right, the bastard's behind you!"

"Copy! Hot damn, where'd he come from! Watch it, Blue Twelve! There's a *Panther* zeroing on you, five o'clock!"

"Break left, Seven! Break left! Oh, damn!"

"Here he comes. Steady, steady! Hose him down!"

"Mayday! Mayday! She's going to blow! I'm punching out!"

Ardan and Fitzgerald hurried their pace.

The two 'Mechs broke free of the forest and entered the battle almost simultaneously. The ground had been rising steadily as they made their way further and further east. Perhaps three kilometers from where Ardan had landed, the forest gave way to an uneven plain covered with blue grass knee-deep on the 'Mechs. The eastern horizon was dominated by the ridge, a low and mostly wooded line of steep-sided hills or eroded mountains, none more than 800 meters high. The plain stretched toward the ridge across perhaps ten kilometers, and the area had become a killing zone as 'Mech struggled wildly with 'Mech.

In the distance, a low line of bunkers with green-mottled, camouflage roofs told Ardan what had happened. There'd been a camp here, probably a full battalion of Liao 'Mechs and possibly an air lance, too, placed well clear of the city and in position to close off the neck of the Highland Peninsula once the counterinvasion was grounded. Instead, part of the Davion drop had come down squarely in the middle of the Liao camp.

A TDR *Thunderbolt* seemed to rise out of the grass 200 meters in front of Ardan, an illusion created by its sudden move from a hidden fold in the ground. Ardan had only an instant to recognize the raised arm-and-sword against the inverted green triangle on the 'Mech's bulky torso. The 'Mech's right arm heavy laser was swinging down in line with Ardan's cockpit.

Ardan dodged left as the *Thunderbolt's* Sunglow Type 2 laser cut loose with a dazzling pulse of green light. He triggered his twin left arm lasers an instant later, but surprise made him miss.

The *Thunderbolt* was known for its heavy armor and even more for being one of the best- and most heavily armed 'Mechs in service. That Sunglow laser could deliver megajoules of raw fury in a single pulse, and the three medium lasers mounted along the left torso were each as powerful as the *Victor's* left arm lasers. And if that weren't enough, Ardan knew that the heavy Delta Dart long-range missile launcher squatting on the *Thunderbolt's* left shoulder could knock out an opponent with a single volley. Ardan's *Victor* might outweigh his opponent by fifteen tons, but the other advantages were all with the TDR.

The Liao 'Mech's LRM launcher blossomed fire. Ardan threw the *Victor* into a twisting, dodging sprint, closing the gap between him and the TDR. At close range, the enemy's LRMs would be useless. He opened fire as he lurched forward, his twin lasers scoring hits on the *Thunderbolt's* torso, cratering armor in explosive gouts of vaporized armor.

At the same moment, a salvo of missiles exploded alongside the *Thunderbolt*, and three of them flashed white brilliance against the machine's legs. The 'Mech twisted to the side, moving swiftly. What...

"I got him, Gold Leader! I got him!"

Ardan had forgotten Fitzgerald's *Crusader*. The boy had opened up with his own LRMs from the edge of the woods, and the *Thunderbolt* was moving now to throw off his aim.

"Steady, Donald!" he replied. "Hang back and keep raking him! I'll try to close!"

Ardan tracked carefully with his lasers and loosed three paired shots in rapid succession. The *Thunderbolt* went down, seeking cover in the grassy slopes of the field.

Ardan ran a hurried check on his *Victor's* main armament. The right arm Pontiac 100 autocannon had the best chance of scoring a crippling hit on the *Thunderbolt*, but he was afraid that his swim in the mud might have fouled its feed mechanism. The autocannon was a devastating weapon. It fired high-speed, rapid-fire streams of explosive, armor-piercing shells from cassettes or carousels fed into the gun one at a time by a complex and occasionally balky autoloader mechanism. Each cassette held 100 shells, and by a widespread but commonly accepted looseness of terminology, each cassette was itself considered to be one round. One cassette round was already loaded. Nineteen more were stored in the autoloader chamber high up in his *Victor's* right torso. He would have to use that single round carefully, because if the loader jammed, he would not get another chance.

Ardan moved swiftly, watching the grass. The *Thunderbolt* had gone to ground...about there...He triggered a control and his IR scanner dropped across his face. The world darkened, lit now in surreal shades of green and blue, with heat sources identified in whites and reds.

A white fountain geysered into the air fifty meters to his right, the heat plume of the hidden *Thunderbolt*. Ardan triggered a salvo of short-ranged missiles. Grass shredded in clots of smoke and flame, and then the *Thunderbolt* was up, swinging past him at a run, its heavy laser already spouting green flame.

The laser caught the *Victor* high up on his left shoulder. There was no shock, but heat flooded Ardan's cockpit. He steadied the crosshairs of his HUD and triggered the autocannon. The weapon bucked and roared, jolting Ardan against his seat. The stream of high explosive chopped and slashed at the *Thunderbolt's* chest armor, smashed across its left shoulder, and turned the LRM launcher into a tangled, black-smoking ruin. It took six seconds for the autocannon to cycle through the cassette, and then the dull thud of a loader failure echoed through the *Victor*. He checked his console. As he'd feared, the mechanism was jammed.

A missile exploded against the *Victor*'s chest, the shock jarring the breath from Ardan's lungs and knocking his 'Mech a staggered step backward. In the same instant, more missile fire washed across the *Thunderbolt*. Fitzgerald had pulled back to a range of 300 meters and was pouring salvo after salvo of long-ranged warheads into the *Thunderbolt*. Ardan triggered his own Holly SRMs and joined in the bombardment. Smoke belched from a rent in the TDR's right side, and its right arm hung dangling, the heavy laser junked.

Something hit Ardan from behind. Instinct brought his hand down on the *Victor*'s jump jet controls. The 'Mech leapt and spun as ravening beams snapped like bolts of fusion-charged lightning at the spot where he'd just been standing.

The *Victor* dropped to one knee as it came to ground. His attacker was now a 70-ton *Warhammer* so much like Sep's that Ardan caught himself looking for her personal crest on the scarred battle machine's left shoulder. The double bolt of lightning had been the discharge from the twin PPCs it mounted as ungainly arms. Those cannons lifted slightly now, their muzzles still red hot and trailing steam in the humid air. One of the 'Mech's medium lasers fired, striking the *Victor* above the left knee. Ardan jumped again, wildly, before those PPCs could be brought into line for another paired shot.

The battle had become a near free-for-all now. The Hussar *Crusader* behind him was exchanging missile fire with the crippled *Thunderbolt*, but the *Warhammer*, baffled by Ardan's sudden jump, was swinging to open fire on Fitzgerald.

If only his autocannon were still working! Ardan opened fire from less than sixty meters with his twin Sorenstein V lasers, savaging the *Warhammer*'s right side. The right PPC dipped abruptly, out of control or unpowered, and the

WHM spun its torso back on its hip swivel to confront his attack. Liquid fire spewed from nozzles set into the machine's chest, up where the twin Sperry Browning machine guns should have been. With a cold touch of fear, Ardan realized the *Warhammer* was a WHM-6L, a House Liao variant on the familiar 6R, which mounted twin flamers instead of MGs. Fire flared close past his *Victor's* chest as he sidestepped the firestreams. Smoke boiled across the viewscreens, obscuring his vision. He fired again with his lasers, not aiming, but laying down a pattern of fire where he guessed the *Warhammer* would be.

The 'Mech's temperature alarms were rasping in his ears, and red and amber lights flickered and winked across his console. The heat inside the cockpit was overwhelming, coating his body with a sheen of sweat and setting the tiny electric pumps in his coolant vest to whining. He had been maneuvering too hard, jumping and discharging his lasers too frequently. The *Victor* could not handle the excess heat much longer.

And neither could he. The high temperature left him gasping, each breath painful. He was weak and dizzy, and only the adrenalin surging through his blood was keeping him moving at all.

He stepped through the fire, and his vision cleared. The *Warhammer* was close, much closer than he'd expected, scarcely thirty meters away. Having turned again to fire at Fitzgerald's *Crusader*, it now had its back to Ardan.

The *Victor's* computer streamed words across his main combat screen: *Heat critical. Suggest immediate shutdown.* He slapped the heat cut-off overrides, then stabbed at the jump jet controls once more. His *Victor* kicked off into the sky, rising on throbbing jets. He kicked in the maneuvering thrusters once, let the massive machine ride against its shrieking gyros. The *Warhammer* turned, looking up, its PPC rising too late...

The impact was deafening. Metal shrieked, and the *Warhammer's* cockpit opened like a flower between the *Victor's* feet. In combat, the *Victor* was a constant surprise to MechWarriors encountering it for the first time, for none expected a 'Mech of its size to be jump-capable. Though the *Warhammer's* pilot had seen the *Victor* jump, he had turned to deal with the *Crusader's* LRM barrage before trying to finish off Ardan's 'Mech. The mistake had cost him his life.

Ardan brought the *Victor* up out of the tangled wreckage, his autocannon trailing streamers of shredded myomer fibers and gutted wiring. The WHM's flamer fuel tanks ignited as he stepped clear, masking the wreckage with a pillar of oily black smoke.

"The *Thunderbolt* shut down," Fitzgerald said. Battle-charged excitement edged his voice. "The pilot ejected."

Ardan swung and saw the TDR still standing, an immobile cast-metal statue now, the blown escape hatch still dangling across the wreckage of its shoulder-mounted LRM launcher. If *Thunderbolts* had a particular weakness in battle, it was their tendency toward rapid heat overloading—the penalty paid for carrying so many heavy weapons.

The battle had turned now in favor of the invaders. Ardan rotated his 'Mech, picked out others he recognized from his own unit moving through the enemy's bunker area. A scattered handful of Liao 'Mechs were withdrawing down the slope into the forested swamps to the west.

He opened a new commlink channel. "Gold Squadron, Gold Squadron, this is Gold Leader. Do you copy?"

"We copy, Gold Leader!" The voice was that of Eric Garrand, whose red-painted *Archer* was the number two 'Mech in Ardan's Command Lance. He sounded enormously relieved. "This is Gold Two, returning command to you, sir! Hell, I saw you fall into a swamp! We thought you'd bought the farm!"

"Not even a down payment, Eric. What's the situation?"

"The 17th is down and scattered. Maybe 40 percent have reported in to me since I took your seat, but there're more coming in all the time. A bunch of us landed smack on this snake's nest, but it looks like we've about got them cleaned out now. Some withdrew toward that jungle behind you. The main body is falling back to the south."

"Good. Any word from the 5th?"

"Not yet, sir. There's no line-of-sight, and we don't have our space relay commlinks in yet. I have a scout platoon moving up the ridge, though, and they'll be able to serve as a lasercom relay station as soon as they get the 5th in view."

"Good enough." Ardan glanced at his chronometer and was shocked to find that less than an hour had passed since he'd touched down, including more than forty minutes he'd spent splashing around in the swamp and hiking back to where the action was.

There were no targets nearby. He locked his controls, pulled the neural helmet from his shoulders, then decided to take a chance and crack his *Victor's* skullcap. The round, topside hatch popped open to admit a gush of cold air as Ardan climbed out onto his 'Mech's shoulder.

14

The air was muggy and hot but so much cooler and fresher than what he had been enjoying in the *Victor*'s cockpit that Ardan sagged back against the 'Mech's massive head in pure relief. He had left the helmet's commlink attachment in place and could hear new reports of additional 'Mechs arriving on the broad and smoke-heavy field. The 17th's ComInt people reported that 85 percent of the regiment had reported in, with more reports still to be processed. Perhaps the 17th had not suffered too many casualties in their ill-advised drop into a bog. It might be days before all of the stragglers reported in, but he was sure now that 'Mechs lost to landing mishaps in lakes or swamp would be mercifully few.

Meanwhile, he opened an access cover, drew his knife, and began working at the mechanism of his autocannon round feeder. The entire assembly had been coated in liquid mud, and the heat spilling from his 'Mech during the battle had baked that mud to the general consistency of tempered ferrocrete. He chipped at the stuff, cursing under his breath but feeling better now than he had in days.

"Gold Leader! Gold Leader!" Garrand's voice cut in from his earpiece. "We got company coming, boss!"

"What is it?" He looked around the horizon. Except for scattered groups of Davion 'Mechs sorting themselves out after the first battle, the area looked clear. A distant thunder rolled down from the eastern ridge, sounds of pitched battle on the far side.

"We got an ASF on radar to the south. Low altitude, high speed. Looks like a ground support mission."

Ardan slapped the access panel back in place, sheathed the knife, and slid back into the stifling interior of his 'Mech. He didn't know the outcome of the tangle between AeroSpace Fighters that he'd seen during the *Exeter*'s approach toward the DZ, but it was logical to assume that the enemy would attempt to hit the Davion DZs as soon as their own units were clear and they had fighters to spare.

"ETA?" He fitted his neural helmet back in place, checked the connections.

"Thirty seconds, Gold Leader. Bearing one-seven-nine, altitude—aw, shoot! He must be plowing the fields! Lost him...No! There! Visual..."

"Target south! *Fire!*" Ardan's command went out to all units on the command override, interrupting Gold Two and triggering a spattering of laser fire from those 'Mechs in a position to target the oncoming aircraft. Ardan's HUD sprang up across his screens, and an autotrack vision enhancer steadied on the ship's nose.

He recognized the squat disk shape immediately. It was a *Thrush*, a favorite Liao air-space fighter, and a battle-torn veteran by the look of the laser scars across its belly and fuselage. For an instant, he saw the head of the pilot through the canopy, masked in a black-visored helmet. A line of silhouettes, thirteen of them, ran along the hull under the canopy, the last of those kill markers still bright and new-painted. This pilot was an old hand, an experienced killer.

The *Thrush's* lasers fired before any of the grounded 'Mechs could lock on. An instant later, a cluster of spinning, silvery cylinders exploded from the fighter's belly, the cloud of objects expanding as the cylinders tumbled down across the field.

Ardan held his position and fired both lasers, launched all of his remaining SRM rounds, and cursed his useless autocannon. As the *Thrush* flashed overhead, the field erupted in spewing, boiling, liquid flame, a chemical fire that splashed across grass and 'Mechs and shrieking men, clinging like some hungry, living thing. Ardan's mind held a seared after-image of Fitzgerald's *Crusader* engulfed in writhing flame, of the 'Mech lifted from its feet by fresh explosions that shredded its legs and hurled it forward in a twisting mass of flaming metal. Fire clung to Ardan's *Victor*. Inferno bombs were a descendant of the napalm of earlier wars, a jellied, incendiary chemical that burned with the heat of white phosphorous. The grass around him was afire.

He turned his *Victor* and lumbered toward the forest, his 'Mech trailing streamers of fire. Once clear of the conflagration in the field, Ardan rolled his heavy machine against the ground, extinguishing the flames and leaving vast, deep-slashed ruts in the mud. The *Victor* stood, blackened and muddy.

He had seen only the one, lone *Thrush* and it was long gone, but that was not reassuring because ground assault tactics always called for multiple aircraft working together as a team. That initial pass would be followed almost immediately by more. He snapped off orders, took reports. Two 'Mechs had been hit in the attack, a *Stinger* and Fitzgerald's *Crusader*. Both machines were total losses and their pilots dead.

The *Thrush* was out of sight now, but others would be coming quickly. His orders called for the 17th to disperse, with Second and Third Battalions spreading out toward the eastern ridge and the First Battalion moving into the swamp. There were still Liao BattleMechs in this wooded slope along the Ordolo Basin. The Regiment would have to take them out or further scatter those enemy 'Mechs if it didn't want to become the target of constant sniping and hit-and-run raids to the rear as it closed on Jordan's Pass. Once inside the treeline, visibility was reduced to less than thirty meters. Unable to see any of the other 'Mechs in the Battalion around him, Ardan used the commlink to organize the unseen formation into a rough line running north and south, travelling west. The tree canopy closed in overhead, shielding them from further *Thrush* attacks. Ardan wondered where the follow-up attack was. Had that *Thrush* pilot truly been acting alone? What did that say about Liao organization here?

The scope of the Liao trap was obvious now. He didn't have the full picture yet and would not until he could compare notes with Ran and Lees. But their guess about a trap had been accurate. There was no reason to keep such large 'Mech forces so far from Steindown unless the plan had been to lure a Davion invasion force onto the broad plains between Steindown and the mountains, trap them on the peninsula, and bomb and shell them into helpless wreckage. The landing north of the peninsula seemed to have caught the Liao 'Mech forces completely by surprise—and even their AeroSpace Fighter support seemed to be operating in a disjointed, undirected fashion.

That confusion meant the Davion forces had the advantage now, but they would have to push to keep it. The battle was not over yet, not by ten thousand light years.

The ground grew broken and steeper. He used his 'Mech's mass to brush aside smaller trees, which fell with splintering crashes. Other massive, age-old lords of the forest grew in greater and greater profusion as he moved deeper into the forest. There was a faint glimmer of water ahead.

Gold Two and the rest of Gold Squadron were further to his right, out of sight, but perhaps 500 meters away. He would have to get closer to them or risk being cut off. Blue Squadron was on his left. Once he caught a glimpse of the company's number four Recon Lance 'Mech, a *Wasp*, moving through the trees. The smaller 'Mechs were better for this kind of maneuver. They were lighter, less likely to become bogged down in mud, and their maneuverability among trees, vines, and undergrowth was impressive.

He cut to the right, then had to detour around an unexpected lake, its surface brilliant with the bright green scum that had nearly fooled him during his landing.

Cannonfire boomed to the right. Gold Seven reported contact with a Liao *Rifleman*. As Ardan hurried forward, his *Victor*'s feet squelching in the shallow mud, he glimpsed movement ahead. The *Victor* shouldered its way between two trees that shuddered and rocked back, roots flailing mud. Dead ahead was a massive, immobile form, hulking and powerful, the Liao emblem bright against its heavy torso armor. Ardan recognized the shape. Originally a House

114

Steiner design, a few of these monsters had apparently fallen into Liao hands. Designated ZEU-6S and called *Zeus*, the 80-ton assault BattleMech resembled Ardan's *Victor* in many respects.

There were differences of detail, of course. The *Zeus* had lighter torso armor than the *Victor*, and heavier armor on its legs and arms. Most critical was the fact that the *Victor* sacrificed a great deal of space and mass to the HildCo Model 12 jump jets set into its back assembly. That meant that the *Zeus*, without jump jets, carried far more in the way of heavy weaponry. Especially since the *Victor's* autocannon was jammed.

The *Zeus* fired first. The monster seemed to have been placed there, waiting for him. A salvo of heavy and medium laser shots flickered across the water. Water close behind Ardan geysered steam, and the tree to his right burst into flame. A dull thud somewhere announced the failure of some piece of machinery. Ardan prayed it wasn't critical.

His own twin lasers were firing in response, but the hits seemed to splash off the *Zeus*'s torso without effect. Then he triggered a salvo of four short-ranged missiles, brilliant pinpoints trailing smoke as they hissed toward the target. There! One of them hit, cratering the enemy 'Mech's shoulder armor but doing no other damage that Ardan could see.

Ardan was scared now. Without his autocannon, he was nearly helpless against the *Zeus*, and among these trees, his much greater maneuverability was useless. The *Zeus* raised its left arm, which mounted a black-barrelled Defiance autocannon. Ardan knew that the *Zeus* carried only five cassette rounds for its cannon, but at this range, with the *Victor* pinned to the ground by trees and underbrush, that would be more than enough.

He pulled back between the trees as the autocannon fired, its muzzle flash an almost steady flicker reflected in the swamp, the roar of exploding shells and splintering trees a drumming thunder against the *Victor*'s hull. He turned. A mistake! He should have turned right! Shells

115

smashed into his left arm, and warning lights flared on his console. One of his lasers was dead, the other damaged.

He loosed another flight of missiles, but couldn't see the result. Smoke drifted across the swamp, masking his *Victor* from the looming shape of the *Zeus*. With so much damage to his weapons system, Ardan's only hope was to disengage in the smoke and attempt to fall back to where he could gain support from friendly forces.

Autocannon fire smashed into him from behind now, pounding at his jump jets, fragmenting armor, chopping into his right leg. The leg froze, refusing to move. Clumsily, he attempted to circle the *Victor* around its immobile leg to face his attacker. The *Zeus* was moving there, looming huge and ominous through trees and smoke. The flicker of that autocannon came a third time, crushing the *Victor's* useless right arm and sending the autocannon spinning away in smoking chunks.

Ardan tasted smoke and blood, mingled with the stench of his own fear. The *Zeus* was taking its time, lumbering closer, picking its steps with care in the boggy ground. Ardan kept up a steady fire with his lone remaining laser, desperately trying for a hit on the *Zeus's* cockpit. His missile racks were empty now. There was a crackle and the sparking of shorted circuitry, and the laser died, though his thumb kept smashing at the useless firing button. His fire control systems were shorting out, overloading as circuit boards melted in the ferocious heat in his 'Mech's reactor module.

The *Zeus* was closer now, thirty meters away. The autocannon was coming up for another rapid-fire round. It was time to punch out—or die.

Ardan thumbed the safety cover from the emergency eject arming switch, locked off the safety, stabbed the full system disconnect, and armed the chair. An alarm hooted, a panel slid back from the bright red eject button, and his palm slapped down with stinging force. The cockpit dissolved in a red blur, and Ardan was smashed down into his seat as though by some mammoth hand. He was not aware of any noise—the explosion had momentarily deafened him—but the skullcap hatch blew away an instant before his cockpit seat blasted clear of the shattered *Victor*.

His flight was a short one. The *Victor* was canted at an angle against a burning tree, and the ejector seat had slammed into a twisted, overhanging limb, then writhed off in a wildly tilting, tumbling descent across the swamp. The seat's landing jets fired to cushion his landing, but their ground sensors had been smashed and so the jets fired parallel to the ground. His harness shackles broke free, and Ardan's unconscious body plowed feet-first into the dank green waters of the Ordolo swamp.

Consciousness returned with a distant, red haze of pain. His arm throbbed with the dull but excruciating ache of a fracture. Cradling the arm against his chest, he stood slowly, swaying against the waves of dizziness that threatened to topple him back into the greenish water. He heard a crash behind him and turned to see the *Zeus* give his ravaged *Victor* a final blow that sent it crumpling into the swamp. The *Zeus* seemed to be scanning for him, its massive head swiveling slowly against the background of green leaves and hanging moss. Ardan's mind groped for a weapon. His Double-O Lancer laser pistol was missing, torn out during his brief flight. That left only his knife—a knife against an eighty-ton 'Mech. He began giggling at the thought, his shock-numbed thoughts on the ragged edge of hysteria. He felt the *Zeus's* gaze upon him and sank slowly down until the water partly covered him once more, but the *Zeus* did not seem bent on further pursuit. The sound of battle was thundering now in the east, toward the edge of the swamp. For one long moment, the *Zeus* seemed to be looking straight at the helpless Ardan, and then it turned and pressed through the dense undergrowth toward the sounds of battle.

He was alone, now. Moving with the clumsy fumblings of an automaton, he found his ejector seat half-buried nearby in the mud. One-handed, he rummaged through a side compartment until he could pull out a preserving sleeve. Once fastened around his injured arm and inflated,

117

the sleeve immobilized his arm and prevented the splintered ends of his humerus from causing further injury. Then he staggered away from the ejection seat, wading through calf-deep mud toward the edge of land nearby.

He staggered out of the swampy water, stiff-legged, scarcely able to move. His throat screamed for water. His uninjured hand fumbled for the survival canister at his belt. It was missing, too, torn free somewhere over the waters of the swamp. It had contained capsules for purifying water, a kit for testing foods...Gone.

Ardan dropped to his knees on dry land. His right leg felt badly bruised, and his head throbbed. Though he didn't remember losing his neural helmet in the launch, it was gone, too, and his head felt as though it had been smashed from behind with a club. Years of training made him automatically inventory what he had—knife, boots, shorts. The tattered remnants of his coolant vest. No food. No drinkable water. A broken arm...

Dizziness and pain rose up, obliterating the defenses that training and his mind had erected. He sagged down to the ground, tears of pain, exhaustion, and pent-up fear streaming down his face. Exhaustion won. For the first time in his life, Ardan Sortek fainted.

15

Maximilian Liao was livid. He stood straight, radiating fury, as Ridzik entered his chamber.

"So. What happened, Pavel? How did our clever ambush go wrong?" The Chancellor was so tense that his narrow shoulders quivered, his hands played games with his rings.

"Davion just didn't follow the plan that our agents had reported to us. They changed at the last minute. Far too late for any word to reach us, even through a Command Circuit. One evening, they were set to hit all the logical targets. The next morning, they came down all over the map. Every place on the *Folly* that could hold up a ship or a 'Mech was busy."

Liao looked bewildered. "But that means Davion himself doesn't know what his commanders have done. How can that be? How could they dare such a thing? Their lives will be forfeit!"

Colonel Ridzik looked grim. "Not every ruler demands the scrupulous adherence to his wishes as do you, Your Grace. Davion allows his commanders much leeway. They can make their own decisions on the ground, as circumstances require. It is not always a bad *modus operandi.*"

Liao's sallow face flushed faintly. "Are you telling me that my ways of operating are sometimes bad ones?"

Ridzik didn't flinch. "By no means, sire. But there are others that may also work extremely well. This time, Davion's method worked. Our only hope of holding the Folly was to surprise his troops as they arrived onworld. Because of their change in mid-operation, we did not succeed in that."

"So, with our lesser armaments, we must retreat. Is that what you're telling me?"

"To Redfield. Yes. Within the next six planetary days, unless we are to lose even more 'Mechs and vehicles, which we cannot afford. We are holding our headquarters and a few other key points, but if Davion makes a concerted effort against those, we will be forced to surrender."

"Surrender? Never. We will pull back, if necessary. But we will never surrender." Liao turned and looked at the starmap. "So near...so near. If only they had kept to their plans!"

Ridzik said nothing, deciding that was the most politic approach for the moment.

The smaller man whirled on his heel. "And we were so close to finding a lever to move Davion! The reports say that Ardan Sortek is with the assault forces. If we had been able to capture him...but that will be unlikely, now. There is no time."

Ridzik looked interested. "Sortek? Yes, it must have been him..." he said almost to himself. "There was a report of an engagement, along the eastern side of the main port city, with a unit commanded by a *Victor*. His methods were similar to those we have known with Sortek." He strode to another map, flipped down the sheet showing the area in question, and pointed.

"A large detachment of men and 'Mechs dropped onto the grasslands to the east of the port. They were met by a group of our own people, including a *Zeus* we captured from Steiner some time ago. The pilot is one of my special informants. After the engagement, he brought the remnants of his command back to headquarters to make his report.

"He personally engaged the leader of the enemy 'Mech unit, whose *Victor* was painted with the Sortek arms below the Federated Suns emblem. Our man disabled the 'Mech, but he believes the pilot was able to escape into the swamp, which was less than a standard kilometer from the battlefield."

Liao's face lightened. "Sortek...afoot. Possibly wounded ...a most interesting possibility presents itself. What is the status of that area now? Can we search the swamp without interference from Davion troops?"

Ridzik nodded. "The units engaged there withdrew to the local command center, after breaking our defense. They don't care about the countryside. What they want is to quash any resistance left in the city itself, as well as around the port."

"Then, have the swamp searched immediately," Liao ordered sharply. "Detail as many men as needed. Watch to see that they don't use heavy equipment, however. We've lost enough in those cursed swamps already. But see that they are thorough."

Ridzik saluted. "Yes, Your Grace. I shall be ready to go as soon as I have obtained all the computer information we will need. You have my assurance that if Sortek is alive, we will find him...Or even if he is not."

After the commander of his troops had left, Liao stood at the window, looking into his garden. This time he saw every vivid blossom, every bright, swift-winged bird. The view soothed him, helped to relieve the terrible tension of the past days.

Though his ruler was finding himself eased, Ridzik was increasingly harried. He had a world full of men and machines to embark for retreat. He had supplies to retrieve, if possible, and to destroy, if not. And now he also had an intricate and dangerous search to put into motion. He cursed the day he had first heard the name of Ardan Sortek.

Nevertheless, upon his arrival at Liao headquarters on Stein's Folly, he called in the leader of a unit that had served him well in many unusual and sometimes shady enterprises.

"Henrik, we have an important mission. The swamp in Sector Five...yes, that one." He smiled as the officer stepped to the map on his office wall and placed a finger on a stretch of green. "We believe that within that area of swamp may be a survivor of our recent battle."

The man nodded, his expression puzzled. Rescue missions had never been a high priority among the Liao troops.

"This man is important to our ruler. The Duke has need of him, even though he is an enemy. We must find him, dead or alive. When you do, bring him at once to the

DropShip being readied for retreat to Redfield. This is of utmost importance, Henrik. Do you understand me?"

The officer had worked with Ridzik often, and he understood all too well. Liao did not accept failure, even in the face of total impossibility. He saluted. "Yessir!"

* * * *

Ardan woke to darkness. His body burned with fever, and ached from head to toe, as though he had taken a brutal beating. Dazed and disoriented, he was not sure at first where he was or how he came to be here. It was his arm, throbbing in its preserving sleeve, that brought it all back...the swamp...ejecting from his *Victor*...the terror that the enemy *Zeus* would finish him off the way he'd finished off Ardan's 'Mech...

He could make out very little in the murk of night, but the trees around him had become raucous with hoots, honks, chirrups, rasps, howls, and other distressing sounds. To his fevered brain, every noise seemed threatening and vicious. When he mustered the strength to lift his head, trying to see into the pitch black of the swamp, some live thing thrashed away into the reeds, making a loud splash as it hit the water.

Ardan moved again, very cautiously. At his side, a tiny voice said "Meep? Meep?" with maddening persistence. He reached slowly for his leg-knife. Once in his hand, its metal reassuringly solid in this murky world, he felt somewhat better. His body screamed for a drink of water, but he dared not slake his thirst on this brackish slime. If only he still had his canister...

That thought brought back the memory of his last moments of combat with the *Zeus*. It had not stayed to finish him off, but had lumbered away toward the sounds of battle in the east. But what if the *Zeus* were to come back for him, after all? How could Ardan defend himself with just a knife, and nearly naked in his shorts and useless cooling vest? He would have to get away from this spot, he thought feverishly, but he dared not venture into the water in the dark.

The night wore on with painful slowness, but the sounds and the slitherings around him did not cease. Whatever those creatures might have been, to Ardan's shaky state of mind and body they were menaces beyond anything spawned in any swamp on any known world.

When a thread of light finally touched the sky beyond the thick treetops, he relaxed a bit. Though he had dozed in the night, some new alien touch on his hair or body had continually jerked him awake. Now he saw that the nightcrawlers had retreated to their burrows. He was alone on the mudbank. Gathering his courage, Ardan made himself slide, headfirst, into the greenish-black water.

It was shallow. He could float along, head above water, propelling himself with his good hand along the slimy stickiness of the bottom mud. From time to time, his palm met something that quivered or throbbed beneath it. That shook him.

He tried to move parallel with the edge of the clear ground. This swamp had to be part of some waterway. Waterways led to rivers. Once he had found a river…then what? He didn't want to think any farther than that. He would find help, or he would not. His head was in no condition to make coherent plans.

The air warmed, but he shivered uncontrollably in the water. His skin wrinkled and grew pale, but Ardan pushed on. The world spun about him, misty with steam over the water, misty with the obscurity growing inside his mind. Eventually, he was shaking so uncontrollably that he had to drag himself onto a mudbank, out of the water. There he saw the imprint of a large body and a wide, dragging tail in the mud. He didn't care.

He lay, face-down, gasping, shivering. Then, his back arched, and he vomited dark liquid. Had he drunk some of the water as he traveled? He must have. Now his belly knotted, and Ardan curled, shaking, nauseated, into a ball. He lay there, unable to move, for what seemed like hours, before he was roused from his stupor by a grunting sound nearby.

He turned to see a fat, pale-skinned shape wallowing in the shallows below him. Its piglike head was cocked upward, watching him. The eyes were black, small, hostile. As he watched, it flapped a wide, leathery tail against the water, raising a shower of droplets.

The owner of the mudbank, Ardan thought dreamily. Then he sank into delirium again.

This time he dreamed.

He was inside his 'Mech, facing hostiles. He tried to raise the arm. There was no response. He tried to scan his surroundings, but the monitors were all dark. He wanted to run...any direction, just to have motion. The legs refused to move.

He was blind, helpless, trapped inside the behemoth, waiting for his enemy to strike him down. He screamed, and the echo went round and round inside his helmet. He was sliding...down, down a chute toward the emergency hatch.

He came out onto a wide plain, stretching away on either hand as far as he could see. No sign of life met his despairing gaze. The grass beneath his feet was burnt brown. The sky was coppery yellow, the sun staring down evilly. His throat was sore; breath came with difficulty into his lungs.

He gasped and sank to his knees. It felt as though a 'Mech were sitting on his chest. What had happened to his unit? Where was Sep? Jarlik? Denek and Fram?

He groaned, and his own voice woke him. He looked up into a pair of round pink eyes, which shocked him fully into consciousness.

Moving with great difficulty, he turned onto his side. The small animal—if that's what it was—sitting beside him seemed undisturbed by the movement. It regarded him calmly, as he pushed himself up, one-armed, to sit facing it.

His head was still reeling, but Ardan felt certain that this was reality. The swamp looked exactly as he remembered it. The mudbank was real. The pain in his arm, legs, head, and back was real.

The creature he was staring at was short. Seated, it came just barely to his shoulder. Its head was as round as its eyes, and it had long-lobed ears hanging to its shoulders. The mouth was thin and straight, creating a prim expression much at variance with its infantile eyes. What Ardan had first taken to be an animal now seemed to him more a being somewhere between beast and human.

Ardan cleared his throat, tasting the remnant of vomit in the back of his throat. "Hello," he said, with some difficulty.

The thing jumped backward from a sitting position with catlike agility. Now it was standing, showing that it had long, thin legs, a stocky body, and a rudimentary tail that twitched with nervousness.

It stared at him for a moment. Then it uttered a high, thin wail that carried through the trees and echoed back from the depths of the swamp.

Bewildered, Ardan shook his head. The creature watched with much attentiveness. It shook its own head, mocking his motion exactly. When Ardan held out his hand in the gesture that meant peace on most known worlds, it held out its own. That meant nothing, Ardan knew. It was purest mimicry.

Then, in the distance, he heard another strange sound. Spattering steps were racing through shallow water. Shrill hoots and chirps accompanied the noise. Before he realized what was happening, he was surrounded by a dozen exact replicas of the creature sitting beside him. They were clad in only their own pale-furred hides, indistinguishable from one another.

The newcomers hooted briefly at their fellow, who chirruped back in a concise burst of sound. They seemed to be communicating in a language of their own, which amazed Ardan. He dimly recalled some of the computer briefings on the swamp life of Stein's Folly, but none of that information had prepared him for the intelligence he sensed among these pink-eyed beings. They turned, with one accord, and fell upon Ardan. Before he could react, he was tied into a sort of bundle with fiber cords. Then the creatures hoisted him on their shoulders, two on either side, and carried him away into the swamp, going deeper and deeper between the increasingly huge trees.

That was when things became hazy. At times, Ardan thought he was back on his father's farm, riding a load of grain to the bins. At others, he felt himself carried away on a berserker 'Mech, running uncontrolled across the country-side.

He burned with fever. He shook with chill. He vomited down the length of himself and all over the creatures carrying him. They dunked him into a pool, splashed water over themselves, and trudged on.

He went out, at last, into a blackness that was a great relief. When he came to, it was to the pitch darkness of the nightbound swamp.

He stirred. There came a twirping sound from somewhere nearby. Another chirrup, more distant, answered the first. A glimmer of light moved toward him, letting him see that he was in a kind of wicker hut, very crude but quite efficient.

He lay on a pallet of tree-moss, still tied up, but much less painfully than before. His mouth felt cleaner. They had given him water, he was almost certain. He hoped it wasn't the terrible stuff from the swamp.

A short figure stumped into the hut with a tiny torch in its hand. It was exactly like every other he had seen thus far, without even any sex differentiation, as far as Ardan could tell.

The thing squatted beside him, tested his bindings, held the torch close, and lifted one of Ardan's eyelids. It grunted. The sound indicated satisfaction, as nearly as Ardan could tell.

126

"I'm glad you're happy. At least one of us is," he said crossly.

The creature sank onto its heels, staring at him. A complex series of grunts, honks, hoots, and chirrups gave him a notion of the source of some of the night-sounds that had troubled him. There was no point of similarity with any language Ardan had ever heard, however. He tried to shrug, but his broken arm made him groan instead.

The creature nodded twice, decisively. It touched his face with an inquiring finger, poked at his bare chest, examined his toes with much interest. Then it took itself and its glow-worm torch back off. The hut was dark again.

Ardan fell asleep, much to his surprise. When he woke, there was light in the hut. Dim green light that was filtered, he surmised, through the interlocking branches and leaves of tremendous trees.

He felt ill. Never in his healthy life, even when injured in battle, had he felt so awful. Fever shook him from time to time. Chills covered him with gooseflesh. His stomach heaved, but lacked anything more to eject.

He smelled smoke. These creatures had fire, then, as well as tools? They were sapient, then. A few other non-human sapients had turned up among the worlds of the Inner Sphere, but these were surely the strangest-looking of any yet known.

He lay still, waiting. The fever cushioned him somewhat from reality. Nothing made much difference now. Whatever happened, he didn't care a great deal.

When the procession came for him, he didn't struggle at all. They lifted him again, still tied, and carried him outside. There they laid him on a litter made of green branches tied together with the familiar fiber cording. When they had him situated, they decked the litter with odorous green, pink, and purple flowers resembling orchids, except for their dragonlike yellow maws.

"Here comes the bride," he murmured, quoting from an old book. Ancient traditions and rituals had always fascinated him. Now he looked fair to become a part of one.

127

One of the Pinks (he decided that he had to call them something, even if only in his thoughts) screeched shrilly. The rest lined up instantly, lifted the litter, and splashed into the water surrounding the hummock holding the hut.

It seemed to Ardan that they walked a long way. He stared up into the vine-clad trees. Birdlike creatures flitted overhead, while other creatures resembling the arboreal primates of Old Earth scampered along the branches and vines, keeping pace with the procession.

He fell into a peaceful state that was interrupted only when his bearers stopped. They tipped the litter up so that he was standing, supported by the wooden frame to which he was tied.

He was on a sizeable spot of solid ground surrounded by dark green water. A number of trees stood about at considerable distance from one another. There were eighteen, which, for some reason, Ardan counted. Bound to all but one tree were skeletons tied with seemingly indestructible cord.

The bones were indubitably of human origin. No Pink had ever grown to such height. The skulls were distinctive, the rib-cages ribboned with climbing vines. The foot-bones were hidden in a light growth of thin grass.

"Oh, wonderful!" he groaned. How long had the Pinks waited for the last victim to complete their set?

"Stein? Is that you, old boy?" he asked aloud. The Pinks ignored him.

"Folly is right. I'll just bet you and your boys and girls tramped off into the swamp, bent on exploration and glory, and wound up as...what?" He turned his gaze to the Pinks, who were very busy about some inscrutable business.

Six approached him, cut away the litter with their clawed fingers, and propped him against the single undecorated tree. They flipped ends of cord about him, then wound them round and round the tree trunk and his body.

Without another sound, they were gone, leaving Ardan to contemplate his fate.

16

Hanse Davion stood beside the holotable, staring down at the nervous blinks that represented ships in transit. The fact that each of the distant craft had already reached its destination and that the table was only catching him up on the most recent information didn't comfort him. He knew his men had retaken Stein's Folly, but the struggle was not over yet. The Prince must now make decisions that might or might not aid those commanders whose instincts had pulled victory from the very jaws of defeat.

He looked up as Ferral, his personal aide, entered the room. "We were lucky, Fer," he said. "If we didn't have the best commanders in the business, our strike would have gone down the tubes. Has the messenger finished his report?"

The younger man looked down. His jaw tightened, and his entire stance showed his reluctance to say the thing that had brought him.

When he looked up, Hanse was staring at him, worry already beginning to wrinkle his brow.

"The report is that…that Ardan Sortek has been lost in action. Not killed…no body has been found, though his *Victor* was pretty well savaged. But there was no trace of him."

"Have searchers scoured the area?" The question was sharper than the Prince's usual even tone.

"No. There has been so much to do, what with the remaining stiff resistance. All available manpower has been occupied in keeping the areas we have taken. Liao troops are pulling off regularly, and we think they are withdrawing to Redfield, but we still have our hands full."

Hanse stared again into the holotable, as if the mechanism might tell him where his friend might be. When he looked up again, he was fully in control.

"Give orders that every effort be made to locate Sortek," he said. "Not only is he an old and dear friend, but he also knows things about me and our methods that the enemy might find most useful. Chemical questioning bypasses the instincts of the most loyal. He must not fall into the hands of the enemy. And if he should, then he must be rescued at any cost."

Davion turned to stare from his arched window into the afternoon sky. "Assign at least one unit to that task. It is of utmost importance, both to me personally and to our security." He did not look around as the aide replied.

Only when the door closed did Hanse turn again to the table. It had been a gamble balanced on a knife-edge of skill and luck. He was the most fortunate of men, lucky to have in his service men of the caliber of Felsner, Hamman...and Ardan Sortek.

He thought of Ardan as a child, riding on Hanse's own strong young back, later learning games and skills from him as they roamed the fields outside the town where they had been reared.

He shook himself and turned to a monitor. He must read the fresh reports. He must make the crucial decisions. He must not think of Ardan again until something concrete could be done about him.

* * * *

The tree was rough against his shoulders. The cooling vest, now much the worse for wear, did nevertheless protect the skin of his back. The Pinks had pulled his arms behind him when they retied him, however, and the ridges of tree bark dug into them.

Ardan, still protected by the fever, giggled softly. This had to be the silliest hallucination ever experienced. The Pinks themselves were ridiculous. This ritual with the skeleton-decorated trees was even worse.

He looked about at the nearest of the bony trophies. Most had turned brown with time, and some were also

130

greenish with fungus. Grungy-looking things. How could his mind, even distorted with fever, come up with something so bizarre as this?

He stared at the adjacent tree. Its tenant grinned back at him absently. The skeleton looked bored, as if the joke had long ago worn thin. A reptile, brilliant yellow striped with mud-green, came into view, crawling up through the rack of bones to coil about the collarbones.

His stomach heaved, and Ardan retched. The motion sent agony through him. The tight bindings had cut off circulation to his extremities, and they throbbed unmercifully.

The pain brought him entirely to his wits for the first time in many hours. This was no delusion. This was real. He was tied to a tree in the middle of a swamp with the remnant of some earlier human expedition. He would rot, as they had done, and snakes would nest in his belly.

He knew there was nothing to be gained by shouting, but he shouted, anyway. To his surprise, he heard a distant but distinct "Halloo!" in return.

Friend? Or enemy? At the moment, Ardan didn't much care.

* * * *

Henrik hated the swamp. His uniform, standard Liao-issue, was too thick, too hot, too constricting for moving about in such country. The foul water soaked through pants-legs and into the boots, making his feet swell and steam. He knew that his men were cursing him silently. He was just as silently cursing his own commander, though he knew that Ridzik had good reason to order this search.

The muck teemed with reptiles and even more evil-looking creatures. The air was aswarm with insects, most of which either stung or bit. He swatted aside a loop of vine, and found himself holding a long green body that wriggled about with terrible quickness to sink fangs into his sleeve.

For an instant, he blessed the same heavy clothing he had been cursing for so long. The fangs did not penetrate the tough fabric, and twin beads of yellow venom were left to roll off into the water about his boots.

He dropped the thing with a yell, and his men scattered to give it room to escape. Most were from worlds that had no serpents, and so most of them recoiled instinctively. Recoiling himself, Henrik stepped back into a deep hole, and fell backward with a mighty splash. The brown-green mud roiled up where his foot had slipped, and he ended up lying on his back, looking up into the tree that leaned overhead.

Henrik found himself staring into a pair of pink eyes, round and frightened in an almost featureless circle of face. Another oddball animal. Its pale fur clung to its colorless hide, and its short, useless tail was quivering nervously.

He was pulled upright again by a pair of his men, who helped him to scrape the foul muck from his uniform. Henrik dried his weapons carefully. What a place! Full of animals, snakes, insects, but seemingly empty of the one he wanted.

Yet they had found, back in the grassy verge of the meadows, a canister of field equipment marked with the Sortek sigil. There had been a clear trail crushed down through the growth, leading directly here. They had even found marks that looked like human tracks on a mudbank.

Sortek had to be here somewhere! Henrik told himself.

The day passed in more discomfort than even a soldier had a right to expect. Darkness came, finding them without any recourse but to climb into a slanting tree like a row of filthy and disgruntled birds, to roost there until the light came again. It was easy to lose men even in a familiar swamp. In an alien place such as this, there was no way to guard against its unknown perils.

His own group of four men had taken this route. Four more had gone the other way. Four more had struck out, as nearly as he could determine from his maps, for the center of the swampy stretch. Surely, among them all, they would find the man they sought!

The morning dragged on with terrible slowness. They slopped and crushed and slithered their way through the terrain, penetrating ever deeper into the wilderness of water and trees. The sun was dropping beyond the thick canopy overhead, when, in the distance, Henrik heard something. A shout. One of his other men? Someone.

He motioned for his group to halt. Then he cupped his hands about his mouth and yelled, "Hallooooo!"

There was a moment of silence. Then the shout again. As well as he could, he took a bearing on the direction from which it came. Then he signalled his men forward.

They moved as fast as was humanly possible, given the terrible footing. Before darkness was total, Henrik stood on a large mound of solid dirt that rose from the surrounding water to hold a stand of tremendous trees.

He saw the man first, squirming as much as his tight bonds would allow.

Two of Henrik's men dashed forward to cut him loose. A more pitiful remnant of humanity they had seldom seen. Almost naked, the man was covered with cuts, weals, bloody gashes, and the marks of the cruel cords. Enemy or not, Henrik pitied him.

The man was so covered with muck and mire that it was hard to tell what he looked like. The eyes, however, were distended, wild, disoriented.

"Folly!" the fellow was saying. "Stein's Folly! Look a-round you, will you? Did you see what I thought I saw? Or was it all in my head?"

Henrik snapped on his light-pack and scanned the surrounding trees. He almost dropped the pack, as he realized what those protuberances that he had taken for viny growths really were.

He heard gasps as his men, too, realized that they stood in the midst of many skeletal human remains. Henrik shivered. He was a soldier. Death was no stranger to him or any

133

of his people. But this was no honest battle-death. This was something strange and outré.

Quickly, the men rigged a litter. This might be solid ground, but no one suggested spending the night here. Only one thought occupied all their minds, including Henrik's.

They had to get out of the swamp. Whatever had done this had been intelligent. Inimical. It was something he had no desire to find or to face.

It was a terrible trek. Periodically, Henrik would pause to sound his audio-signal, telling his other searchers that the quarry had been found. That would set the denizens of the swamp to making greater efforts, and the noise that followed the signal was deafening.

The brilliance of the light-packs didn't really help much. Indeed, it brought into being terrifying shadows, and revealed myriad eyes shining malevolently about them every step of the way.

Before dawn, Henrik and his men rejoined the rest of the search party, but even that did not dispel their feeling of horror. When light came at last, bringing the misty surface of the water, the shadowy hulks of the trees, the mysterious deeps of the brush-clumps into sight, they breathed a mutual sigh of relief...and walked even faster through the nasty water and nastier mud.

They were not surprised that their captive had lapsed into unconsciousness. The thought of being alone in that swamp, tied to a tree among the remains of the long-dead, filled Henrik with an emotion he didn't examine closely.

By the time they reached the meadows, Sortek was thrashing violently in the litter, making it difficult for his bearers. He shouted and wept, by turns. Nothing in the Medkit seemed to relieve him, and so it was a relief when they finally loaded him into their land transport.

The party reached the main base without difficulty, for which Henrik was devoutly grateful. From the start, this had been the worst of assignments. He turned the captive over to Ridzik, with proper procedure, and then watched curiously as the MedTechs wheeled him away.

"I will be surprised if he lives to be useful," he said, almost to himself.

Ridzik turned with a glaring look. "Oh, he will live, Henrik. We will make certain of that. You have done well. Now prepare your unit for transport to Redfield. We will be pulling out over the next two days."

"What about him?" Henrik nodded in the direction taken by the Meds. "Sir?"

"He can't be moved. I can see that. He will be among the last to go. That will give us time..." Ridzik's voice dwindled, and he seemed to be seeing something inside his own mind.

"No time to speculate," he snapped. "Get ready, Henrik. And thank you."

Dismissed, Henrik thought about those last words. It must be important, the capture of that sick man. Ridzik was not known for thanking his subordinates.

17

"Culture thirteen, negative. Begin test of culture fourteen."

The voice seemed to be inside his head. Ardan tried to open his eyes to see who was speaking such odd words, but he couldn't. No muscle in his body seemed willing to move. Even his will was not working. He didn't want to move, to speak. Even to breathe.

He felt his chest moving. He knew that he was not expanding and contracting it...he was through with breathing. With everything. But the air pumped into and out of him inexorably.

He sank into black depths...like swamp water. He tried to scream, but nothing worked any longer. Then he was deep in the darkness, seeing swirls of light that were evil colors. Eyes with no bodies. Bodies without eyes.

Pink eyes. Eyeless skulls.

Tied to a tree was a child, its entrails dangling from a wound in its belly. A snake was trying to crawl in...to take the place of those lost intestines. And that would make the child into a monster! An alien monster, capable of any atrocity!

Ardan writhed and moaned. Hands touched him. Something burned along the vein in his left arm, and oblivion seemed to follow it. Yet that turned into nightmare again.

He was walking in his *Victor* through a beautiful countryside. Before him were trees bearing ripe fruits, their boughs bending to touch the delicately colored flowers blooming in the grass beneath them. Houses stood in neat gardens, their walls covered with vines heavy with ripe bunches of grapes.

Croplands spread away from the road he followed. Birds sang as they flew in formations, catching insects. It was so beautiful! He took care to keep his 'Mech in the exact middle of the paved strip, so as to avoid damaging anything.

He entered a forest filled with deep green shadow. A sense of peace was upon the place, and he would have liked to stop and rest, but the 'Mech plodded onward. No matter what Ardan did, it was as though the Victor had a will of its own. He could not make it obey the controls.

At last, the 'Mech paused. It swayed...and then it turned on its metal heel.

Ardan gasped with shock. Behind him, there was complete devastation. The forest was splintered, ruined, with only stumps and charred remnants showing where it had been. The road was buckled. Weeds grew in cracks, and small trees were sprouting in the middle of it. The houses were gone. The croplands were barren, seared, brown. No fruit tree was left, no bird, not even an insect gave life to the empty landscape.

"I am a destroyer!" he said aloud. "I am a sword, and I work havoc, wherever I go. Even the most subtle dagger is no worse than I."

And with those words, he awoke fully for the first time in two days.

He looked about, his vision a bit hazy but adequate. There was nobody in the tiny room, though the curtain over the door was still moving as if someone had gone through recently. A tray beside his bed held medications in applicators, waiting, Ardan supposed, to be used on him.

He focused his eyes with some difficulty. On the containers was the tiny green triangle, crossed with armored hand and blade, that was the mark of House Liao.

He was a captive.

The thought sent adrenalin through him. He stirred. His muscles responded.

He lay for a moment, astonished. He had been so weak for so long...how was it that he could move now? The MedTechs in charge must be masters of their craft.

He squirmed and sat up very cautiously, letting the reeling in his head subside before trying for more. He glanced down to see that he was neatly clad in a white smock, hospital garb that hadn't changed in millennia. Below the edge of the litter on which he lay was a pair of flat slippers.

He swung his feet about carefully. Not too bad...a bit of dizziness, but it seemed to be subsiding. The slippers fit his big feet.

When he stood up, Ardan almost fell. His head began its interior rocking, like a vessel on a stormy sea. But he was determined to stand, to walk. To get away while his attendant was gone.

Even as he made his legs cooperate, Ardan wondered about his situation. He was a captive. Surely the MedTechs knew what their medications could do. Why had they left him alone just when he would be regaining consciousness?

He shook his errant mind back into order. Whatever the reason, he had to get out. Find his unit again. See if his Tech could repair his *Victor* or scrounge parts to make a hybrid 'Mech of it. There was so much to do...and he had no idea how the attack had gone.

Beyond the curtain was an empty hallway. At the end of it, behind a closed door, he could hear voices. He crept into the corridor and turned in the opposite direction. Doors lined the way, some open into empty chambers like the one he had left, some closed. Pushing one open, Ardan found himself staring at a bandaged shape spreadeagled on an orthopedic rack.

He moved on, trying a door from time to time. At last, he found one that led into another passageway. This was dark, as if little used. Glass-windowed doors on either side let dim light into the corridor, and he stepped to the one on his left and peered through into the room beyond.

It was a big chamber, filled with unusual and somehow disturbing equipment. Glass-fronted cubicles lined the side wall, and there was the throb of motors, as if compressors were operating beneath the floor.

He leaned against a metal table in the middle of the room. His head...his head was whirling again. Pictures were forming behind his eyes. As disturbing scenes bubbled up from some hidden place inside him, he put his hands to his eyes and moaned.

The sound was echoed faintly from one of the cubicles. He turned awkwardly, trying to see through the faint frost that covered the glass.

Someone was inside. Someone...familiar...? He moved closer, pressed his hands to the glass, and set his face between them, peering hard at the dim shape. As if summoned by his attention, the light intensified around the body inside.

"Hanse!" he whimpered, scrabbling at the glass with his numbed fingers. "Hanse, what have they done to you?"

The familiar face was blank. The eyes were closed.

As he stared, he began to see subtle differences. The lines of thought and humor that marked Hanse's square face were lacking in this version of it. The unique expression that made of Hanse's features something special and precious had not set its seal upon these identical features.

This was a blank, waiting to be finished. Waiting to be used...for what?

His head throbbed, and his brain seemed to whirl, like water sloshing about in a bucket. Ardan moved away from the cubicle. He had discovered something of terrible importance. Someone, surely, could interpret it.

But first, he must get away. Find the forces of Davion, wherever they might be. He turned blindly, his tiny hoard of strength expended. In a daze, he staggered back to the room in which he had awakened.

* * * *

Lees Hamman took the assignment enthusiastically. "I'll get him out," he told Felsner. "If the spy's report was correct, I'll find him and bring him back. But he must be in pretty bad shape, if your information is to be believed. We've done harder things than breaching the Liao base."

"According to our information, there's not much armor or staff left there," Felsner agreed. "I wonder why they took

139

the trouble to capture Ardan, only to leave him with such a light guard? Seems strange."

"Let's be grateful for small favors," said Hamman. "I'll take an infantry unit for backup. This calls for something more subtle than a straightforward 'Mech attack. They might kill him before we could find him."

"I agree. We have a scout available. He might come in handy." Felsner thrust out a hand to his subordinate. "Good luck, Lees. A lot is riding on this."

"I know. Let's get moving, eh?"

Hamman found the scout, a man named Rem, waiting for him with the other six men assigned to the operation. When he reached his own quarters, they knelt on the floor and spread the detailed map of the Liao headquarters compound on the floor.

"Your man is in bad physical shape. The informant saw him brought in. Delirious, dehydrated. Starved. Injured ...Broken arm, bad cuts, and bruises all over him. And the Meds think he ingested some sort of organism that is playing havoc with his body chemistry and digestion. He is not going to walk out of there under his own steam." Rem pointed to an L-shaped extension of the main building.

"That is the main hospital area. At least, that's what our commanders used it for, and it has all the necessary equipment, beds, everything. So that's what they use it for, too. He'll be somewhere along this corridor, I'm pretty certain."

Hamman measured the distance from their present position to that of the Liao base. "How long will it take us to get there? And can we slip into the area unseen?"

"Six hours, by hovercraft," Rem replied. "And we can set down in the middle of this strip of woodland...see?" He touched the map. "Right there. We can go into a drainage tunnel that ends in this stream. It is one that serves the reactors, so we'll need radiation-shielded suits and boots. They won't expect anyone to come that way—even if they know about the tunnel at all."

He grinned. "They haven't been in control all that long. I doubt they've found it, yet."

"Good," said Hamman. "Can you get the necessary equipment issued within the next two hours? That will put us in the area just about sundown. A good time for this kind of foray."

"Done," the scout said. "Oh-nine-hundred hours for set-down?"

"Just right," the subcommander said.

They didn't quite make it, but their timing was close enough. It was dark when they set their hovercraft in a clearing in the forest. They donned their rad suits, then began creeping through the trees, on the lookout for the stream. They found it gurgling between narrow banks that were half-filled with rank growths of ferns and other vegetation. The stream would hide the eight of them until they reached the point where it met the mouth of the tunnel.

They moved as silently as possible through the water until a splotch of deeper darkness loomed beside them. The tunnel mouth.

They carefully removed the grating that covered it, using the special wrenches that Rem had thought to provide for the purpose. The flow of water was shallow, once they were inside. Their rad-counters began to click faster, as they made their way up the vaulted conduit.

They used little light. There was only Rem's glimmer, which provided just enough to keep them from bumping into walls when the tunnel curved.

When they reached the shield-wall from which the main artery drained, they were faced with another grating. It, too, yielded to the wrenches. This time, they were so careful that almost no sound accompanied their work.

Then they were in the lower tier of the building. Hamman, having memorized the maps, turned to his right and climbed to a catwalk. Now was the time when luck would be with them...or not. He could only hope.

18

Ardan had somehow managed to get back into his bed before passing out. Now he began to move again, trying to speak, and a hand touched his face. A muffled voice spoke to someone outside his doorway. He strained to hear, but the sound was too garbled to make sense.

He recalled something...a solid fact that he knew he could trust. He *had* seen the medications. They *had* been marked with the Liao insignia. So he was in the hands of the enemy.

He stopped trying to speak, to warn those around him about the duplicate Hanse he had seen. His memory of wandering through the building was becoming dim and unreal to him, but the recollection of that blank face in the cubicle was sharp and clear.

A hand shook his shoulder. The voice outside the door became clearer. "Did he see?"

See what? wondered Ardan, as he joggled limply under the moving hand. He didn't want to come back to full consciousness now. He was too groggy...and he had too many questions waiting for him. He drifted deeper...

Then there was a noise outside. Not a voice. A thud. The crackle of a hand weapon. A scream that was cut off in the middle. The hand was gone. The room seemed empty, except for himself.

With a tremendous effort, he opened his eyes. They felt gummy, sticky, unfocused. He saw shapes in pale suits covering them from head to foot. Two were pushing into the room. He tried to move, to sit. One of the shapes whipped off the head-covering.

"Lees!" he whispered. "How?...Where?"

"Not now. Here, let's get you into that coverall hanging in that cupboard over there. Don't try to help me. I can see that you're out of it. Rem, you take his other side. O.K., Ardan? We're leaving now." The voice paused, and the two men lifted Ardan and bore him away down the corridor he had seen once before.

Even as they covered the distance to the double doors at the end, he drifted into and out of consciousness. They burst through the doors and pounded down stairs just beyond.

Ardan gritted his teeth, coming back to himself. The pain had cut through his disorientation for a moment. His arm twinged sharply as his weight shifted.

"It won't be too long," grunted Lees. There was a crackle as a weapon discharged, and the three came to the floor of another corridor.

"O.K." That was an unfamiliar voice. "We've cleared our run to the main entrance. There's just about no staff or guard left here. This is spooky."

"Now!" That was Rem.

Ardan was pulled upright again and swung along swiftly, his toes dragging. He couldn't make his legs move properly, and so he just relaxed and let the other two men do all the work. He hoped they knew what they were doing.

Flashes from side passages told him that there was at least some resistance left in the complex, but they shot past too quickly for him to know what was being done about it. Then they were outside.

It was raining. He was soaked through instantly, which made him sneeze so hard it shook both his bearers.

"We'd better get him into shelter fast. He could get pneumonia awfully easy," said Rem.

"We've located the ground vehicles they've been leaving behind," came a voice. "Over here. We've found a troop carrier that should take us all. Just hope that it's powered up and ready to go."

After some jostling and tugging, Ardan found himself lying flat on a hard surface. Men were tumbling in around him haphazardly. There was the sound of power and a vibration of the surface on which he lay. Then motion.

He cried out, "Hanse! Why?"

Lees reached down to touch his face. "Fever," his voice said. "Cas, you have the medkit?"

There was the familiar touch of a spray-shot on his arm. Then he went into a blackness as deep as that of the swamp.

* * * *

The messenger always hurried when he came into the room. Hanse supposed it was to impress him with the urgency of the news he carried, as well as the devotion of the man to his duty. It always irritated him.

"Well?"

"The mopping-up on Stein's Folly is complete. The last of the Liao forces have retreated to Redfield. Our casualties have been heavy, but not as heavy as we had originally expected. And your friend Ardan Sortek has been recovered from a hospital unit in the base used by Ridzik while on the planet."

Hanse felt relief surge through him. The tightness that had seemed to bind his heart so painfully now eased. He had dreaded other, worse news of his friend.

"I want a detailed report of his injuries and his present condition. The unit caring for him. Everything."

The messenger obeyed his gesture to sit. Hanse made himself settle into the deep chair behind his desk. He quieted his hands, breathed deeply, and concentrated on the words of his messenger. With his learned discipline, he would not forget a syllable that he heard.

"Ardan Sortek," said the messenger, going into his automatic-report mode, his voice sounding almost mechanical, "has suffered recent dehydration, starvation, broken left radius, badly stressed ligaments, right leg. Surface bruises, cuts, scratches, fungal infections." He paused for breath.

"Systemic infection, probably from contaminated food or water ingested. Mental disorientation is persistent, characterized by repeated reference to injured child, to unusual fauna in the swamp on the world in question, and to some sort of doppleganger complex he has developed."

"Doppleganger? Doesn't that mean ghostly double..." Hanse said thoughtfully. "That is a symptom of mental derangement, is it not?"

"It can be, the MedTechs say. This is very deeply impressed upon his mind. He keeps linking it, strangely enough, with the Prince of Davion."

"Strange," said Hanse. "I have known that Ardan was not completely comfortable with many matters, but I hadn't thought it to be serious."

"The medical people are most concerned about his mental state. Their facilities are focused upon battlefield casualties, and they haven't the psychiatric staffing to deal with this sort of problem in the most effective manner. They suggest intensive care as soon as possible."

Hanse motioned for the man to pause, while he thought carefully. There were things Ardan knew concerning his own affairs that were best undisclosed, even to the most faithful MedTechs. If Ardan were seriously unbalanced in his mind, it was perhaps best to keep him away from New Avalon for the time being. The Court on New Avalon was rife with spies and informers, he knew, and Ardan could seriously compromise many affairs of state if he were to speak of them while not in his right mind. Hanse considered distances, facilities...and he had an idea.

"Is the Steiner DropShip still docked on the Folly?" he asked.

"It is scheduled to leave in three planetary days. The supplies have been unloaded, and a number of the badly wounded have been placed aboard for transport to the medical facilities on Tharkad," the messenger concluded.

"You are scheduled to go back down the Command Circuit tomorrow," Davion said, "and so you will arrive in time. Have Ardan Sortek placed in the care of Steiner. Their psychologists are among the best in any sphere. If anyone can help him, they can." He felt reassured, relieved. "Is there anything else of importance?"

"Only a minor matter," the messenger replied. "The officer leading the rescue mission was puzzled at how easily it

145

was carried out. He insisted that I report to you his suspicions that we were intended to recover Sortek. He wonders if some sort of biological might have been used to infect him in order to bring a danger into your presence when he returns to New Avalon. With the uncatalogued infections already in his system, this would be quite possible."

Hanse sat forward, frowning. "If we got him back easily, after Liao took the trouble to capture instead of killing him, there is something beneath it. Not necessarily that, but something. Do warn the Steiner Meds to use utmost caution as they care for him. Assure them that we appreciate their faithful adherence to our treaty. Anything else?"

"All the technical data is being entered into the computers. You will receive a printout shortly. For now, that is all." The messenger looked a bit pale.

Hanse had a twinge of conscience. Jump was a strain on the system, and it showed on the messenger. He smiled at him and said, "You will find that your good work has earned you a fitting reward. I think a promotion and a grant of land to your family will be in order, later, when there is more time for such things."

The man looked surprised. Then he grinned, the first expression Hanse had ever seen on his tight face. He left the room less pale than he had entered it.

Before the man was out of earshot, Hanse had touched a button on his desk. "I need an Adept, please," he said to the ComStar Tech who replied.

While waiting for the arrival of the Adept, Hanse composed a terse message to Katrina Steiner, asking her not only to take good care of Ardan but to take care that he did not reveal information sensitive to both their Houses. He was just finishing when Adept Ara tapped quietly at his door.

"Enter," he said at once.

Ara was assigned as liaison to the Federated Suns by her Order, and so she was not Hanse Davion's subject and had no need to salute him. Ordinarily, this irritated him, but he had no time for that now.

"I want a message to go through to Katrina Steiner on Tharkad. It is of great importance and secrecy. How soon can I expect it to reach her?"

Ara's smile was gently reproving. "You know as well as I that the HyperPulse Generator signal travels the distance from New Avalon to Tharkad in three weeks. No more, no less. Impatience, Highness, is no virture in a ruler."

He sighed. She was right, which was the most irritating thing of all.

"Of course." He handed her the message he had been working on while waiting. It was dated Third Quarter, Tenday, 3025. It would be on Tharkad before the ship bearing Ardan could possibly reach there. No need to worry about that.

Ara glanced at the message, which was coded. She smiled faintly. "A message to the fair Melissa?"

How did they know these things? Hanse shifted in his chair, but remained expressionless. Good thing he had used the new code. "You can see that it is addressed to the Archon," he said. "Only to her."

She took the message and nodded. "This will be sent at once. Good evening, Your Highness."

Hanse stared after her. Secrets were the leakiest of matters. If his own ComStar Adept knew of his secret engagement to Melissa Steiner, who else did? The union of their two Houses would form a formidable barrier to the ambitions of the Liao-Kurita interests. And that information could be of inestimable value to any of a number of other powers.

He sighed. One could only trust that ComStar was still the unaligned, impartial body it claimed to be.

19

The first jump, added to his existing condition, made Ardan very ill, indeed. While the group in transit waited for recharge, he was entrusted to a Doctor Karn, who kept a close check on him.

Ardan had waked fully for a time after the jump. He had been visibly distressed, trying to convey some information that seemed terribly important to him. It had required a sedative to quiet him, and now Ardan knew that Karn was peeping into his cubicle often.

He liked the young doctor. For one thing, the man was not talkative. The cool, clean feel of competence he brought with him was also extremely reassuring. And right now, Ardan needed a lot of that.

For the fifth time, Karn was saying, "Yes, Commander Sortek, you are on your way to Tharkad, as a guest of the Archon herself. Others of the expeditionary force are also being sent to our facilities for treatment. You are definitely out of the hands of the Liao forces. Please relax. Everything is all right, now. Sleep. Rest. You need that if you are to heal."

Ardan closed his eyes. They sprang open again as if his eyelids were on springs.

"There is something I must tell someone. I am not often as clear in my mind as I am right now, Doctor. But you must listen."

The young man nodded, a patient expression on his dark-browed face. "Yes. I am listening."

"There was a duplicate of Hanse, back there where I was. I take it that was the Liao base?"

Karn nodded.

"I woke up. Someone had just left the room. I found, unexpectedly, that I could move, though I hadn't been able to before. Or even to hold onto any single thought for more than a moment. But I seemed suddenly much better. I thought that I would escape, if luck were with me."

Ardan paused, as Karn held water to his lips. He sucked gratefully on the tube.

"I went down the hall. Someone was talking in the other direction, so I went the opposite. You see?"

Again the doctor nodded.

"There was a door at the end of the hall...on the side. I'd tried others, but they led into rooms with wounded men in them. This one went into a dark hallway. Halfway down were big glass doors on either side. I looked into one, and saw some sort of laboratory.

"I went into it. I don't quite know why, but I did. There was a table in the middle...I remember I had to lean on it for a bit to get my breath. There were glass boxes along one side." He shivered, and the doctor put a hand reassuringly on his shoulder.

"I looked into one of them, and Hanse was inside. Or someone just like Hanse, only...only different. His face... he had a face that never had been *used*. Do you understand what I'm saying?"

"You saw—you think you saw a double or a duplicate of your Prince of House Davion? Interesting. Most interesting."

"The other doctors told me I was hallucinating. They talked about doppelgangers, whatever those might be. But I did see that. Everything else is hazy, but I remember that, without any doubt. You do believe me?" He looked anxiously at Karn.

The young doctor bent his head. "I think that you did see something. Whether you are interpreting it correctly, I have no way of knowing. There must have been something there, to convince you so deeply. But now you must rest."

Ardan caught at his hand. "Why wasn't I put into cryogenic stasis for travel? That's the way we always brought home our wounded before."

Karn smiled. "You were in such a strange physical state that it didn't work on you. One of those strange infections,

149

I suspect. But we have those under control now. Don't worry, though, you won't have to sweat out every stopover. The next time you wake up, you will be on Tharkad."

Ardan relaxed against the foam pillow. "Thank you, Doctor. You have helped me a lot. I needed to tell someone what I saw. You will pass it on?"

"Of course. Now sleep. The shot I gave you should put you out. When you open your eyes again, we will be at the palace in Tharkad City. In winter, of course, which is not much fun, but it will, indeed, be Tharkad."

* * * *

And that was just the way it happened. Before he opened his eyes, Ardan smelled the rock-firs that tanged the air of the capital of that stony world. Even inside a building, as he obviously was, the crisp scent of green things managed to sneak through the ventilators to liven up the hospital's antiseptic smell.

He sighed heavily. Now he knew that he was safe. The Steiner dynasty had become a staunch supporter of the Federated Suns...and Hanse. He smiled secretively. In a few years, Hanse would marry Melissa, daughter of the Archon, Katrina Steiner. After all, fifteen was still a bit young to take on marriage with a man so much her senior.

He had known her well, and her mother, too. The last time Hanse had visited Tharkad, Ardan had commanded the Guard unit assigned to the Prince. He had loved that assignment more than most.

The world was a bracing one, not too lush and easy, as so many of the most populous ones tended to be. Tharkad held challenge for its inhabitants, and danger. As Hanse had wanted him to see the countryside and get to know the people, Ardan had spent much time mountain climbing, especially with men and women of the Lyran guard.

It had been during that visit that Hanse had arranged with Katrina for her daughter's hand, a clause that was

150

worked into the intricate treaty they were negotiating and that was later signed at Sol.

Ardan stirred. For the first time in what seemed an eternity, he felt able to sit. He pushed with his right arm, trying to raise himself.

"None of that!" It was the Archon herself, bustling in through the curtained space serving as a door. "Be still, Ardan, and get well. I have particular instructions from Hanse to take special care of you."

Ardan found himself smiling. She was a woman after his own heart, strong and determined. Now she stood in the narrow space between his bed and the screen dividing it from the next cubicle. Her hair was coiled about her finely shaped head, and her color was ruddy from the brisk weather.

"Ardan, how are you?" she asked, perching on the edge of his bed and taking his hand in both of hers. "I have had word from the Prince, and he is most concerned about you. We are taking you with us, back to the palace. Melissa is going to learn nursing, tending you."

The young man tried to sit, but the woman pushed him back gently. "I am so happy to see you," he said. "My duty on Tharkad was the most pleasant of all my service, I think. But do take care, ma'am. I have had some very odd infections and viruses. Don't risk infecting yourself or the Archon-Designate."

She laughed. "I have had a full report from your doctors. Don't trouble yourself about anything. We are going to bring you back to health so quickly it will astonish you. Now sleep a bit more. We will move you when the snowstorm ends—or tomorrow, whichever comes first."

He closed his eyes, only to open them again at the sound of a quiet voice at his side. Melissa stood there, wrapped in a long fur robe with a round fur hat on her smooth hair. She regarded him intently with her gray eyes.

"How do you feel?" she asked softly. "Don't worry about us. The doctors say they have eliminated the bugs from your system. It's quite safe to be around you now."

She was still the tall, slender girl he remembered. At fifteen, she was not yet the stunning woman she looked to become, but her understated loveliness was unmistakable. He thought that Hanse could have done much worse in the choice of a wife, even without the political considerations.

"Then I'm ready to go! I remember the palace well. Is it as comfortable in the winter as it is in the spring?"

"Not quite," she said, wrinkling her patrician nose. "You have to wear long underwear, unless you want to freeze stiff. But it will be some time before you are allowed up. We will read together, and you shall tell me stories about...about your Prince. If you don't mind?"

He understood her curiosity. She had last seen her intended husband several years before. She had been a child then, unaware of many things that must now have her wondering.

He nodded briskly. "Indeed, I will. I can remember Hanse from the time he must have been about fifteen, and I was only five or so. We were neighbors, and good friends were rearing him. Though he was almost a man, he was very patient with me, even as a tiny child. I loved him like the brother I never had. We have been close, even when we were great distances apart."

Even as he spoke, Ardan realized how true were his words. Why had he stopped trusting Hanse? Why had he questioned the ethics of the man he knew better than anyone else? A surge of sorrow went through him.

"What is it? What is the matter?" Melissa asked, bending over him to place her small, chilly hand on his forehead. "Are you worse?"

Ardan managed a sick smile. "No. Not physically. I have just realized that I've been a fool, and that is never a pleasant experience. For some silly reason, I began to think that I knew more about running a system of worlds than those who have been trained for it. Somehow, I thought that my personal standards must, of necessity, be those that everyone must practice. Ridiculous, eh?"

152

"Well, you look worse than you did when mother left. I think I'd better call for a doctor." Her tone was decisive. In that moment, Ardan saw the ruler in the making. Melissa would be just such another as her mother. Perhaps not a warrior—she had, after all, not been trained for that—but as a statesman, a manager of human beings, she was going to be something to watch.

She left in a swirl of flowery scent, with an after-tang of pine. In a moment, a Med came in to administer a shot. Ardan drifted away on a wave of drug, yet a part of his mind was still alert, inquisitive, ready to rejoin the world. And so it was that he heard the quiet voices outside in the corridor.

"He is still delusional?" That was Katrina's tone.

"Only in certain matters. He has put the injured child into perspective. Our psychs have delved into the roots of that fixation. A nasty experience, too…one that would give anyone a bad time. This illness and injury just brought that out into the open. Probably, in the long run, it will be a good thing for him."

That voice belonged to another woman. Her tones were higher, less cultured than those of the Duchess of Tharkad.

"No, it's the other thing that still has a hold upon his mind. The double of Hanse Davion. We are a bit worried about this. He should have been able to get a grip on that, the way he did the other problem."

"I have read, in tapes of old books, about such things," said Melissa. "There was a book called *The Prisoner of Zenda*, about a man who was the double of the ruler. He went through the coronation ceremony in the missing man's place, foiling a plot of some sort. And then they took their own places again. There are several books about such a substitution of a double for a controversial person of importance."

Katrina pushed aside the curtain and glanced at Ardan. He had his eyes closed, remained totally relaxed, breathing deeply. His body was asleep; it was his mind that was still alert.

153

"When you study military history, you come up with many strange matters. Once, a very long while ago, there was a war on Old Earth. The Commander of one side—I believe his name was Montgomery or something similar—reviewed troops and traveled about the battle areas, misleading the enemy totally. That man was a double. The real Field Marshal was helping to plan a major attack, which succeeded partially because of that ploy. Such things have happened more than once," she said.

"Well, this cannot be such an instance," said the doctor. "The time for such play-acting is surely in the distant past, not in our civilized present."

Another voice chimed in, deeper, assured. Doctor Karns. "He is deeply troubled by that vision. But it's hard to tell whether he really ever left his bed at all. It is quite possible the entire sequence of events was an hallucination. Yet he repeats it with utter consistency. That is unusual with a true hallucination. It is a troublesome problem."

"We shall remove him from any reminder of such matters," said the Archon. "Melissa will entertain him. We shall take his mind off anything painful or distressing."

"That should be of great help. He is most fortunate to have the friendship of the ruler of the Lyran Commonwealth," said the woman doctor. Her sycophantic tone disgusted Ardan.

He twitched his hand, trying to move, but the drug carried him away, deeper and deeper. The voices were silent, or perhaps the speakers had moved away. It was just as well. He needed sleep.

But as he sank into that darkness, he saw the face of that other Hanse before him. Still. Uncommunicative. Unused.

20

Outside the double-glazed and insulated windows, framed in the graceful arch, a snowstorm was doing its worst. Melissa Steiner sat on the cushioned windowseat, gazing out into the blizzard. From time to time, a wayward gust would sweep the curtains of snow aside, giving a brief glimpse of the deeps below the crag where stood the favorite seat of House Steiner.

Melissa enjoyed the violent climate of her homeworld. The distant glimpses of Tharkad's snowswept crags and peaks, the tumbles of lesser eminences with their heavy wigs of white, filled her with a sort of fierce joy. She hoped Ardan was awake to look from the window beside his bed. He liked this world, too, she recalled.

At the thought of their guest, her face grew sober. From her first glimpse of the trim young officer in charge of Hanse Davion's personal Guard, she had liked him. He had always treated her with respect, but the two of them had also developed a conspiratorial pleasure in hatching practical jokes for which they were never blamed.

That was probably because nobody ever suspected that the bookworm Melissa would indulge in such pranks. Ardan Sortek was the first person ever to tap the repressed mischief in her nature. Remembering all that now, she smiled and subdued a sudden urge to do something silly.

She was fifteen now, almost a grown woman, too old to indulge in foolishness. But she was happy, indeed, that Ardan had returned. Winter could be very long and boring on Tharkad. It would be diverting to pass the time with him.

That reminded her of what she had meant to check in her Reader. Ardan's insistence that he *had* seen a double for Hanse had reminded her so much of that ancient novel she had read. Melissa rose and went over to the Reader, intending to review the computer records for anything similar.

She keyed in 'Impersonations' and touched the command key. The monitor asked: Historical? Social? Literary? Economic?

That surprised her. The computer's response seemed to indicate that history was full of such things. She decided to start with the literary references, as it was *The Prisoner of Zenda* that had set off her train of thought in the first place. A list of titles and authors began to scroll down the screen.

She printed out those she thought might be most interesting. There was *The Prince and the Pauper*, *The Man in the Iron Mask*, as well as a number of others that were unfamiliar to her. Next, Melissa asked for the historical data.

Those results astounded her, too. It was not only in ancient history that such things had occurred. In 2381, a double had succeeded in impersonating the Elazar of Trimerrion so successfully that his world was plunged into a war that almost destroyed it. The true Elazar had not been able to win free of his captors until it was too late to prevent the catastrophe.

Melissa's gray eyes narrowed. The situation among the ruling Houses of the Successor States was now unstable, making a treaty between Davion and Steiner a major irritation to both Kurita and Liao. Therefore, anything that disrupted the planned union of the Lyran and Federated Suns systems would be of great benefit to the Draconis Combine and the Capellan Confederation.

She read further. In 2738, one of the pivotal allies of the Lord of the Star League had suddenly changed his policies so drastically that it affected the decisions of several of the other states later involved in the Succession Wars. Only later, after the man's death, was it learned that he had not been Faillol Esteren at all. His fingerprints had been altered to match, of course, and his retinal patterns were sufficiently similar to trigger various security devices. What they found, however, was that the false Esteren had broken some bones in his youth, but his appendix was in place. The true Faillol had undergone an appendectomy at age 15, but had never broken a bone.

The mystery of who had been the imposter was never solved. Nor was it ever learned who was behind the substitution, nor how it had been done.

She read closely the detailed history of that era, learning that the false ruler's decisions had furthered two different interests. Neither appeared to be involved in the plot, but it was strange that the two closest friends of Faillol had vanished from the scene at about the same time. One had suddenly become so ill that his mental processes were affected. He was hospitalized and later institutionalized, but never recovered.

"Drugs," said Melissa. "No doubt of it."

The other was accused of treason when certain state secrets were leaked. What must have been the false Faillol had spoken half-heartedly in his behalf, making matters worse, not better, for the unfortunate man. Eventually, he was tried and found guilty. The fact that an innocent man had been dishonored and executed came out only after the imposter's death, years later. The dead man had been so completely in the real Esteren's confidence that he would have immediately detected an imposter.

Ardan, too, was the close confidante of his Prince, Hanse Davion. Could there be some devious reason for his sudden recovery at just the right moment to see that shape in the laboratory?

For the next week, Melissa read everything she could find. The novels, the historical records, even the accounts of social substitutions. This only reinforced her first impression that impersonators were not and never had been rare. It was more that they were seldom uncovered. How many more had been totally successful, so that the imposter had gone to his grave without being detected?

When she had absorbed as much of this background as her mind could hold, Melissa went to see her mother. Katrina was, as usual, immersed in the affairs of her worlds and those of her allies and enemies. But she swept a clear spot on the carpet beside her, always glad to make time for her daughter.

"And what have you been doing all week, my dear? Is Ardan able to be up and about, yet?"

Melissa shook her head. "Almost. Doctor Karns says tomorrow he may get up and sit in the garden room. I already have a pile of books there, waiting for him. But it's about Ardan that I came, Mother. I think there may be something to his tale about the double of Hanse that he saw in the Liao base."

Katrina twirled a lock of hair about a finger. It was a sure sign that she was uncomfortable about something.

"I truly doubt that, my dear. The doctors say that the alien infections Ardan suffered also affected his mental functions. That, combined with the stresses our young man suffered, was enough to unbalance him, just a bit. Only temporarily, though. They assure me of that. Nothing that can't be healed by a long rest on Argyle, while the Prince is there in his summer palace."

"But mother," Melissa insisted. "I've just gone through everything I can find in the comprehensive computer files on impersonations and substitutions. You would be astonished to know how many there have been…and, of course, those are only the ones that were discovered. In fairly recent times, Mother, there have been leaders and rulers replaced by doubles who made profound changes in events." Melissa put her chin on Katrina's knee. "Do think about it a bit. Doesn't it seem odd that Ardan recovered his wits at just the right time to find himself alone?

"And isn't it strange that the voices at one end of the hall determined that he would go the other way? Right to the only door that led someplace? Right to the lab where that body was waiting in its cryogenic cubicle? I think it is straining coincidence a bit," said Melissa.

Katrina put her hand on her daughter's hair. "I can see that you have been troubled by the situation. I understand that. You say there have been cases in recent history?"

"Within a couple of centuries, which isn't a lot, as history goes. And at times when the decisions those people made were unusually important. It seems to me that carrying out our treaty with Hanse might well be a similar situation. Think about it, Mother!"

"What you say is reasonable," her mother admitted, "but I must consider the expert opinions of those who care for the mentally or physically ill. It is not only the word of those doctors directly involved in the care of our guest that sway my thinking. I also have called in specialists from the foremost institutions on Tharkad." She tipped Melissa's head with her hand and looked into those intelligent gray eyes.

"They are unanimous in their verdicts. He is convalescent. He has suffered serious traumas, both physical and mental. He is overcoming those, slowly. And that story about the double is, without any doubt, simply a delusion."

Melissa sighed.

"You still do not agree?" asked Katrina.

"Something feels all wrong. Ardan isn't one to keep insisting if there's any possibility at all that he might be in error. But Mother, at least please inform Hanse that his friend has this belief. If nothing is in the wind, then no harm will be done. But if there *is* some sort of plot, then perhaps it may help him to guard against it."

"Good thinking," said Katrina. "When the next message packet goes out, I shall see to it. Now you go and cheer up that young man. He was staring at the wall and mumbling curses the last time I looked in on him. The nurse had tried to give him a full bath in bed."

Melissa laughed. "I can imagine how that would suit him if he is able to do anything for himself at all. Thank you for hearing me out, Mother. I'll let you get back to work now." She stared about at the confusion of papers, printouts, and micros.

"One day I'll have to deal with all of this. How will I do it? You should have made a MechWarrior out of me! I don't know if I will ever become an administrator."

"You'll handle it, as I do—as well as you can. Now, off with you, and give Ardan my affectionate regards."

159

Melissa moved through the chilly stone hallways on fur-clad feet, keeping her hands curled in the deep pockets of a fur-trimmed woolen over-robe. The palace was constructed solidly, insulated as well as possible, but Tharkad's bitter winter winds managed to creep in by crannies known only to itself.

Fires burned on hearths in the luxurious rooms she passed. The heating system, powered by a reactor deep in the bedrock below the house, murmured, sending out warm currents that seemed to lose themselves against the chilly stone.

"I wish I lived in a wooden cottage with ceilings less than six meters high," Melissa muttered, turning down the corridor toward Ardan's room, which Doctor Karns had just entered. She reached the door and paused outside, waiting for him to finish examining his patient.

Though Melissa was no eavesdropper, she couldn't help hearing the murmur of voices. She was astonished to hear the doctor encouraging Ardan to hold onto his belief in what he had seen.

"Nothing that is completely a delusion could grip you so strongly," Karns was saying. "So, don't let anyone make you feel that you are mad for insisting on it. You are as sane as I. I'm sure of it."

She stepped away, back up the hall, thinking hard. This was the exact opposite of what she had heard him tell her mother, only the day before. Something was very wrong, someplace. Was it possible that a conspiracy might reach even into Tharkad? Worse, into her own house?

As the door opened, Melissa moved back toward Ardan's room.

"Oh, Doctor...how is our patient this morning?"

Karns smiled, his dark face creasing charmingly. "Much better, indeed. He will be able to get up for awhile, if you promise to put him back to bed at once if he becomes tired. We must take care...he is still in a delicate state."

Melissa smiled sweetly in return, but all the while she was thinking: *I will watch you, my friend. You are not exactly what you seem.*

21

Ardan looked up to see Melissa entering his room. For the first time that day, he smiled. "You look like a Winter Queen," he said. "I wish I were up to going out for some cross-country skiing. Remember how the members of the Court took to that, when I was here before?" He sighed.

"It's blowing like anything outside," she replied. "Here, let me open the curtain. See? Nobody but an idiot would go out if he didn't have to. But the doctor says you can get up for a bit. I have books and games in a nice warm spot in the garden room. Will you join me?"

He sat up straight and looked about for the heavy robe Katrina had provided for him. Melissa was already handing him a pair of furred slippers.

In a few moments, they were making their way up the corridor toward the moist warmth of the conservatory, where plants from every sort of world lived together, loops of orchidaceous blossoms hanging from entirely unsuitable trees from the swamps of Stein's Folly. Ardan shuddered as he recognized a slender, straight-trunked variety whose umbrella of rubbery leaves flared almost to the top of the distant skylight. The orchids had found purchase among the clusters of pinkish blossoms that furred the smooth skin of the plant.

There were two cushioned chairs set near the vent of the heating system. Also waiting for them were a pile of valuable printed books, which lay in waterproof coverings.

Exhausted by even this brief walk, Ardan sank into a chair and covered his knees with the light embroidered coverlet waiting for him. He gazed up into the heights of the conservatory. All manner and color of hanging vines and air plants crisscrossed the domed skylight from the room's support columns.

"This is the place for getting well," he said. "My father always says that there's nothing like growing things to pull you together and make you feel better."

"I remember when your Prince was here. To make the …the arrangements with Mother. He came here often and would sit just looking up as you are now. I thought then that he was a lonely man. Does he have many friends, except for you?"

Ardan looked down at the girl, who seemed so wistful now. He wondered suddenly what it would be like to be wed, as she would be, to a stranger she had seen only briefly and about whom she knew virtually nothing.

"No, he doesn't. Not really. People who want to get close are usually those hoping to use him in some way. Politicians, bureaucrats, sycophants, all of them. And those he really cares for are people who are too useful to waste at Court. He has to send them away as ambassadors or commanders of armies or representatives in all sorts of ticklish negotiations." Ardan realized that he hadn't truly understood this about his friend until this moment.

That was why Hanse had seemed so sad to have Ardan ask for transfer. Of all the many people at Court, Ardan was the only one Hanse Davion could call friend, without any qualifications.

He sighed. "I didn't understand that when I asked to go into action. Not that I didn't want to…I just didn't realize how alone it would leave my old friend."

Melissa's eyes were filled with concern. "You love him, then? He is a man who is easy to love?"

Ardan considered that question carefully. "I wouldn't say he is easy to love. To love him, you have to know him well. He can seem very harsh and stern, when need be. But inside he is a caring man. Even when I was a tiny lad, and he was so much older, bigger, and stronger, he was always patient, even tender—for a boy—when it came to me. He never made me feel like a nuisance, though I must have been one often."

"What did you do together? When you were boys?" Melissa was sitting cross-legged on the carpet, looking up with the starry eyes of a child. Ardan didn't smile.

"We went fishing and caught whales that turned into minnows, once we got them home. We trapped grassbirds for the farmers, to keep them from spoiling the fields of grain. We picked fruits from my father's farm, and we helped the family that had the care of Hanse with the work there, too. Hanse's father didn't believe in bringing up a Prince to behave like someone above and beyond ordinary people."

"Like Mother!" Melissa exclaimed.

"Very like," Ardan agreed. "We went boating on the river...almost drowned, too. I understand now that the convenient fishermen who pulled us out were there just for the purpose of seeing that the younger son of their ruler survived to grow up. And a good thing it was, too. Otherwise, when Ian was killed, that slimy Michael would have managed to seize power. Hanse's sister is no Katrina. She is easily swayed."

"And when he went away...to be trained as a Mech-Warrior...did you miss him?"

"Terribly. If it hadn't been for my father's promise that I would go, too, as soon as I was old enough, I might well have pined away. Like a pet whose master has left it behind."

Melissa set her chin on her fists. "I have heard that Hanse was a brilliant warrior. Brave and resourceful. Did you ever go into battle with him? When you were old enough?"

"Only once, just before his brother was killed. I was young. Just trained. Hanse used to see to my training personally when he could find the time and opportunity. We were attacking an enemy position from two sides. I was on the left flank, he was on the right of the center line in a *Warhammer*." Behind his eyes, Ardan could still see the battle. He felt his blood warm at the memory.

164

"There was a unit of 'Mechs there, backed by infantry with hand-weapons and tanks armed and ready. It was the last stronghold of the enemy onplanet, and we had to root them out.

"The position had been dug into a cliff with a heavy overhang of granite, where sandstone had been washed out beneath it by some ancient stream or sea. An impossible position, believe me. We were taking heavy losses, for we had to bunch up to rush the only entrance, and that brought us into the line of fire of everything they had."

Melissa had straightened, her eyes huge as she listened raptly.

"As Hanse came through our ranks, he signalled for us to fall back. When we did, he walked right up to that hellish entryway and threw in everything he had at it. Then he stood there, taking fire from every direction, every kind you can imagine, while his PPC hammered at the pillar of sandstone at the edge of the portal."

"What happened then?" demanded Melissa, when he paused for breath.

"Hanse must have felt like a piece of cooked meat—with his 'Mech getting hotter every minute. But he kept right on firing until the granite roof caved in on the entire enemy installation—men, 'Mechs, tanks, and all. We dug them out later, but only a few men survived. We got 'Mechs and replacement parts out of there that we're still using." He recalled his ruined *Victor* and sighed.

"He is brave, then. And an original thinker...I like that," the girl said. "I don't think I could be happy with someone who went by the book all the time."

Ardan chuckled. "Never accuse Hanse of that!" he said. "He writes a new book whenever he has to, and never limits himself to what's been done before."

"He was so kind to me the one time we were together for any length of time," she said. "We had seen each other when he met with mother and the Councillors, but we'd spoken only once or twice. Mother gave an entertainment ...do you remember it?...when the treaty was finished.

Everything formal and elegant and dressed-up. It was my own engagement, and I insisted on going, even though I was too young." She giggled. "I also insisted on doing my hair up on top of my head and wearing a black dress. I must have looked a fright!"

"I was on duty that night, so I didn't see you. But you never look a fright, even when you're acting like one," Ardan grinned, recalling some of their antics when he had first known her.

"Anyway, Hanse had brought a fantastically ancient and valuable vase for Mother…one of those that really belong in a museum, you know. It was lovely, too. All iridescent peacock-blue with pinkish lights all over it. Gorgeous." She sighed.

"I was really too young for such an entertainment. I was overexcited and trying to make an impression. You know how young people are."

Ardan hid his smile.

"Anyway, I insisted on looking at the vase, holding it in my hands." She paused, remembering. "And I dropped it …A world's ransom in antique vase, and I shattered it to flinders on the parquet flooring of the ballroom. I was mortified.

"Mother was really angry. It's one of the few times I have seen her so furious. And I could see everyone whispering and murmuring behind their hands…I felt like a worm. A veritable worm!"

"I can imagine," Ardan said, picturing the scene.

"I started to cry. Just like the child I was at the time, of course, but it embarrassed me even more than the accident did. I stood there in my sophisticated black dress, my hair beginning to tumble down, and my face wet with tears. I remember thinking that the Prince, mature and at ease and in control of everything around him, would never accept such a complete failure as a wife."

Melissa smiled. "I found a dark corner and was trying to sort myself out and clean up my face, when I felt someone

166

touch my shoulder, and give me a kind of pat. When I looked up, it was Hanse. He was smiling at me."

"That's so like him," Ardan murmured. "He hates for others to be uncomfortable through no great fault of their own."

"I found that out. But I was still mortified to be caught crying like an infant. I said to him, 'I suppose you *never* cry, do you?' And his answer comforted me instantly, though I have never quite understood what it meant."

Ardan gazed down at her. "And what did he say?"

Melissa's gray eyes were seeing into the past as she replied, "He said, 'The Starbird weeps inside.' Do you know what that means?"

For a moment, Ardan caught at an errant memory that evaporated the moment he tried to seize it in thought. "No, though I suspect it means something quite deep and important to Hanse. And I do know that he hates much of what he must do to maintain the balance of powers and influences that hold the Federated Suns stable. I wish I could tell you more..."

She rose. "You look tired. Back to bed with you!"

He found, to his astonishment, that she was right. The short walk, the brief time spent sitting and talking, had drained his energies.

As she accompanied him back to his room, Melissa whispered, "That was when I knew that I would not object ...not at all!...to becoming Hanse Davion's wife."

Ardan thought of that later. It might, of course, have been policy...or Hanse's exquisite sense of the decent thing to do. But he suspected otherwise, that Melissa's story revealed a gentle man comforting a stricken child. There were worse beginnings for political marriages.

22

As he grew stronger, Ardan took advantage of the Palace's excellent facilities, exercising to the limits of his ability every day. Sometimes Melissa joined him. Though there was a fragility about her, she had grown into a tall girl who was tough as whipcord.

They laughed and joked as they worked out in the gymnasium, using the computer-controlled exercise machines. But when they were alone in one end of the huge space, out of earshot of the trainers and other exercise enthusiasts, they often talked seriously.

Winter was on the wane when Ardan made a crucial decision. He knew that he had to return to Stein's Folly, but it would have to be done secretly. And for that he would need help. For one thing, he had to get a message to Sep. He hoped she had forgiven his harsh behavior and words during their last meeting, and that she would keep her promise to help him, if ever there was a need. He clung to that promise, which was his only hope of accomplishing what he intended.

He found Melissa an attentive listener, when he gasped out his conclusions between surges of effort on the Total Musculature Machine. He had felt, all along, that she alone of the people on Tharkad believed his story about that weird double of Hanse. Now he felt her agreement, though she said nothing while pumping the handles of her own exercise machine.

"I am just about back to normal," Ardan began. "Strong enough to hold up under long periods of effort, if the computer readouts are to be believed. That means that I'm going to have to find some way to look into…that matter."

Melissa nodded, her cheeks pink with exertion.

"I've got to go back to the Folly. Things have quieted down there since the enemy pulled back. All the mop-up has been done, too, from what your mother says. The

168

garrison at Main Port has been beefed up, but all the lesser ones have been closed and booby-trapped. Hanse doesn't want anyone else to be able to use our own installations against us."

He paused to change machines and also to catch his breath.

"I have to have assistance. I need my junior officer, Candent Septarian. She said she'd come any time I called, and now I need to contact her as quickly as possible. Have you access to ComStar?" he asked Melissa.

She smiled secretively. "I have made close friends with the Acolyte here. She is very bright and most dutiful. She doesn't go by the book, either."

"She can access the HPG system? I need to get word to Sep as quickly as possible."

"Three weeks," said Melissa. "The laws of physics are pretty immutable. But in three weeks she will have word. What should I tell her?"

Ardan thought intensely for a few minutes. "Is there freighter service now between Tharkad and the Folly?" he asked finally.

"Kerrion has gone back into service there, since the restoration. His freighter DropShip is in port right now. But a freighter is too slow. You need your own JumpShip. A small and unobtrusive one that can get you there unremarked. They're not going to want you back on the Folly, you know."

"But I haven't a JumpShip," he said patiently. "And I must do with what I can manage."

"Mother doesn't believe in your doppelganger," said Melissa, "but if I ask her, I know she'll lend you a ship."

He signed with relief. "Then tell Sep to rendezvous with me at Point X-r-23, behind the larger moon of Stein's Folly. The transit time for the message...plus time for getting herself ready and whoever she can recruit...plus the eight jumps from New Avalon...We should rendezvous fairly well together, timewise."

He sprang for the hanging rings and swung himself into a handstand. "Tell her to bring anyone who can manage some leave-time. And their 'Mechs, too, if possible. We may have a hard time breaking into that installation."

"She can ask Hanse for help," he gasped. "But make it private. Even secret. We don't know what's going on, or who is involved."

Melissa rose from the machine and reached for a towel. She wrapped it about her shoulders, put another over her sweat-soaked hair, and said, "I'm glad you're doing this. I've had a bad feeling about the whole situation from the start. Something is going on that I can't quite figure out."

She turned to add, "I'll send the message first. Then I'll ask my mother for the ship. She hasn't lasted this long as Archon, much less as a MechWarrior, by hanging back when action is called for. I don't think she's entirely comfortable with your 'delusion', either. Now, work hard!" Then she was gone.

As he pushed his still-painful body past its limits, Ardan thought deeply. There might not be anything left on the Folly to give him a clue to his weird vision. But if there were, he would find it.

And then what? His only hope was to have an impartial and dependable observer present. Not Sep...it might be said that she was prejudiced in his favor, having been his junior officer in their unit. He hoped that she would bring friends, but he also prayed that she would find someone who knew him only casually.

After finishing his exercise routine, Ardan showered and returned to his room, where there was an invitation to dinner from Katrina Steiner. Ardan rather suspected it meant that Melissa had been persuasive, and the first step in his enterprise was in the works. The loan of a JumpShip, even a small one, was no small matter—their being among the rarest and most prized remnants of the Star League era. Katrina Steiner must have much love as well as much confidence in her young daughter to grant such a tremendous favor.

He dressed carefully in the formal attire Katrina Steiner had thoughtfully provided. The Archon was never able to dine privately. There was always business to be done, as well as dignitaries to pacify or potentates to impress.

She did it well, too, he decided. He had attended such affairs before, but only as a member of the Guard. As a guest this time, he found the difference interesting. Here he was, mixing with a flower-garden of brightly clad people, men and women from every corner of the Lyran Commonwealth, as well as representatives of lesser systems.

Indeed, tonight Katrina had a full house. Also present were Klefft, the ambassador from the Capellan system, who was talking intensely with Hardt, his opposite number from the Draconis Combine. And there was Baron Sefnes from New Syrtis...Ardan hadn't even been aware that Michael Hasek-Davion maintained his own diplomatic relations with Steiner. As head of the strongest economic force in the Inner Sphere, Katrina was a pragmatist who tried to keep trade and military matters from interfering too much with one another. No matter that her House was in conflict militarily with Kurita and Liao—business was business. Indeed, it was House Steiner's innovative economic and trade policies that had nurtured the continuing economic growth and strength of the resource-rich Commonwealth. Its military fortunes were another matter, of course, which was one of the reasons the ever-practical Katrina had wooed and won Hanse Davion as an ally and future son-in-law.

Ardan moved among the guests, talked idly with Melissa's cousin, the Margrafin Kelya, and watched intently the interactions of those on differing sides of the present conflict between Davion and Liao. There were undercurrents in that spacious chamber that he found it impossible to read.

When the gong announced dinner, Ardan found himself beside Melissa, who took his arm and steered him toward the tall arch of the doorway. "We are seated together. I arranged it with the *arbiter elegantiae*. He kicked a bit, but I know where a few of his skeletons are buried, in a manner

171

of speaking. He daren't risk my blowing the whistle on him," she said, her tone smug.

An elegantly attired gentleman stood beside the dining room door announcing the entry of the important guests. Pointedly ignoring Ardan, he cried, "The Archon-Designate Melissa Steiner. And escort."

Ardan tried not to grin. Feeling Melissa quiver lightly against his arm, he knew she was stifling laughter, too. They were of one mind when it came to formal occasions and the haughtiness attending them.

Once they were all seated at the long, richly covered table, Ardan watched Katrina discreetly, pondering once more the ways of life at the royal courts of the Inner Sphere. He had never been able to play the elegant and treacherous wordgames that passed for conversation there. Rarely did anyone say what he meant, and even the most innocuous comment might have some sinister double intent. Tonight, Katrina sat between the Kurita and Liao ambassadors, smiling, nodding, and interjecting a comment from time to time. Ardan couldn't always hear what the three were saying, nor could he read their bland, diplomatic expressions.

Just after the servants had brought out the first course of creamed aspergrot soup, Katrina glanced around at all her guests and lifted her voice so that all might hear. "Honored guests," she began, mustering her most gracious royal tone, "may we say what a pleasure it is to have you here. And may we add how especially gratifying it is to welcome several distinguished representatives from our neighboring Houses to our midst as well." Katrina smiled at Hardt, Klefft, and Sefnes before continuing.

"We live in uncertain times, but House Steiner continues to forge strong bonds of trade and commerce wherever and whenever possible. This has ever been our strength. Our merchants are gifted and resourceful, and make us friends in even the most unlikely places."

"House Steiner's great gift for commerce is the envy of the Inner Sphere," said the ambassador from Liao, perhaps too smoothly. "All admire this talent..."

"...and would do well to emulate it," said Katrina, playing the game. "We have even had news of late that our free traders venturing into the Periphery have fared well among the outlanders there, prospering themselves and our House. As my scholarly daughter put it"—Katrina smiled down at Melissa—"our merchants seem to have the Midas touch!"

"Ah," said Kurita's man Hardt, "Your Grace refers to the old Earth tale of the king who so loved wealth that he asked the gods to turn everything he touched into gold."

"So, the ambassador from Luthien is familiar with the old stories, too," said Katrina affably.

"Well, if memory serves, the story tells that this Midas almost starved to death when his magic touch also turned his food and drink to gold."

Katrina ignored the hidden sarcasm, and laughed easily. "Well, one thing is for certain, and that is that no one shall starve this night"—and she gestured at the mounds of delicacies piled up and down the table—"Let us enjoy this bounty, one and all, for it is the real thing, untainted by the Midas touch."

The servants continued to bring in course after course of viands imported from all over the Steiner sphere. The plain dishes Ardan accepted, but passed over the impossibly furbished and sauced ones. Now that he was getting better, it was no time to get sick again from sampling rich dishes from distant worlds.

When servants brought in silver basins for the convenience of guests who had indulged in finger-foods, Katrina took advantage of the pause to tap a cut glass bell with the handle of her knife.

"We have had, for the past few months, a most welcome guest here on Tharkad," she said, gesturing at Ardan. "Please meet Ardan Sortek, friend and subject of Hanse Davion, Prince of the Federated Suns. To our joy, he is now recovered from the wounds that brought him here. To our sorrow, he is now ready to rejoin his ruler at his summer retreat on Argyle."

She raised her heavy wineglass. "I propose a toast to this brave young officer. May we all command such devotion in time of trial!"

There was a polite murmur as the guests raised their glasses. Taking a sip from his own cup, Ardan noted that Klefft, from Sian, and Hardt, Kurita's man, seemed inscrutable, yet Ardan knew there was discomfiture in their very rigidity.

He smiled, stood, and bowed. "My thanks to my gracious hostess. A warmer welcome and better care have never been extended to anyone. I am anxious to rejoin my Prince, but I am desolate to leave the company of those here present." He sat amid polite applause.

It was the diplomat's art to disguise what he thought and felt, yet Ardan was sure he caught surprise, even anger, flickering momentarily across the faces not only of the Liao and Kurita ambassadors, but over that of Michael Hasek-Davion's man as well. He was sure, too, that the trio exchanged a look among themselves that was neither casual nor diplomatic. Ardan might have expected some kind of reaction from Klefft and Hardt, but what had Michael's man Sefnes to do with any of this?

Melissa leaned to whisper in his ear, "My mother never does anything without a good reason...and perhaps more than one good reason. You saw?"

He smiled, as if replying to a casual comment. "Indeed, I did. Unexpected. Watch, Melissa. There may be rot at the root of more than one tree."

Without changing her gay expression, his friend twitched her brow slightly. She had thought of that already, he saw. What a ruler she was going to make!

As the meal finally wound down to its end, the servants brought in decanters of fiery Atrean brandy, which they poured into snifters that resembled bubbles of light, each cut from a single crystal and ornamented until it refracted

174

every beam blindingly. The arrival of the brandy seemed to relax the gathering even more.

Ardan turned down his glass, however. His body chemistry was still disturbed, and the doctors recommended that he abstain for some months more. Melissa accepted a finger of amber-brown brandy and sipped it slowly while talk of everything from trade relations with the Free States to the recent retaking of Stein's Folly swirled around them.

Finally, though, Katrina Steiner rose from her chair. "If you will join me in the ballroom, those who wish to dance may do so. Oldsters like me may prefer to play at games that we have set out for your amusement. And, of course, those with duties or early rising hours may feel free to retire."

This was one of her most civilized habits. Many rulers required everyone to remain in attendance until they themselves had decided to retire. Katrina's leave gave Ardan the opportunity to return to his room and his preparations to leave Tharkad on the morrow.

He had barely had time to change when there was a light tap on his door. Melissa waited outside, clad again in her warm day-gown.

"What a deadly business that was," she said, "but we learned something valuable, don't you think?"

Ardan had been thinking of little else. "Yes, it seems strange…If my glimpse of that double had been accidental, you would think that whoever is behind it would hope that it remained a secret, and that no one would believe me. But tonight it looked as though some powers are disappointed that I seem to have accepted the doctors' verdicts and have ostensibly given up insisting upon its reality.

"I had expected…them…to be glad of my going to Argyle, to be with Hanse. But they weren't. They seemed shocked, as though expecting me to take some other step. Liao's man Klefft looked appalled."

"I saw it," said Melissa. "Did you know that Doctor Karns used hypnotherapy while you were so very ill? He said that it was to help you to deal with your fixations. And

175

nobody was allowed to monitor, because he claimed it would be dangerously distracting."

Ardan stared at her, his mind going in circles, speculating, discarding theories.

Melissa looked grave. "He might have implanted something. Be very careful, Ardan...This next move of yours may not have originated with you."

Though he rejected that thought at once, it had shaken him, troubled him. "Did your mother agree to lend me a ship?"

Melissa nodded. "Not without a lot of argument, I must say. The doctors have almost persuaded her to their way of thinking. But she respects my judgment, too, thank goodness. The *Atlan* is charged. She is small but dependable. After your final jump, her DropShip will get you into synchronous orbit with the Folly's larger moon and keep you there until your friend Sep arrives. If, that is, she doesn't get there first."

The girl shook out and refolded neatly the clothing he had crammed into the case she'd provided for him. Her hands busy, she continued, "The ship will be ready for jump just after sunrise. We thought it best to get you away quickly, just in case..."

Ardan dropped onto the edge of the bed and stared out the window. With the snow almost gone now, the rocks of Tharkad showed through like bones through tattered flesh. He turned his mind from the darkness of that thought, and bowed to Melissa, saying, "I am forever obliged to you, Your Highness."

She laughed. "None of that! Just plain Melissa is good enough for fellow rogues. But I will be eternally obliged to you, Ardan Sortek, if you save my future husband from disaster."

23

It had been a grueling day. The transshipment of all the personnel, 'Mechs, and supplies for the Guard to Argyle was always an unwieldy process, and Sep had just begun to get her unit back into shape after the move. She was well aware of the reason for the summer sojourn, however. Argyle was important to the Federated Suns, and its inhabitants were a crucial factor in the Prince's constant need to walk a tightrope to maintain his balance of power. Nevertheless, it was hell on the Guard, not to mention the servants of the Palace.

Sep had just now put things enough in order to begin drilling the unit again. The summer Gauntlet was in operation, and she had spent the morning putting MechWarriors through its inhospitable bag of tricks. They needed to get back their edge after the enforced inactivity.

She was tired. Tired and a bit sick of pushing resisting men and machines. She needed leave, but Ardan's departure had delayed her scheduled R and R. Jarlik, too, as her new second-in-command, was ready for some free time. She wondered if he might not like to join her. It would do Denek good to be in command for a time, as a MechWarrior never knew when he would have to take over without notice. And Denek was her own successor, as she was Ardan's.

These were the thoughts occupying Sep as she returned to her quarters and stepped into the Cleaning Unit. With the sweat and grime removed from her skin, she felt infinitely better as she stepped out to don a light robe. Already Argyle was balmy.

There was a message capsule in the drop inside her door. The messenger must have come while she was freshening up. It looked...it was!...a ComStar transmission.

Sep felt her heart thud warily, dreading bad news. The worst possible news had been Ardan's disappearance during the battle on Stein's Folly, but it had been wiped away by that of his recapture. What now?

. Picking up the capsule, she felt for the seam, and cracked it open. A hiss of air guaranteed that the sealed message had not been tampered with upon receipt by the local ComStar Adept.

The code was familiar. Ardan needed her! The thought sang through her like a fresh breeze.

She had known, of course, of his illness. Even word of his obsessions had been transmitted to her and Ardan's other friends, for Hanse understood the value of personal devotion among MechWarriors.

She reread the message, thinking all the while of the things she had been told. When she finished going over it for the third time, she knew what her old friend intended. She would have done the same.

Ardan was too sound a person to insist upon something that might be unreal. He believed he might uncover some evidence on the Folly. She knew fairly certainly that no search had been made of the facility where he had been found, for Davion's troops had been busy subduing the invaders and putting things back into order.

The planet's civilian population was scanty, principally employed as service personnel about the cities and the ports. The few others were farmers, intent on growing enough to supply the needs of the cities. She could see no reason for any of those people to go poking about in sealed bases, either.

No, if what Ardan had seen was real, some clue might have been left behind. The Liao forces had, after all, retired in considerable disarray. She and Ardan would need 'Mechs for their investigation, though. Davion's booby traps would make short work of any unarmored intruder prying into the installations.

All she needed do to gain an audience with the Prince was to move her name up the list of personal guards. Tonight, he was scheduled to consult with representatives of the New Avalon Institute of Science, and that was always a long, drawn-out affair. It had been a week since her last such duty. As she was the one making up the duty-rosters, there was nothing remotely unusual about her drawing it again.

Sep took quite seriously Ardan's request that she keep this matter secret and private. That night, she waited patiently while the Honorable Doctors of Science talked endlessly on abstruse subjects that did not seem to bore the Prince as much as it did his guard.

She could see the alertness in his eyes. He understood what those persons were saying, no matter how technical and puzzling. From time to time, he made a suggestion or an objection, and always it was one the men and women from NAIS had to consider seriously. She found herself with increased respect for the strictly intellectual side of this complex man.

When the last of the Doctors had gone and Hanse was preparing to leave the chamber, Sep gestured for him to remain, without speaking.

Hanse could have given lessons to the most subtle spy in existence. He sighed, closed the window against the sudden breeze from the river beyond the garden, and turned down the glow of the lamp above his desk.

Sep swept the room yet again with the electronic device that spied out any bugging element. She activated the stronger one that could intercept any signal from a distant amplifier that might pick up what they said. Nothing registered.

"Your Highness," she said finally, "I have had a message, via ComStar, from Ardan Sortek. To save time, I would like for you to read it." She handed it across the desk.

"Thank you, Major Septarian." He took the capsule, opened it, and rapidly scanned the contents, nodding several times.

When he finished, Davion looked at Sep and said, "The Archon sent me word, some time ago, about this claim that Ardan saw my double on the Folly. The doctors insist that it is delusional. I know Ardan. If he wants to check it out—which I guess to be the motive for this message—then he must have the chance. If not for my sake, for his own."

He turned to the computer console beside him, and quickly punched up the records of Septarian and Jarlik.

Sep almost grinned. The Prince's mind was running along the same channels as her own.

"I see that you and Captain Jarlik have not had your regular leaves. We can't have our officers overworked in peacetime. How would you like some time, Major? You might even like to choose several of your fellow officers to accompany you. I know how close you become, in a unit. And you have no family nearby, I see."

"I'd like that very much, Highness," she said. "I have been wanting to see Stein's Folly, ever since our reconquest of that world. There should be some valuable learning there for a commander, both defensively and offensively. I'd like to take Jarlik and Ref Handrikan with me, if you approve. With our 'Mechs. We might get tired of relaxing, and want to get in some training, too, while we are there."

"It happens that I have a small JumpShip waiting to convey a...message...to Stein's Folly. It will also be convenient for your purposes. I shall put it at your disposal." His eyes twinkled at her in a conspiratorial fashion.

"Find out for me," he said, his voice so low as to be nearly inaudible. "And take care of Ardan."

"Thank you, Highness," she said, saluting. "And good night. My relief is in the hall. I can hear him already."

She moved rapidly after that. Jarlik was already asleep when she pounded on the door of his quarters.

"Whoozat?" came his bearlike growl. "Betterbe'n' emergency!"

"Jarlik! Septarian, here! Let me in at once!"

The door clicked, and a suspiciously yellowed eye looked out.

It widened, as did the gap in the door. "Sep! Come in. I thought it was that triple-damned Fram playing a trick on me again. What's up?"

"We're going to take a trip," she said. "To Stein's Folly. But no more now. Just get yourself and your 'Mech ready to be loaded on a DropShip waiting to rendezvous with a ship at our jump point. Get Ref. He's going, too. I don't want to say anything else until we reach our first recharge."

Jarlik was now fully awake. He was fumbling for his case, pulling gear from drawers and cupboards, and cramming it in without folding or even looking at what he grabbed. The excitement he seemed to feel thrummed through the room like a high-powered generator.

Sep grinned. Her own packing would probably go something like this.

"I've got to alert Denek, too. He'll be in charge of the unit until we get back. We have, by the way, two standard months, excluding recharge time, and two more months discretionary time. We're both well behind in leave-time, so there will be no question about it. Be ready, though. We're leaving as soon as I can get things in hand."

She hurried away to Denek's quarters, which he shared with his bosom enemy, Fram. A tap at that door was never enough to wake the pair. She used her override key and walked in.

Sep pulled the covers off Denek and turned up the cooling unit. He shivered. His eyes opened.

"Hey!" he protested. "What goes?"

"You're in charge," she said briefly, "until Jarlik and I get back off leave. We've been working our tails off while you dopes goof off. Now we've got the chance to take some time off and a way to do some traveling, and we're grabbing it. Oh-six-hundred hours tomorrow, my friend. Don't be late, and don't forget the drill, or your tail will be in the fire when I get back." She stepped to the door and turned to grin at the sleepy officer.

"Don't think I won't know if you pull anything stupid. No pranks, now. No practical jokes. No great ideas. Just do your job, Denek, the way I know you can. Now, goodbye."

Doing her own manic version of packing a bit later, Sep shivered with excitement. What was it that Ardan thought

181

he would find, there on that embattled world where he had so nearly died?

She puzzled over that thought while overseeing the storage of their 'Mechs on the DropShip that would take them to the JumpShip waiting in deep space. Her Tech had been joined by those of Jarlik and Ref, and all three were yawning. Their standbys were being left behind, however. This was no trip into war. A holiday jaunt, even with some training purposes, did not require taking along an entire battle-ready group.

The ship embarked a few minutes after sunrise. Only a sleepy guard-'Mech and a handful of troopers saw it go, and none of them thought twice about it. DropShips were in and out of the Prince's private port at all times of the day and night, as he sent and received messengers from all over the system, and beyond.

Sep found her billet and closed her eyes for a nap. When she woke at the jump point, she would tell her companions what was afoot. For now, she intended to catch some sleep. There would be plenty of time for everything in the long transit to Stein's Folly.

24

The weeks of jump didn't bother Ardan as much as usual. Nor did the long wait for recharge at each intermediary jump point afflict his nerves. He was too busy thinking about what he might possibly find upon return to Stein's Folly. Their final jump point was one of the irregular ones for that system, and from there, he could go by DropShip to the rendezvous point on the far side of the Folly's larger moon. He knew Sep would come, and though the JumpShip captain argued that the Steiners would never forgive him for leaving their guest alone in such a perilous situation, Ardan insisted.

The DropShip's scanners gave him a fair view of the desolate contours of the rocky planetoid as it orbited. The sky was black, for the vessel was in the shadow. Ardan's drop into the system had been invisible from the scanners on the Folly, hidden by the moon. Now he could see brilliant sparks against the midnight sky, other worlds and suns he probably would never visit.

The tiny lump of rock turned toward the sun, which sent long shadows along its gritty stone surface. Ardan began to relax, even to doze a little. He was in place, and knew without a doubt that Sep was on her way. Things would begin to happen soon.

He woke with a start as a clang told him his capsule was being reattached to another ship. When he looked out, the moon had turned again and this side was dark. His scanners revealed another sleek DropShip in position. The hatch opened as he turned toward it.

"Sep, you made it!" he almost shouted, rising to meet her.

"We came as soon as we could, Dan. The Prince sent us." Sep caught him by his shoulders, and studied his face with concern. "But how are you? Are you all right now?"

"We can talk about me later," he said. "If Hanse sent you, I guess that explains how you got a ship. But who else is with you?"

"Jarlik and Ref Handrikan. And our 'Mechs. Too bad about your *Victor*—they had to scrounge the parts. It couldn't be repaired. But we've a lot of armor...my *Warhammer*, Jarlik's *Crusader*, and Ref's *BattleMaster*. What we can't knock down, can't be knocked down, I suspect."

Ardan felt his heart sink. Without a 'Mech, he would have to stand back and watch the others break into the installation. Yet there was no way Hanse could have sent him a machine. The neural helmet had to be constructed with painstaking care to the attributes of the wearer.

"Well, I may not have a 'Mech, but I've got a way to get us onworld without anyone detecting our approach," he said. "I don't want to go in officially right away because I just don't know who to trust anymore, even among our own people...There are still too many unanswered questions...And nothing's going to prevent me from getting into that hospital and searching for some proof of what I saw while I was there!"

"I'm with you, but how do we get past the system's traffic controllers? Their computers are going to be looking for our ID codes, you know, and they're probably watching the air like hawks since all this trouble with Liao."

"That's just it," Ardan told her excitedly. "The traffic controllers read off what the transponder tells them and what shows on their displays, but I've got a code that will tell the computers: 'Ignore me. I'm not here.' We simply won't show up on the screens and they'll ignore our beacon.

"This code is pretty top-secret stuff. Few people know about it, much less suspect it exists. I learned this one straight from Hanse, and then only because of a high-secrecy mission he had me carry out once."

"But what about visual sighting?" Sep asked.

"We're still vulnerable to that, but it's a million-in-one chance that we'll be spotted. Especially if we take care with our approach."

"Well, the pilots that brought us here are the best," Sep said. "Davion's finest."

"Good thing, too," Ardan laughed. "Since we won't be in the traffic sequence, we'll definitely have to look out for other traffic."

Sep laughed, too. "This I gotta see," she said, and the two of them crossed through the exit hatch into her Drop-Ship, their spirits high.

* * * *

Sep was right. The Prince's pilots were expert. Using Ardan's high-secrecy code, they bypassed the traffic controllers, and were able to land unknown to anyone onworld. They dropped by night in the eastern hills along the Highland Peninsula.

The pilot had picked the nearest secure spot to the coordinates they'd given her, which put them about three kilometers away from their target.

Ardan and his three comrades climbed down from the DropShip to get their bearings and to decide their next move.

"The only thing between us and the facility are those rolling hills," said Ardan. "It won't be too bad going in that way."

"I guess the groundcar we brought for you will come in handy," Sep said, her face thoughtful. "We can recharge it with one of our reactors if necessary, but I don't think we'll need to."

It was getting close to dawn as Sep, Ardan, Jarlik, and Ref stood looking across the few kilometers they had to cross.

"No civilians detected with the body-heat scanners within ninety klicks," said Ref. "We should be able to use our own searchlights safely. Here's the chart. We can pick the best route now, then we'd better head out."

The four of them knelt beside the DropShip, peering at the unrolled plastic chart by the handlights they carried. "I never saw the thing from outside in my right mind," said Ardan, "but I studied every installation onworld before we attacked. This one is strong in every direction." He drew a line with his finger on the map. "This is as good a way as any."

He pointed to a dot on the chart. "The east portal was the one we intended to go through, if we got that far."

"Well, we won't have to fight any 'Mechs," commented Sep, rolling up the chart again and slipping it into its case.

"We hope," rumbled Jarlik.

Within half an hour, they had unloaded and serviced the 'Mechs, checked out the ground car, and were headed toward their destination across the starlit grass of the hills. Ardan led, his lights on the car being lower to the ground. He could pick out dustpits or other obstacles that weren't apparent from above.

The installation came into view much sooner than he had expected. The comm-tower was still in place, thrusting its thin spire into the dark heavens. It made a good object to home in on.

Approaching cautiously, lights off, he geared his ground car into silent mode. At ninety meters, Ardan came to a full stop and signalled the huge 'Mechs stalking behind him to pause. He had learned never to trust anything that looked safe or easy, and so climbed out of the ground car to creep forward on foot.

The building was so heavily constructed that it looked more like a bit of a mountain than something shaped by human hands. The ferrocrete curved with the terrain, each successive story inset from the one lower. The few windows were multiple-stress duraglass. The door was a monolith of metal and heavy-duty plastics.

Ardan knew better than to approach further. When Davion's troops booby-trapped a building, it was well and truly done. He had known times when even small wild animals had triggered the things by going too near in their nightly prowlings.

186

He checked out the circumference of the installation, moving at a distance all around it, looking through his night-sight glasses to make sure the portals were the standard variety. So far, everything looked good.

At last, he signalled for his reinforcements to proceed. They came thudding up in line, Jarlik taking the rear, as usual. Anyone trying to approach from behind them would find more than one nasty surprise waiting.

Sep's voice came over the comm. "All clear?"

"I wouldn't sign any guarantees. But everything is quiet. I don't get a warm-body reading on any of the instruments. That isn't to say there isn't something automatic waiting for us inside there," he replied.

"Then get back...I mean way back," said Sep. "There isn't any way of knowing what we'll set off when we knock down the door."

Ardan knew that. He ran to the ground car and dropped behind its bulk. He had seen men and women sliced into ribbons by some of the nasties left for them to find. Inside a 'Mech, you didn't have to worry, but a man's skin was very little protection.

Sep strode up to the portal to test the door with the great foot of her *Warhammer*. The metal gonged protestingly, and something within gave a nervous pop.

Ardan peered out from under the ground car. In the distance, he could see the *Warhammer* bring back its leg for a devastating kick. When it came, Ardan started involuntarily.

With simultaneous crash, thud, gong, thump, and shattering, the armored doorway caved inward, taking with it the ferrocrete surround into which it had been set. The 'Mech sprang backward.

Ref took his turn also, hammering away at the debris left in the doorway. Dust rose pale in the starlight. Ardan saw the gap in the facade grow wider. Ref's shape disappeared into the blackness, and more dust came boiling out behind him.

Sep went inside. Jarlik came near to the opening and stood with his back to it, scanning the terrain on all sides.

Ardan, hearing no disturbance, made his way closer, waiting for the signal to proceed into the building.

At last Jarlik's huge arm rose, beckoning. Ardan ran forward to stand beside the 'Mech.

"Sep says it's all right to come in. We'll stand guard while you check things out."

Ardan nodded and worked his way among the splintered shards of ferrocrete into the main hallway of the installation. Except for the places where the 'Mechs had wrecked it, it was still solid and sturdy. He recalled the memorized plans for such installations. Hospital wing…there!

He hurried off in that direction. In such a large building, it took some time to find the corridor he could recall only dimly. He tried higher and lower ones, but always something was not quite familiar. When he hit the correct one, he knew it at once and began moving down the hallway, checking each room. He was almost certain that the third on the left had been the one where he had waked.

He looked back. The doors through which he had come had concealed the people whose voices he had heard. Ahead …yes. There were the doors on the right, the ones he had passed through before.

He raced down the passage and burst through the swinging doors. The hall beyond was dark. No light from the lab now shone through the glass. But this time, he had his own source of light. Switching on his belt torch, he pushed the heavy doors apart.

The place was just as he remembered it. The table in the middle, the equipment standing about or hanging from the ceiling. The cubicles on the wall…all as they were. All except one.

He stepped into the space left by the removal of that one. Yes, it had been just here that the duplicate of Hanse had lain, suspended…waiting for what?

He hadn't really expected it to still be here. It was for use, and the enemy would not have left it behind. But he might find something else, if he looked closely…and if he recognized it when he found it.

188

Ardan began checking systematically, first at the door, then moving to the right. File cabinets. Small equipment cupboard, still stocked with flasks, test tubes, pipettes, and probes. He turned the corner.

There was a cabinet filled with holos. On the desk that formed the lower part of it was a Reader. Ardan felt excitement build inside him. Was this something useful?

He checked the machine, and saw that it was operable by either current or battery. Surely he had seen batteries in that equipment cupboard!

He had, and a pair of them fit. He put them into the compartment and switched on the machine. A beam of light fanned against the pale wall.

Starting at the top of the ranks of holos, he worked his way down to the right. There were dozens of nasty-looking things that he presumed might be viruses and bacteria. Cultures? Maybe.

There were more dozens of indecipherable schematics. He was sure of only one thing—they had nothing to do with weapons or 'Mechs.

Then he hit the third vertical row. The first made him gasp. It was a study of Hanse as he had seen him hundreds of times, sitting at his desk, leaning forward with the force of his intensity, talking, moving his hands as he always did. The next was of Hanse walking in a garden. The third of Hanse at a formal dinner.

Another, and another, and another, all of Hanse Davion as he went about both his everyday routine and formal and official matters that were a part of his duty.

Studies! By damn, they were studies! Whoever would wear that false body had to know how to make it behave, and this had evidently been part of his training.

Ardan flipped rapidly through the sets of studies, looking for some clue as to the one to be trained, or the use to which the image would be put. The last row held studies of the summer palace on Argyle, from every angle, inside and out.

There were close-ups of all the royal staff, the Guard, the intimates of the Court, the officials with whom Hanse came in contact. A thorough bunch, whoever had done this.

And then he saw the false Hanse...still just a body, waiting to be used. In the cubicle, just as he had seen it the first time. Measurements were noted beside it, with coded symbols he could not decipher.

Ardan felt that he could be certain of one thing only... whatever was going to happen would happen on Argyle. Why else make such careful studies of a world and a house that Hanse inhabited for only a few months a year?

He turned away, ran back down the maze of corridors. He had to call Sep, to get witnesses to this discovery!

25

Sep had descended from her 'Mech and was waiting for Ardan when he reached the central corridor past the entry. Ref, too, was ready.

"I brought Ref for the unimpeachable witness you wanted. You look excited, Dan. What have you found?"

Ardan turned back the way he had come, calling over his shoulder as they ran, "Holos. A bunch of them that show Hanse doing everything you can think of. And others showing the Summer Palace, not to mention still others that give a good view of that substitute Hanse in his cubicle." He felt something slap against his side and put his hand in the pocket of his uniform.

"I must have put one in my pocket, but we don't need to stop and look at it now. The good stuff is in that lab."

They pounded up the corridor, climbed emergency stairs, turned and cornered at top speed. They had reached the right corridor when there came a slight tremor underfoot, a vibration in the ferrocrete that seemed to quiver through the building's whole structure. Sep caught his arm and pulled him to a halt. Ref raised his head and motioned toward the other end of the passageway.

"Listen!" he said.

Then they heard it...a series of dull pops beneath and ahead of them. As if someone had set charges along the supporting pillars at one edge of the building where they stood.

"Out!" yelled Sep, pulling Ardan frantically by the arm. "It's going to buckle toward us! We can make it."

"No! I've got to get those holos out of here. Nobody will ever believe me if I don't." Ardan turned to run forward, but found himself seized by two sets of strong arms that dragged him bodily along the way he had just come.

"You don't understand," he moaned. "They think I'm crazy, all the doctors. Hanse won't have any alternative but

191

to believe them. I wasn't in very good shape when I last talked with him. He'll think I'm crazy, too."

Neither answered him. Behind them, the floors tilted, the walls crumpled into dust. They were staying ahead of the demolition, but only by a little.

They descended the stairs in two leaps and flew along the lower corridor at top speed. As the curving walls overhead began to buckle, the huge figure of Jarlik's *Crusader* stomped through the shaking structure and reached with irresistible arms toward them.

Sep grabbed the autocannon on the right. Ref leaped onto an armored foot and hoisted Ardan so that he could reach the left cannon. The 'Mech then backed swiftly out of the self-destructing building, which collapsed in on itself as they retreated.

The air was full of dust and deafening noise. As the last walls buckled, the debris shifted, trying to find repose within the heaps of shattered ferrocrete, wall paneling, and ruined equipment.

Jarlik let his passengers down onto the cool grass beyond the reach of the dust. Then he opened his cockpit and climbed out of his 'Mech to join them.

"Some booby trap," he grunted. "What did they think was in there?"

"I suspect they thought the Liao forces might try to use it again. If they had, it would have wiped out a bunch of their Techs and staff people. A nasty little surprise, that one," said Sep.

Ardan was silent. Sitting on the grass, head buried between his hands, he felt that his last hope of proving his story was irretrievably gone. How could he protect Hanse from a takeover if he couldn't prove his story? The only hope now was that there would be enough proof on the holodiscs he *had* been able to retrieve. They'd look at them later in the DropShip.

Jarlik came and sat beside him. "I don't know why you're so down. Sep told me just what I had to know about all this, and not a word more. Give, Ardan. Maybe I can help out."

Ref sat on the other side of him. Sep sighed and also dropped to the grass. "Your message was necessarily brief. Now's the time to fill us in on what you're trying to do. We've all heard odd things about your mental state. You seem all right to me. But we need to know what's going on. Now."

Ardan stripped the green from a blade of grass as he spoke. "You're right, but don't think I'm crazy until you've heard me out. Then tell me honestly what you think." He reached into his pocket. "I did save one block of holo discs. When we get back to the ship, you can see for yourselves what's on them...I haven't an idea. I don't really remember putting them in my pocket."

There was the sound of wind in the grass. A lonely insect cried, "Zeet! Zeet!" somewhere nearby. The 'Mechs stood about, a monstrous trio, seeming to listen as they rested.

"I was in bad shape when they brought me here, as I guess you've heard. Broken bones, contusions, infections of undiagnosable kinds from the swamp where I'd hidden. I'd been through some very odd experiences, and was hallucinating. I will admit that. When I came through those doors, I was just about totally out of it. I didn't know anything for a long time. It might have been days. I haven't any way to tell.

"When I came to, I could see that someone had just gone out of the little room where they had me. The curtain was still moving. I thought of only one thing—that I had to be in the hands of the enemy. I remembered the Liao uniforms on the men who had cut me down from the tree where I was tied up in the swamp."

Sep's head came up. Jarlik growled, "Tree? Tied?"

Ardan shook his head. "That part's not relevant right now. I'll tell you about it later, if we get the chance. No, I knew I had to be a captive of the Capellan forces. The one thought in my head was escape. So when I heard voices at

193

the end of the corridor—where we were just now when the explosion went off—I went the other way. There's a set of doors on the right, down the hall, and through there is the lab I found.

"Inside were cryogenic cubicles, and in one was the body of a man who could have been Hanse Davion. I went right up to it and looked closely. The face was exactly the same. Except for one thing. Hanse wasn't behind it."

Sep nodded. Jarlik rubbed his chin, and Ref narrowed his eyes.

"Like a life-mask? When someone wears it, he looks just like the original, but the expressions are never quite right."

Ardan looked at Ref. "Yes. Exactly. The lines were right, the shapes were correct, but the total impression was wrong. That face had never been...been lived in."

"O.K. That's what you saw. What sort of condition were you in when you saw it?" Sep, as always, was down-to-earth.

Ardan considered carefully. "I had been terribly ill, but I was recovered enough to be able to walk quite a long distance. Nothing hurt very badly. I was alert. Unusually alert, as if I might have been given some sort of stimulant. I've wondered...Indeed, Melissa Steiner and I both wondered, if I was *supposed* to see that substitute Hanse." He shook his head.

"I was tired, of course, after moving about so much. I quickly grew weak, and barely made it back to bed. I went out at once, and the next thing I knew I was being rescued by Lees Hamman."

"So the Meds thought you were crazy. It doesn't quite make sense," said Jarlik.

"Well, there were more problems than that. I'd had a bad experience, back a way, and it had been preying on my mind. That was all mixed up with the thing I'd seen in the lab, and they decided that everything was hallucination. Part of it was, and I admit that freely, but the rest was real. As

194

real as the three of us sitting here. As real as those 'Mechs." He gestured toward the waiting trio.

"And you can't prove it, unless there's something on that set of holos you made off with," mused Ref. "So what are we going to do now?"

"We'll return to the moon before anyone knows we've been here, and then come back here tomorrow, *officially*. Or, I should say, I want *you* to come back tomorrow and formally request a salvage operation from the officer in charge of the garrison. I'd better stay in the drop and keep quiet. If I'm connected with the request, they're not going to cooperate, even with an officer of the Guard in Hanse's own private courier ship."

"You think there's any chance of finding anything at all in that mess?" Sep asked, gesturing toward the pile of rubble.

"It would be at the farther edge. The thing was falling in on itself and slightly leaning this way. It should be some fifty meters from where the back wall was, fairly in the center of the left wing. The holos were in a cabinet that should have protected them well. I remember snapping the lock of the door—a very nice double catch. The entire cabinet was built together with a desktop below. The whole thing must have been about two meters wide by three tall. Made of solid metal with duraplast doors. It should be easily detectable with a metal detector. Of course, there's a lot of metal in that pile. But just maybe..."

"We'll give it a try," said Sep. "And if that doesn't work, we'll think of something else. I trust your judgment, Ardan. If you say you were alert, then, by damn, you were alert. You say you know where the hallucination left off and the reality began, and that's good enough for me." She rose and dusted the dried grass from her uniform.

Jarlik groaned to his feet, too. "Better make tracks before it starts to get light. We need to skip out of here so we can come back all nice and tidy and official."

Ref offered Ardan a hand up. "I never expected anything like this when Sep volunteered me for this duty. I wonder what sort of reception we'll get from the commandant tomorrow. Duke Michael's men are back in charge of garrisoning the Folly, now that the counterinvasion is over."

It turned out that Ref had hit the nail on the head. The commandant, a Hasek-Davion officer detached from the Syrtis Fusiliers and commanding a combination of Eridani Light Horse and Davion regulars, seemed indifferent, if not actively hostile.

"I have a world that has been fought over, trampled, detonated, and otherwise disrupted within a centimeter of its life. The civilian population is devastated, and there are more demands on my time and manpower than I can possibly attend to. And now you ask me to go dig in a booby-trapped installation for something you think might be there? I beg your pardon!"

He looked simultaneously irritated and nauseated.

"Then you will not object if we borrow some detection gear and go look for ourselves," Sep half-asked and half-stated.

The commandant looked startled, but gave in with a weary shrug. "I suppose not. But do be cautious. Those engineers are good at their job. The booby traps are not to be taken lightly."

Assuring him that they would take care, Sep led her companions on their way as quickly as was polite. It seemed safe to add Ardan to their group when they stopped at the DropShip for their transport, an all-purpose ground-effect machine. They hid him beneath a pile of probes and detectors, and nobody gave them a second look as they left the port city.

They travelled quickly, talking very little. It was lucky that the commandant had not insisted upon sending one of his officers along as a precaution. It would have been rather awkward, trying to explain how they came to be investigating an installation whose booby trap had already gone off. The coincidence would hardly be overlooked.

They drove south this time, circling around the southernmost finger of the Yaeger Mountains, then up through the foothills along the eastern coast of the peninsula. The marks of the war were everywhere, having left great burnt slashes of black on the green-tan grassfields. Houses broken like dropped eggs. Fields gouged out with the tracks of 'Mechs who had battled it out.

Ardan found himself thinking of that other ruined landscape, and the child in the valley. The memory was sad, but the horror had gone. The wail of the child had grown faint, and the pain, though never to be lost entirely, had become bearable.

They came around a low growth of trees. Before them should have been the ruins of the installation, but where the piles of debris had been, there was now a deep depression.

"Damn!" grunted Jarlik. "Was that part of the booby trap, or did the bedrock cave in under the shift in weight?"

They pulled up and piled out of the vehicle. A gigantic, saucer-shaped hole lay at the spot where the building had stood. They ran to the edge and peered over it.

Twenty meters below them, the ferrocrete and everything else had been returned to something like their natural state. Nothing recognizable remained among the dusty tumbles of dirt and rock.

Somehow, Ardan was not surprised. He was beginning to feel like a pawn on a gigantic chessboard, moved here and there, his perceptions a part of the game, his will irrelevant.

"I think this was deliberate. Some secondary effect meant to occur if the primary booby trap was triggered. Someone wanted that building entirely lost to human examination." He laughed harshly. "They did a damn good job."

Sep put a hand on Ardan's shoulder. "Not as good as you did in rescuing those other holos you showed us aboard ship," she said. "They'll make damn good proof!"

197

26

Ardan believed there was only one thing to do. Hanse was in residence on Argyle, and he must join him there. Sep, Jarlik, and Ref, however, must follow through with their 'holiday' if they were not to arouse suspicion. They had to spend at least a short time in study and rest on Stein's Folly.

We'll take you back up to your DropShip," said Sep. "From there, you can catch up with the Steiner JumpShip that brought you."

Ardan nodded. "But I don't think I'll return openly. Something tells me that the people behind this whole thing want me to run straight to Hanse, in full view of everyone, as soon as I find a way.

"If I seem to disappear—which I have now effectively done—and cannot be located on any observable ship or freighter, maybe it will force the conspirators into moving faster than they had planned. They'll be uncertain about me. Did I accept my own disability more than they had intended? Have I become depressed and done away with myself? They won't know for certain." He grinned.

"Steiner is totally safe. Neither of the Archons will breathe a word about the how and when of my departure. And nobody could possibly know about your leaving Argyle, Sep. Only you and Hanse and the pilot were in on that. So I should be able to slip into Argyle and lose myself there.

"I know the Summer Palace like the back of my hand. There are ways of getting in that others may not be aware of. I can get to Hanse without anyone knowing I'm near. Come as soon as it looks reasonable."

Sep started the vehicle, which rose quickly on its cushion of air and headed back toward the port city.

* * * *

Ardan landed openly at the commercial port on Argyle, then spent the rest of the morning making his way to the palace grounds.

It was just after noon, and there were few workers visible about the storage sheds and in the gardens around the Summer Palace at Argyle. Wearing some clothes he'd found aboard the DropShip, Ardan aroused no more curiosity than any other Tech coming in to work. He ducked into one of the sheds and found the ranks of lockers assigned to workers around the private port.

Though he hated doing it, he went through each one until he found a clean overall of the dark blue favored by Personnel for garden staff. After changing into it, he left a coin worth two of the suits.

Now, for the next step. He went into the lavatory, which, to his relief, was empty. Staring into the mirror, Ardan pondered his light brown hair with its hint of curl, his narrow amber eyes, the high cheekbones. What could he do to alter them?

Glancing about at the antiseptic room, his mind quickly hit on an idea. He gathered together a dispenser of boot-blackener, the box of towels for taking grease off the hands before washing, and a dispenser of eye-protectors for those about to do welding.

Ardan put a dab of the blackener into the palm of his left hand. With the fingers of his right, he worked the sticky stuff through his hair. It was nasty to work with, but once he had it well applied, he scrubbed his hair fiercely with some of the towelling, rubbing away the excess greasiness.

When he ran his comb through his altered locks, they lay flat and dingy. The change in his appearance was astonishing.

He nodded with satisfaction. Next, he ripped off a strip of towel and rolled it tightly. One of those in each jaw changed the line of his face remarkably. With the goggles bent to a less identifiable shape, their clear frame blackened

199

to resemble glare-glasses, his eyes and cheekbones were adequately concealed.

Studying himself in the glass, Ardan realized that his own father might well pass him by without recognizing him. Now he could see about finding and warning Hanse to take care.

There was no trick to making his way through the gardens. His authorized thumbprints would permit him to move about the Summer Palace. After all, the mechanisms made no distinction between the thumbs of warriors and those of servants.

He found the thick hedge of flowering shrubbery that he had picked as his access point. Looking about and seeing no one, Ardan dropped to hands and knees and crawled through the drooping fronds. He knew that behind this shrubbery was a narrow space leading to the corner of the wing.

About three meters in, he found the crawlspace he remembered. Its grillwork yielded to his all-purpose pocket tool, and then Ardan found himself standing in the shadows of the upper winecellar.

He moved briskly toward the steps leading up into the service wing. Reaching the top stair, he heard a woman's sharp voice: "I say! What are you doing inside the palace? You gardeners have strict orders to remain outside at all times! Explain yourself, if you please!"

He groaned silently. Fani Lettik was the proverbial pain in the butt, whether you were a MechWarrior, a noble, a gardener, or a cook.

Ardan turned, his attitude expressing outrage. "I am in the process of inspecting a defective grillwork for the Maître of the Household," he snapped. "I have entered the palace through a totally unauthorized opening, which must be repaired at once. It's a good thing I was checking the shrubbery for root-rot!" He glared, nose-to-nose with the woman who knew him so well.

She stepped back. Fani was, he knew, a flaming snob, keeping her distance from anyone below her in rank. Her yellowish face turned faintly pink.

"Then do so at once, and return to your duties!" she snapped. "Root-rot, indeed!" Fani mumbled, as she turned away, no doubt to search out some other poor bastard whom she could give a hard time.

Ardan restrained a chuckle. It was the only time in his life that he had bested the woman, and it had to be in the guise of a Palace gardener!

He moved through the service wing by the least traveled corridors. At this time of day, the living quarters were empty, and he cut through those, climbing narrow service stairs and scooting through cubbies known only to the staff of the huge household.

At last he came to a passage that intersected the main corridor, where Hanse's study was situated. Ardan didn't know the guard at the door, and he would never pass as a gardener, that was certain.

He retreated down the hall. There was a spare room he had often used on those nights when duty kept him too late to return to the barracks. Would it still be unused by anyone else? Knowing Hanse, Ardan felt almost certain his friend would have appointed the room for him, whether Ardan were present or not at the time of the move to Argyle.

He had to lurk behind draperies and behind tall furniture more than once, as he made his way to the familiar door. He set his thumb against the plate.

Hearing the familiar click, Ardan sighed with relief. If the room was ready, he was almost certain to find at least one change of clothing there.

The chamber looked no different than at any other time he had seen it. Indeed, he might only have left it the day before. Uniforms were lined up in the clothing-cubicle, and there was soap and shampoo in the Cleaner. He was in business!

The grubby gardener disappeared in minutes, his coverall stuffed down the Disposal, along with the goggles and wads of towelling. When Ardan stepped out into the corridor again, it was as his most resplendent self.

201

"I might as well impress the hell out of them, while I'm at it," he had told his reflection in the mirror. He wore his best uniform, the one trimmed with gold, decorated with bright rows of medals, and with the Federated Suns emblem worked in gems.

Ardan strode up the corridor now, paying no heed to the startled glances of those he passed. Nobody could get to Hanse ahead of him, he knew. He was almost at the door.

The guard stiffened to attention. "Sir!" he barked.

Ardan nodded pleasantly and set his thumb against the identity plate. At once, the familiar voice called out, "Ardan! Come in!"

He stepped inside and closed the door behind him, setting in place the bar that prevented automatic unlocking. Hanse met him with outstretched arms, and Ardan returned the bear hug fiercely. "I was wrong," he said, as they stepped apart. "I know now that you do only what you have to do. So much has come into focus for me these past months. Forgive me, Hanse."

Hanse Davion was beaming down at him, his ruddy face bright with relief. "Oh, stow it! he said. "Just let me look at you. What happened out there, Ardan?"

It was to be, of course, a very long tale. They sat together before the window that gave a wide view of the land around the eminence where the palace sat. This was a soft country, the cornucopia of this part of the system. Wide fields were edged with walls to prevent erosion. Flocks of birds wheeled overhead.

Ardan sighed with pleasure at the view. "How good it is to be here! I never much liked Argyle before…too quiet and peaceful. But now I can stand any amount of that, and then some more." He turned to his Prince and began the account of all that had recently happened.

When he fell silent at last, Hanse sat still, staring at him. Ardan could feel his old friend weighing his story, assessing his appearance and his attitude. The Prince had doubtless been advised that Ardan Sortek was mentally ill. Now he had to make his own decision.

202

Ardan rose and moved to the window. A shuttle was moving downward onto the private port. Messengers or bureaucrats, he supposed. He turned back to Hanse.

"I am convinced that there is a conspiracy of some sort afoot. Why else would I have been allowed to see the double and then to escape? Even Lees thought that escape was suspiciously easy. I suspect that he must have reported that to you."

The Prince rose and came to stand beside him. "I have been hearing many wild things about you," he said slowly, thoughtfully. "But I know you too well. Whatever happened out there, you are quite sane. But someone has done a remarkable job of trying to destroy your credibility. Why? I cannot imagine how anyone could expect to substitute another man for me."

Ardan set his hand on his friend's shoulder. "Your betrothed has quite a head on her young shoulders. She is the one who found the records of former impersonations. She is the one who set me to thinking about the suspicious ease of everything leading to my escape. She is the one who got her mother to lend me a JumpShip. Without that, I could not have hoped to leave Tharkad City without being seen and reported.

"She thought at least one of the doctors in attendance was involved in some way, and particularly asked me to warn you to be careful." Ardan smiled. "I believe that you have linked yourself with a woman who will be a joy to you. And not only politically."

Hanse looked at him quizzically. "A bit in love with her, yourself?" he asked gently.

The thought surprised Ardan. He was fond of Melissa, true, but that particular part of his heart seemed to be already occupied.

"Very fond of her," he said. "But there might be someone else. Some day. When things are suitable."

Hanse chuckled. "I can guess..." he started to say, before being cut off by a disturbance audible even through the thickness of the study door.

"What the...?" He went to the doorway and unlocked the portal, opening it with a jerk. "What on the Great Green Runway is going on?" he demanded. Then Hanse Davion stopped dead, his face turning very pale.

He was looking directly into his own eyes.

27

It was not easy for the Archon-Designate to do anything secretly, but Doctor Erl Karns never suspected Melissa's quiet surveillance.

Ardan had left Tharkad City at the dull and dreary tag-end of winter. With the snow too soft for skiing and too deep for hiking, there were few other entertainments left. Nearly everyone in Tharkad was bored and restless, now that the end of winter's rule seemed so near at hand. And so Melissa's ceaseless, seemingly aimless prowling about the great house of the Steiners did not seem strange. The computer system was, of course, her most valuable ally.

The Steiner library was comprehensive, updated constantly. Data files from every conceivable source poured into its unlimited capacity every day, including personal dossiers for anyone on Tharkad who had any dealing, however remote, with the royal family, the staff, the military, the diplomatic corps, known and suspected criminals, spies, and agents for commerce. There were few things that didn't find their way into that system, sooner or later.

Melissa knew her way around a computer system. She had learned her letters when she was two from such a source, and had been burrowing her way through all manner of exotic, boring, and unusual files ever since. She knew, too, how to cover her tracks after having sought out the dossier on Erl Karns. Not a trace remained on record to reveal that anyone had been asking questions about him.

She had, of course, told her mother what she intended doing. Katrina, loaded down with overseeing the many matters vital to the Commonwealth, had assented without giving the matter a second thought. So it was that when Melissa tapped on her study door early one morning with a hint of spring in the air, Katrina was astonished at the news the young woman brought to her.

"The good doctor Karns has had dealings with our enemies," Melissa told her. "More than once. He was on Luthien for four years, ostensibly to track down a virus that was plaguing the troops Kurita had stationed on Raselhague. Some sort of mysterious tropical disease."

"That's reasonable enough," said Katrina. "A doctor investigates many matters. A virus on one world, even an enemy one, can become a threat to many others, if left unchecked."

"Then he moved on to Capella, where he took an advanced degree in internal medicine, with emphasis on unusual viruses. From there, he went to New Syrtis, where he became an intimate of the Liao consular official. This was during a period of particular stress between the Davion interests that control that world and those of Kurita and Liao."

"I still do not see anything suspicious about a doctor who is obviously interested in unusual viral diseases pursuing them to their sources and studying them in places where they are most commmon." Katrina was beginning to look impatient.

Melissa unfolded a printout. "Here are the people with whom he was friends in all those places. His regular companions and his occasional haunts. Read them and then tell me there is nothing suspicious about our dedicated physician!"

Katrina scanned the sheet. At first, her eyebrows were quirked skeptically. They straightened. Then they rose in an arch. She looked up, her eyes wide and angry.

"Why hasn't Security picked up all this?" she asked Melissa.

"I wondered about that, too. I checked through the system, running down everything I could think of. But without an override code, I could never have traced Karns' activities at all. There's a lock on all his files. Nobody of less authority than you or me could possibly access this material. Security, for all its power, hasn't that ultimate override. And nobody, I suspect, ever thought that we would look into such a minor medical person's record."

"Nor would we, if he had not been sent to the Folly to attend the wounded in their transit to Tharkad," mused her mother. "I wonder...if that was the normal rotation of staff, or if it was efficiently managed. The other doctors seemed almost in awe of Karns. There has been interference on his behalf, perhaps?"

They stared at each other.

"It was Karns who encouraged Ardan to insist on the reality of that double. That seems strange, if there is some sort of conspiracy in the offing," Melissa said. "And yet, when I checked out the historical records, I saw that the close friends of other men who had been impersonated were simply removed, sometimes rather obviously." She stared at her mother.

"I think they intend to get rid of Hanse and Ardan both at the same time. Probably they intend to play them off against each other. Those two didn't part on the best of terms, and everyone knows it."

"It would be possible to do strange things, if you had an imposter and a dear friend of the original who showed visible signs of insanity," mused Katrina.

Melissa was a bit pale, her eyes big with worry. "Do you think there may truly be a plot against Hanse?" she asked. "Do you believe they might hurt him?"

"How can I answer that, Melissa? Without knowing who might be involved or what might be in the wind? But I am going to send a message to Davion now. It will take weeks, but I must warn Hanse, if I can," Katrina said.

When she signalled for the ComStar Adept, Melissa rose, knowing that Katrina would want privacy to compose the coded message for Davion.

Leaving her mother's chamber, she returned to the library, where she had been working. Melissa rechecked every file she had accessed, making certain that no trace of her investigation remained. Then she set her own lock on the entire dossier concerning Erl Karns. Anyone else trying to check up on Agent Karns would find a rude surprise in store for him. She felt that might be a good thing, all in all.

* * * *

Sep and Jarlik had exhausted the possibilities of Stein's Folly, along with themselves and Ref. They had gone through the motions of a combined educational and relaxation leave, but both were impatient to return to Argyle, where they felt they would be needed.

Ref, when consulted, had the same notion. But when they tried to get clearance for their DropShip, the way was blocked. Not a single military JumpShip was scheduled for transport to Argyle.

"It's not natural. That's where Hanse is. I know he's keeping track of what's taking place here and on adjacent worlds. But as far as I can tell, not even the Command Circuit is operating in this sector. What's happening?" Sep complained to Jarlik, after a particularly infuriating interview with the coordinator of travel out of the port city.

"I've been checking into freighters, too," Jarlik said. "There's not...a...single...one scheduled for a planetary month. A frigging month! Can you believe that?"

"No, I can't. And you don't, either. We are, for some obscure reason, getting a royal run-around. Somebody doesn't want us back on Argyle any time soon. And I don't know what to do about it."

"I do," said Ref. "I've been looking into the situation. It's time for a bit of bribery and corruption. Some of the hair of the dog, so to speak.

"I've made a new friend, down at barracks. He's been telling me some interesting rumors. For instance, I've learned that our friend, Sallek Atrion, the garrison commander, has passed the word, very quietly, that we're to be held here for at least a month."

"And does rumor hint at the source of that word? There's no reason for the commandant to care where we are or what

208

we do. It has to be coming from somewhere higher than him," said Sep.

"Oh, it hints at all sorts of things, from Steiner double-cross to Liao bribes. One even suggests that Michael is in on it, which is ridiculous on the face of it. But it's obvious that nobody really knows. I have found out one tangible bit of information, however." Ref looked smug.

"Atrion has suddenly come into quite a large inheritance from a distant relative. He's brought his family to Stein's Folly and installed his wife and children in an expensive home in the hills, as well as his current mistress in a plush apartment in the port city. He's also acquired a wardrobe that would be the envy of a Successor Lord."

Jarlik grunted. Sep looked quizzical. Ref nodded.

"Too pat, don't you think? Someone has bribed this gentleman to keep us here. So it's time for us to bribe someone to take us offplanet."

"I agree, if it's possible. But why should our presence or absence from Argyle make any difference to anyone?" Sep asked.

"I can think of but one reason. We will stand with Ardan Sortek, if any sort of disagreement arises, which assures Hanse Davion the support of at least one group of MechWarriors. And Hanse Davion will be, to us, whoever Ardan says he is."

Jarlik rose to stand, arms akimbo, staring at Ref. "Ardan is there right now. Whatever's happening will be long past by the time we can get back to our posts. But we've got to go, nevertheless. And how I wish we had a Command Circuit at our disposal!"

Sep rose to stand beside him, her slender strength a contrast to his bulk. "We'll hijack transport. Here. At Dragon's Field. At Hamlin. At Ral. At every jump point between Stein's Folly and Argyle."

"Impossible!" said Ref.

"Such a thing has never been attempted!" growled Jarlik.

"That's why it will work," Sep said, her eyes glinting dangerously. "What hasn't happened is never guarded against. A bribe at this end, to gain access to a JumpShip and its pilot. Then we'll either bribe or raid for every jump in between.

"We'll have the 'Mechs armed and ready to move before we leave the Folly. If we're fast enough and keep our wits, we'll get to Argyle in time to do some good...maybe."

"And go to prison for the rest of our natural lives," groaned Ref.

"Maybe that, too. It's worth the risk if we can help Ardan and the Prince, though. Don't you agree?" She looked about at the two.

They nodded, very solemnly. It was, indeed, worth the gamble.

28

Ardan, standing behind and to one side of his Prince, looked from one to the other of the men in the doorway. His mind reeled. For a moment, he felt a return of that terrible disorientation that had plagued him before his recovery.

The man in the corridor stepped inside the room, followed by Cleery, the Maître of the Household, and Ekkles, Hanse Davion's aide-de-camp.

"There! That's the imposter. And even Sortek! We have caught both the prime conspirators at once," the newcomer said.

Hanse backed up several steps to stand beside Ardan. "It looks as if you were correct, all the way," he said quietly. Then, more loudly, "I'd like an explanation of this charade. Cleery, who admitted this man into my house?"

The Maître looked perturbed. "No one admitted this man to the Summer Palace. He emerged from the Prince's chambers and rang for assistance, after receiving an unexpected messenger just arrived by shuttle." The man's discomfort was obvious.

Ardan felt for him. Dressed exactly alike, with the same bodies, faces, gestures, and voices, the pair could not have been distinguished by Hanse's own mother, if she had still been alive. Yet Ardan knew with his heart as well as his mind that the man at his side was his old friend. He needed no more proof than that.

"I have known the Prince since I was a boy," he said, with all the confidence he could muster. "This man is my old friend. I will vouch for that."

"You!" Ekkles snorted. "You, too, are a part of the plot!" he said. "It is well known with what bitterness you left New Avalon and our Prince. Now you appear from nowhere beside a man pretending to be Hanse Davion...The connection is obvious. Not only are you mentally unstable,

211

but you are a traitor as well!" He turned to the guard beside the door. "Arrest these two!" he ordered.

Hanse, however, was not outwardly disturbed. "Let us consider this matter a bit further," he said calmly. "For example, there are affairs, secrets of state, of great importance for the future of the Federated Suns. I have in mind one, in particular. Can you tell me what it is?" he asked the man who was his double.

The other Hanse wrinkled his nose in a manner all too familiar to everyone in the room. "You presume to question me in my own house? But I will answer, if only to reassure my people. You can only mean the secret treaty between the Houses Davion and Steiner, which includes promises of mutual aid, as well as my betrothal to Archon-Designate Melissa Steiner. And how you came to know of it, I cannot imagine!"

Ardan cleared his throat. "What happened on the day Hanse and I almost drowned?" he asked. "Over twenty years ago, it was, on New Avalon. Can you tell me that?"

The false Hanse stared at him sorrowfully. "Ah, yes, that was a time when we were, indeed, almost brothers," he said. "Well do I remember that day…and the two fishermen who pulled us from the river, wet as frogs, and took us to your mother. She dried us out, scolded us well, and didn't inform my father." He laughed.

"However, those fishermen were not the chance-comers they seemed to be. It was from them that my father heard of the incident. It turned out that those two had been set there to guard my life, as I was the second in line for the throne. Does that satisfy you, who have returned to my house as a traitor and possibly a spy?"

Ardan refused to concede defeat. "What did you give me for my twelfth birthday?" he asked.

The other turned on his heel and walked to the window. He was jiggling the fob attached to his belt with Hanse's own nervous habit. Ardan felt sick.

212

"The warrant admitting you to the Battle School. And my promise to oversee as much of your training as I could possibly manage."

Ardan turned to look into the eyes of the real Hanse, who still stood beside him. There was deep shock and growing concern in those familiar gray eyes. Hanse was just now realizing what kind of trap had been sprung for him.

The young warrior had one last weapon. It was a slim hope, but he had to try it.

"And to whom did you say, 'The Starbird weeps inside'?" he asked the newcomer.

The man did not turn, did not answer, but his hand twitched jerkily at the fob. Hanse, however, gasped with astonishment. "Melissa! I said that to Melissa! How did you know?"

But the aide and the Maître were not convinced. "Arrest these men," Ekkles said once more to the guard beside the door.

The new Prince of Davion turned sharply. "You cannot drag them through the palace as they are. We can't have the servants babbling about seeing their ruler arrested and thrown into the detention cells beneath the house. And we certainly can't let it be known that Sortek is involved. That could be awkward, as he is a favorite of House Steiner.

"No, they must be concealed, disguised...You think of something!" he said to the aide. "I have other important matters that await me."

Ardan had donned full-dress uniform for his reunion with Hanse. That included a light laser pistol, a sidearm that was now in his hand as the guard approached.

"I don't really want to kill anyone, but I cannot allow you to arrest the Prince of Davion," he said. "Step aside. We are going out through that doorway."

The guard, the aide, and Cleery had no choice but to step aside, to stand with the man who was now, at least temporarily, the ruler of the Federated Suns. Ardan was sorely tempted to kill the imposter where he stood, but Hanse read the thought in him and shook his head.

Then they were outside the door. It could not be locked. The computer in the study gave those inside instant access to the entire complex, anyway. Forgetting dignity, the pair ran pell-mell down the corridor.

"Here!" panted Ardan, pulling Hanse aside into a niche containing a small fountain and green plants.

"You're going to try hiding me under a philodendron?" asked Hanse. He came into the shallow curve of the wall unwillingly and stood listening intently for sounds of pursuit.

Ardan didn't reply. He pushed aside the woven-reed tapestry covering the section of the wall from which the marble arm and hand poured water from a silver pitcher. A push sent the entire segment pivoting on some hidden central point, so that the pouring pitcher and the basin to catch the water moved aside as they slipped through a narrow crevice.

"Help me push it back," whispered Ardan. "The curtain will return, just as it was."

Hanse was muttering quiet curses under his breath, but he put his shoulder to the smooth side of the stone and lent his strength. The pivot moved back silently.

Now they stood in a narrow space barely wide enough for Hanse's powerful shoulders, which was lit dimly from above.

Ardan gestured upward to indicate the slit that evidently went from this floor of the palace all the way to one of the skylights in the roof. "This is a ventilation duct. Lets the moisture from all that marble in the walls dry out...feel the breeze? It has slits into the outer air on several levels, and the marble behind the fountain is pierced to allow the freshness into the corridor."

Hanse looked stunned. He had lived in the Summer Palace almost every year since ascending to the throne. Before that, he had come here with his father on many occasions. Never had he suspected that behind the fountain alcoves in each floor of the house was what amounted to a secret passage.

"I never knew!" he said. His tone was rather wistful.

"You didn't have to design a defense for the house. We did. The architect's records are in the computer, ready to be called up at any time. But the only ones likely to do that are those charged with your personal safety."

"Where does this come out?" Hanse asked quietly.

Ardan turned to follow the cranny out of the dimly lit portion into blackness. "In the wall above the kitchen wing. We'll have to wait for darkness before we try scaling the wall to the roof."

Hanse's eyes lit up. On the roof was, of course, his personal air car. With it, they could be away before the imposter and his crew could finish searching this tremendous and complex structure.

They crept like mice through winding, impossibly narrow spaces. Ardan's impressive uniform acquired a coating of dust and cobweb that added nothing to its appearance. Hanse, attired in plain clothing for work in his study, fared a bit better. Brown woven stuff showed the deposits of debris far less than did the buff and gold, slashed with scarlet, that Ardan wore.

From time to time, Ardan paused. Lateral spaces crossed their path, even narrower than the one they followed. More than once, one of those ran away at an oblique angle, and Ardan had to recall to mind the plans he had committed to memory years before.

"What are those?" asked Hanse at last, indicating one of the dark tunnels.

"They go between the walls. Keeps the walls from sweating and rotting the paneling and tapestries on the inside. Stone is terrifically sweaty stuff, particularly in such a humid climate," Ardan whispered.

Hanse seemed unsettled by this warren of passages between the walls of his summer home. "Why, anyone who knows the plan could slip into the place at will," he murmured.

Ardan glanced back over his shoulder. Hanse's bulk was a deeper black against the darkness.

"They could…but I know where the traps are that keep them from succeeding. We've passed three, so far. Another is just ahead. Want me to point it out?"

"It wouldn't do any good. How could I see it?"

Ardan chuckled quietly. A few more paces and he paused to take Hanse's hand. "Feel, as I hold back the trigger," he said.

Their hands moved together to feel along the wall to their right. A slender rod extended out into the narrow passage. Even a man with some sort of handlight would not be likely to see it, for it was at shoulder height.

"It's painted black," murmured Ardan. "If you went staggering along here without knowing it was there and then brushed against it, a metal panel would slide into place before and behind you. You'd be caught here, while an alarm went off in the guardpost. You'd be neatly trapped. Here, let me move it aside."

He caught the rod in his hand and gave it a twist, at the same time lifting it straight up. After Hanse squeezed past him, Ardan let the rod down gently and twisted it back into its original position.

"Why didn't I have to squeeze past you before?" asked the Prince.

"Oh, the others are all different. You have to know where each one is and also WHAT it is. Else you're in bad trouble. The next one is a dilly…and I'm not quite certain where it is, either."

"Oh, wonderful," grunted the ruler of the Federated Suns.

29

No one had ever accused Hanse Davion of being tight-fisted. Sep blessed that fact as she counted out the store of C-Bills he had provided for their rendezvous with Ardan. She had spent relatively few, leaving plenty for bribes and other emergencies.

Jarlik was the one who found them transportation with a pilot named Dahl, skipper of an *Invader* Class JumpShip. The two shared a few mugs of ale in the local bar, where Jarlik learned that Dahl had a grudge against Sallek Atrion, the garrison commander. The man would be happy to secretly pilot them and their DropShip to Dragon's Field if it might eventually mean trouble for Atrion.

Once aboard Dahl's *Invader*, with their DropShip safely attached, Sep said, "When we hit Dragon's Field, we'll get our bearings first at the deep-space station. There's bound to be another 'cooperative and discreet' pilot looking to make a few extra C-Bills."

Dahl said, "Why don't you let me check things out for you? As a pilot, I'd never be suspect. And once you're gone to worlds distant, I'll just be sitting here nice and innocent-like, recharging my ship."

Dragon's Field was a snap. Dahl found some friendly pretext for inviting another pilot aboard the DropShip, where Sep, Jarlik, and Ref were waiting.

"These folks need to use your ship," said Dahl reasonably. "They'll pay you well. And if anybody asks, just tell them you were kidnapped. How about it?"

Dahl had chosen well. Within fifteen minutes of docking their DropShip to the new pilot's JumpShip, they were on their way. No hue and cry was raised, nor would any be until someone wanted to board the charged ship that had vanished so mysteriously.

The jump from Hamlin was a bit more difficult. Their last pilot had been willing to be 'kidnapped', but not to compound a felony by helping them hijack another ship. Again, it was Jarlik who did reconnaissance in port, where he strolled about, observing the possibilities. When he learned of a JumpShip that was currently idle, he told Sep and Ref, "I'll persuade the pilot to transport me to some phony destination, while you and the crew hide snug in the DropShip. Once we're aboard, we'll introduce ourselves and our real destination to the captain."

As the new pilot was making ready for jump, Jarlik approached, his hand laser drawn. "What we really need is a lift to Ral," he said, his tone as mild as a rumble can be. The pilot came up swinging, but one shove of Jarlik's big hand convinced him that the bigger man outdid him, armed or otherwise.

They popped into being near the Ral system, where four JumpShips were charging not far beyond their position.

Jarlik patted his captive on the shoulder. "Nice work. Here's a bit to make it worth your while, and also enough to pay for the extra charge. You'll have to report this, but you don't have any idea who has taken you for a ride, do you?"

The pilot shook his head. He didn't, and that was the truth. He barely understood what had happened, as such a hijacking had never been tried before.

The three companions then selected one of the Jump-Ships waiting nearby, and had their current pilot signal that he wanted to board to get some assistance with a minor mechanical problem. Then Ref, Sep, and Jarlik got into their DropShip, and had their crew pilot them over to the new ship. In less than half an hour, they had jumped again, with another JumpShip pilot wondering if it were all a bad dream.

The last jump, from Vincent to Argyle, was accomplished in much the same fashion. "You won't know where you've been," Jarlik told the pilot, handing him a wad of C-Bills, "and you won't know who took you there, now will you?"

The pilot shook his head. "But I'd like to know how you made out when this is all over," he said. "Here's my call number. Get a message to me when you can."

Jarlik nodded. "Will do...if we live."

They landed their DropShip in a meadow outside the city of Stirling, which housed Hanse Davion's Summer Palace. Not wanting to be seen in port, they had chosen a spot that seemed safe for a private landing.

This early in the morning, mist was rising from the streams that made a webwork of waterways through the countryside. The 'Mechs stalked from the DropShip, and stood like prehistoric monsters in a dawn-world. The Drop-Ship crew, meanwhile, had orders to keep quiet and stay undercover.

"We'd best stow the 'Mechs in the woods and check out the palace on foot," said Sep. "One of us can stay to watch them. The other two can split up to see if we can find out what is going on."

They thudded through the summer grass toward the towering forest that stood between the meadow and the grasslands around the Summer Palace. There was enough cover there for an army of 'Mechs. Stowed in a thicket of heavy-leaved bushes, the heads and shoulders of the 'Mechs were screened by arching boughs of the trees overhanging the thicket. From a distance, nothing was visible to anyone who didn't know to look closely.

It was decided that Ref and Sep would probably be able to melt into the palace background fairly easily, but that Jarlik would probably be recognized instantly. They decided that he would remain behind.

Sep and Ref went to separate entrances, where their retinal scans admitted them through the portals into the complex. Almost reflexively, Sep found herself headed toward the barracks.

Denek was coming down the steps as she mounted them.

"How goes it Den?" she asked. He looked up, startled, then grinned. "Sep, by golly, it's good to see you back. I

219

never knew managing a unit could be so much hassle. Come with me and tell me what you've been doing!"

She turned companionably and moved with him toward the Palace. "Everything going well?" she asked again.

He looked doubtful. "I don't know about well. Not that there's any trouble, but with getting the guard ready to move back to New Avalon and all, it's been confusing. And the trouble with Steiner, too, right on the heels of that."

Sep stopped in her tracks. "Trouble with Steiner? What trouble? I've been on R and R, remember?"

He nodded. "Come on, then. I've got to hurry. Final inspection before jump. Davion's already gone. We all registered a protest that it was a bad move, but he insisted that he must attend to some important business on New Avalon. So off he went, with just a skeleton guard, his aide, and one unit."

"But what about Steiner?" she asked impatiently.

"We'd all thought there was some sort of agreement between the Commonwealth and the Federation. You remember, we used to talk about it. Well, just a week or so ago, Hanse went up by Command Circuit to meet with Katrina on Sol. Came back in a towering rage, saying he'd rather tie up with a she-bear. All connections have been severed."

Denek turned abruptly into the gate of the drillground. "And it puts us into a real bind, if Liao tries to retake Stein's Folly. We'll be standing alone now, with all the major systems against us."

Sep digested Denek's words as he checked out the unit and sent the 'Mechs to their DropShips, the warriors to quarters. When Denek was done, she pulled him aside. "We have to talk. Now," she said, and began at the beginning. Denek listened, but his expression grew more and more skeptical as she spoke.

"Sep, Ardan was out of it. The doctors, the Meds, everyone said so."

She stared at him sternly. "So just about the time Ardan would have gotten here, Hanse just happens to change drastically. Not to mention the fact that there's no sign of Ardan and hasn't been, even though he was using the Jump-Ship Hanse Davion assigned to us so that we could get to the Folly and meet him."

She set her hand on his shoulder and shook him gently. "Ardan got into that installation where he'd been held. He found a holo set up with pictures of Hanse in every sort of situation. Also of Argyle, in detail. When he brought Ref and me back to see it, the booby-traps began to go, and we had to get out or die. But he had put a set of holos in his pocket."

"He what?"

"Just what I said. He had a packet of them in his pocket. When we put them in the viewer, we saw the Palace at Argyle. There were holos of everything, in so much detail that if you studied them, it'd be almost like having lived here most of your life. From the Prince's private can to the bird sanctuary, with the names of all Hanse's favorite birds marked onto the case of the holo. It told *us* something. Doesn't it say anything to you?"

Denek might behave as if he were a foolish young fellow out for a good time, but he was a MechWarrior, and a good one. That meant he was no fool.

"They were training someone to take the Prince's place. And he's done it. If Ardan did show up here unannounced, he was probably either killed or is in hiding or has been ...detained."

He looked steadily into Sep's eyes.

"I have to get the unit offworld right now. You stay here and learn what you can. There's a ship, for emergencies only, stashed in Hangar Twelve at the private port. Old Sarnov lives in the village north of the grounds. He was one of the best pilots ever. When you find something...if you find something...you come to New Avalon. You're due back off leave, anyway. Nobody is going to ask how you got onworld, once you're there.

"I'll put your impending arrival on the incoming chart, as soon as I get in, with the notation that you are allowed recharge time and your exact time of arrival is unknown."

She patted his shoulder. "Good thinking. And put it as 'Candent Septarian and group', will you? We just might be able to slip Ardan in that way. Not to mention Hanse, if he should still be around."

She turned back to the forest, her mind busy. Where would the false Hanse have put his captives? Would he be naive enough to put them in the cells beneath the palace?

Where?

30

Ardan found himself at the outlet of the ventilation slot while the sun was still high. Hanse, behind him, was silent, and Ardan recalled suddenly that the Prince had a tendency toward claustrophobia. He felt a twinge of guilt at bringing him through such a tight place.

Then he chuckled.

"What's so funny?" asked Hanse.

"I was feeling sorry about getting you into such a smothery position, when I remembered that the alternative was the detention cells. Have you ever taken the tour? It's enough to make your gorge rise. I wonder why your whatever-it-is-great grandfather built them as he did."

Hanse sighed and crouched beside Ardan in the narrow passageway. "Old Lucien was a complex character, I suspect. He had, among other things, a mania for the antique. Not what we call antique, mind you, but the really ancient. He was an able administrator, a wonderful organizer, but he had several important screws pretty loose, indeed. He made his detention cells just like the dungeons in the ancient records. Odd thing. We've never used them much for any but important prisoners who were in danger of their lives."

As the sun set, Ardan watched the line of light work its way along the wall. Only a shoulder's width of space marked the slit on the outside wall, he knew. It was decorated around its edges with carved stone and looked like a high-set window.

"Well, I'd rather be here than down in those ghastly deeps," he said. "It'll be dark before too long. Then we can get onto the roof and take off."

The sky darkened gradually. The slit of warm gold was gone, and the sky turned to lilac, then to gray, and then to midnight black. Stars sprinkled the expanse when the two fugitives worked their way from the slit and began climbing the sheer wall.

Lucien had liked stone-carving. His decorations, old as they were, were still firm, and they gave finger and toe-holds to his descendant as Hanse and Ardan made their painful way up the wall toward the roof. From time to time, they froze in place, as the thud of giant feet announced the presence of a 'Mech guard on the paved terrace below.

At the top of the wall was an overhang. That posed a problem, for there wasn't firm enough purchase to allow one of the men to swing his foot over the ledge above them.

They clung there for many minutes, trying to think of a way to go upward without falling from the wall. Then Hanse whispered, "You move toward me along this string-course. Yes, like that. Now. Set your near foot onto my knee. I have it braced between the stone and the wall. See if you can get high enough to put an elbow over the top."

Ardan moved as directed. Once he had his foot set firmly on Hanse's knee, he found that he could give a spring upward. It took him far enough to catch the lip of the crowning ledge with his right elbow and his left hand. In a moment, he was over onto the roof. Anchoring his body against a chimney, he then reached down.

"Hanse! Can you reach me?" he hissed.

A big hand slapped into his palm. Another hit his other hand. Heaving with all his might, Ardan swung the big man sideways to clear the overhang. Hanse's leg hooked over the lip. Then he was beside Ardan on the roof.

"Whooo!" the Prince said. "I also hate heights, in case anyone wonders. But I have a new liking for my many-times-great Grandpa. If he hadn't decorated his palace like a wedding cake, we'd never have been able to make it."

They crept around the bulk of the chimney stack and started toward the blister that sheltered the air car. The closure opened to Hanse's thumb, and the two pulled the light craft free onto the roof. While Ardan was checking it over, Hanse unlocked the stubby wings and put them into vertical takeoff position.

"Very pretty," a voice behind them said. "We knew you would probably come here."

Cleery stepped from behind another chimney stack, accompanied by six heavily armed guardsmen. "Ekkles was really puzzled by your disappearing trick. You will tell me how you accomplished that, before we are done."

"I prefer to deal with Ekkles than you," said the Prince. He sounded calm, but Ardan felt the undercurrent of frustration in him.

"Impossible, I'm afraid. Ekkles has accompanied Hanse Davion to New Avalon. An unexpected emergency demanded the presence of the Prince. You are now in my hands." The note of gloating in the man's voice startled Ardan.

He had known Cleery for years, ever since the man had become Davion's Maître of the Household on Argyle. Neither of them had suspected that there might be a power-mad sadist lurking beneath that suave and polite exterior. A shiver moved through Ardan's body. What had they gotten into now?

Cleery took no chances. He had the guards shackle Ardan to Hanse, and their feet linked on short chains so they couldn't possibly run. Then, the Maître stepped forward and snapped his fingers. One of the young pages brought him a bag, from which he took two thick robes, like those worn by inhabitants of some desert worlds. They had deep hoods.

Once the captives had them on, neither could possibly have been recognized, unless an observer were to stand face to face with them and look directly into the shadowy recesses of the hoods. Cleery was definitely no fool, Ardan decided.

The Maître had, of course, ordered that both men be disarmed immediately. Cleery himself had run his hands down the arms, sides, and legs of his prisoners to make doubly sure. Then the guards led them down and down beneath the huge palace, into the dank corridor that led into Lucien's genuine, old Earth-type dungeons. Even the steps they descended had been artificially shaped to hint at millennia of wear.

The bottommost corridor ran crosswise. Rats scampered away from the handlight of the guards. Drips sounded, echoing hollowly through the maze of tunnels leading from the main artery. The smell was not pleasant, and it got worse as they moved deeper into the complex.

"Here we are," said Cleery, mock cheerful. "The Royal suite. Designed, no doubt, for Pretenders. Suitable enough. We'll even leave you together to grieve over the failure of your plot."

Ardan felt sure at this moment that Cleery was part of the conspiracy. How else could the false Hanse have gotten into the Palace and into the royal quarters so easily without being detected?

"Cleery, I never really knew you," said Hanse quietly. "And now that I'm beginning to, it's certainly not a pleasure."

The Maître smiled, his fat lips stretched obscenely over his square white teeth. "I think that you will now have time to plan all sorts of vengeful schemes. And that is all you will have—Time. It can break the hardest will, I am told. It will be interesting to put the theory to the test."

Hanse did not reply. They watched the heavy door slam to. Bars were slid across from the outside. Locks snapped, the harsh echoes resounding crazily.

A torch had been left in the corridor, and its dim flickers gave only the barest illumination to the cell, the light making its way through some slits in the stone wall. Ardan examined those at once, but they were obviously for the purpose of placing food and water within reach of prisoners, without taking the chance of opening a door.

"No hope there," he said, testing the solidity of the stonework. "I think it must be cut out of the bedrock the house sits on."

"Damn Lucien!" said Hanse. "That's exactly what it is. I've read his journals. He was very proud of his authentic dungeons, from which no prisoner would ever escape." He shivered in the dank, chill air. "Cold in here, isn't it? At least we can be thankful for these havy robes."

Ardan nodded. With his mind racing frantically to think of some way out of an impossible situation, he hadn't even noticed the cold till now. He shivered, too, hoping the torch would hold out for a while. He didn't like to think about how it would be when they also were faced with total darkness. Ardan huddled against Hanse in a corner. Evidently, no prisoner had ever been kept in the place, for there wasn't even straw to cushion the hardness of the stone floor.

At first, Ardan and Hanse had expected that their captors would kill them immediately. As long as they remained alive, the two of them were a grave threat to the plot to replace Hanse Davion with an imposter.

Instead, the days passed, empty, dark, cold, and interminable. Hanse and Ardan no longer knew whether it was night or day, though Ardan had pulled the wire from a pocket charm the guards had not removed, and he was using it to scratch out the passage of time in the stone wall. There wasn't much else to do, except think. But when the routine suddenly changed, Ardan would gladly have gone back to the torture of boredom.

One day, several guards came into the cell, seized Hanse roughly, and dragged him away protesting. "Hanse!" Ardan screamed, grasping the bars and pressing his face against them as the footsteps retreated down the corridor. When the silence descended once more, Ardan dropped to the floor, overcome by his sorrow and despair. He was sure Hanse had just gone to his death.

What seemed like hours later, Ardan again heard heavy footsteps approaching down the stone corridor. "My turn now," he thought grimly. But the guards merely opened the cell door, and threw Hanse bodily back into its gloom. Ardan crawled weakly over to his friend, and found him drugged senseless. It was a relief that Hanse was still alive, but what had they done to him?

He did his best to make Hanse comfortable, holding the Prince's head on his lap, and laying his own robe over him

227

for extra warmth. The two of them sat that way for hours, Ardan with eyes closed, his back propped against the damp stone wall. When Hanse mumbled something finally, and stirred as though trying to get up, Ardan restrained him. "Hanse, no…you must rest now and stay warm…"

"Ardan…you…" Hanse murmured. "They took me…" he said with great effort. "Cleery was there…and some others…doctors maybe…Gave me something…an injection…"

"Not now, Hanse," Ardan said. "Later…you can tell me later."

But Hanse was never able to remember anything more than that. The guards came back for him frequently now, and when they returned him hours, even days later, Hanse was usually so drugged or his mind so numbed from exhaustion that he might as well have been. Whatever they did while Hanse was semiconscious, it would take him several days to break out of the mental fog and confusion. Then the guards would come for him once more, and the whole cycle would begin again.

Huddled like an animal in the cavelike damp of the cell, Ardan could never be sure whether Hanse would come back or not. Though Hanse could never remember anything afterward, Ardan was sure their captors were interrogating him, using mental taps and drugs. In spite of the nicks he etched into the wall, Ardan had no idea whether it was day or night or how much time had passed since they had been led down into this dungeon and the horror of their uncertain fate. It was small comfort, but he was beginning to understand what was going on, at least.

When he and Hanse had confronted the false Prince, what baffled Ardan was how the imposter could have known so many details about the past…things no one but he or Hanse could have known. The betrothal to Melissa, for instance, or the long-ago day when Hanse had almost drowned or the gift he had given the child Ardan one birthday. Now it was starting to make sense. For one thing, the imposter had *not* known about the starbird, which was a story that Melissa had told Ardan *after* he had been rescued

228

from Liao hands. While he had lain delirious in that hospital on Stein's Folly, the Liao doctors must have been probing his brain with drugs and mental taps just as they were doing with Hanse now.

Ardan was sure that his captors were systematically probing Hanse Davion's mind for every last memory so that they could transfer it all to their puppet Hanse, and authenticate him beyond the shadow of a doubt. These men were as desperate as they were ambitious, and so Ardan was certain neither he nor Hanse would survive long once they had all they needed.

Sep found Jarlik alert but fuming at the delay in getting to the business at hand. "We have to know where Ardan is before we can spring him free or help him escape from Argyle," she said.

"If he's been captured, he's in the dungeon. And if he hasn't, he'll be in our old hideaway in the woods. But I've already looked there, so it's the dungeons, Sep. And we can only get into those with 'Mechs. Ardan can sneak around the Summer Palace like a mouse, but I don't remember the architects' plans the way he does."

Ref, rejoining them, agreed with Jarlik's assessment. "There's no word of anyone being captured around the palace. Nothing out of the ordinary. The only person who was suspicious was Fani Lettik. Awhile back, she saw someone in the kitchen area who shouldn't have been there. The man told her he was a gardener investigating a defective grillwork behind the shrubbery. But when she asked the Maître if it had been reported to him, he denied it."

Ref looked at Sep, his eyebrow quirked. "And nobody else saw that man at all. When she described him, he sounded terribly fishy, too. Flat, greasy-looking hair. Very dark goggles that hid his eyes. A blue coverall, which was proper for a gardener. But she said he looked as if he had a swollen tooth. His face was lopsided."

"Ardan," said Sep. Jarlik nodded.

"Put something on his hair to change its look. Stuffed wadding in his jaws. Got hold of some goggles someplace to hide those amber eyes and those sharp cheekbones. No doubt about it. He got into the house. Then Hanse Davion changed his mind about staying his usual time on Argyle."

"I'll bet anything you name that Hanse and Ardan are down below the Palace, locked away in those barbaric dungeons old Lucien had built. Dammit!" Sep pounded her fist softly against her uniformed knee.

"Wait a minute, Sep. Think about it..." said Ref, who was sitting on a fallen tree trunk and gazing idly at the high canopy of leaves overhead. "Where's the problem? The Prince is gone, right? And he's taken most of the guard with him. All that's left around the Summer Palace in the off-season is a skeleton crew. I say we go in tonight and get them out."

Sep thought for a momenet, then grinned suddenly. "Good thinking, Ref. You're right...Tonight's the night. I've got the security codes to disarm the Palace defenses, for one thing, and the retinal scanners'll recognize me as head of the Guard. That'll get me and Jarlik past the automatic defenses easily enough. In the meantime, Ref, you'll go over to the old fuel depot. I bet there are still enough combustibles lying around there for you to set off quite a big bang. And while you're over there drawing off most of the Palace Guards by making as much noise as possible, Jarlik and I will spring Hanse and Ardan from the Palace."

Jarlik chuckled deep in his throat. "Any 'Mech who doesn't get diverted will wish he had."

Sep nodded. "But what about getting into the lower level, where the access corridor is?" she asked the big man. "I've never been on personal duty for the Prince. I usually pulled shifts at training the Guard, not at guarding the Royal residence."

"Well, I've learned a lot of the ins and outs from working with Ardan so long. Back in the service area, there is a cul-de-sac serving the doors to the laundry rooms, the kitchens, the catering services, and the butler's pantry. At night, it's deserted down there." After sweeping aside dead leaves to clear a space, Jarlik sketched a rough diagram in the dust.

"There's the service floor. Here's the corridor that gives access to the lower level where the dungeons are. There"— he sketched a rapid series of crossbars—"are the ventilators. Even prisoners have to breathe. We can batter through those easily. I see no problem, unless some hotshot 'Mech guard tries to liven things up."

It seemed to take a year for the sun to set. The forest rustled and whispered about them. From time to time, some small animal peered from branches above or from the snakelike roots of one of the big trees, but the trio sat so quietly that the creatures soon lost interest and went about their own business.

When the sky was black and the treetops lost against the starry expanse, the three mounted their 'Mechs. Ref headed for the fuel depot, while Sep and Jarlik moved across the vineyards and then the public gardens that stood just outside the Palace walls. As expected, the two passed through the automatic defenses with no problem.

"Well, getting in was easy," Sep said into her com, "but getting out could be another problem entirely. Denek gave me access to the emergency DropShip, but who knows how we'll get to it. Much less how we contact the pilot he suggested. This may be our last burst of glory, old friend. Let's make it count!"

They strode closer to the Palace, which was dark except for a few glimmers of light from windows in the servants' wing. That startled Sep until she realized that she had always seen the Summer Palace ablaze with the lights and activity that swirled around the Prince, with all the comings and goings that attended his affairs of state, visitors, and minions. Now those same tiers of rooms stood in darkness.

Just then, an explosion boomed to the east of them, and a huge fireball rose into the night sky.

"Looks good," said Sep, and she heard Jarlik's grunt of agreement, as they halted at the edge of the courtyard that led up to the Palace. Standing in the shadows, they waited, hoping most of the guard 'Mechs had gone to investigate the explosion, according to plan.

Though they had no way of knowing, the fact that everything was so quiet close to the Palace seemed a good sign. "Looks like we're home free," Sep said, "but let's wait another minute. I don't see anything, do you?"

"Coast is clear," Jarlik replied.

"All right, let's move while we've got the chance!" she said, and the two began striding forward on the giant legs of their 'Mechs. At that moment, something caught Sep's eye to their right...something coming around the western flank of the Palace. It was a *Wasp* on patrol. She was about to warn Jarlik, when she heard the *Wasp* pilot sounding an alarm over the general frequency.

"Halt and identify yourselves!" the *Wasp* challenged, as Sep and Jarlik continued moving forward. The guard then lifted its right arm in an accusatory gesture that spat fire from its medium laser.

"Hostiles on Palace grounds. Engaging!" they heard him report frantically over the crackle of the general frequency. The two heavy 'Mechs dodged, and the shot missed.

"Concentrate fire!" Sep yelled into the com. "Right leg! Give him everything you've got." The combined fire from their lasers, autocannon, and SRMs was deafening, almost blinding. Then they saw the *Wasp* fall to the ground, its right leg totally disintegrated. The huge machine was now effectively out of commision.

"One down," said Sep, "but he's put out the warning now, and it won't be long before the rest of them show up. We better get done with this now!"

They sped down the deserted walks toward the palace. With the main Guard gone, very few troops lived in the barracks. It was more economical to have the entire staff living in the big house, which had to be heated and cooled, whether tenanted or not.

No one challenged them until they came abreast of the kitchen wing.

"What is going on here?" came the cry.

Sep groaned. Fani Lettik had a habit of showing up when she was least wanted. Confronted with the two giant forms of a *Warhammer* and a *Crusader*, however, Fani froze in her tracks, an expression of terror on her face. As Sep and Ref continued to lumber forward, Fani let out a scream, then turned and ran. It was the first time Sep had ever seen

Fani intimidated, and it had taken two heavy 'Mechs to do it.

Rounding the corner, the two 'Mechs stalked on into the cul-de-sac, which was just where Jarlik had said it would be. Sep kept watch as Jarlik set one of his armored feet against the ventilation grid. It, too, was solid stone. With a mighty swing, he kicked forcefully and struck the rock with a resounding crash. There was the rattle of stone chips falling away into the darkness below.

Again Jarlik kicked. More stone fell, and a gap opened in the grill. Sep chanced a flash of light from her torch. The wall was beginning to give, sure enough.

She aimed her laser and gave the spot a long blast. Hissing and spitting, the beam melted the rock into taffy-like puddles that dripped down the sides of the hole. Another blast, and the hole caved in bodily, leaving a huge pit in the paving that floored the niche.

"I'll go," she said to Jarlik. "You just keep anyone from coming in after me."

Sep dismounted, leaving her *Warhammer* ready for instant use when she returned. The stone was still hot, and she had to wait for a moment before she could spring down into the blackness below. But lights were coming on inside the house now. Voices cried out. They would have company long before she was ready for it.

She dropped through the hole and rolled with practiced ease, coming upright in darkness. Hitting the switch of her belt light, she looked about. It was a nasty sort of place, damp and chilly, and seemed to be a warren of tunnels and cells. She ran along toward the interior of the block. "Ardan!" she shouted.

There was a moment of silence. Then, muffled with stone and distance, came a welcome reply.

"Sep? By God! Sep!"

She homed on the sound and ran, watching closely as she set her feet. If she tripped and knocked herself out, it wouldn't help any of them. Rats scuttered away in front of her, and she could hear their chittering behind her. Her skin crawled.

"Ardan!" she called again, pausing at a three-way corner.

"Here!" His voice was nearer now. Down the right angle. As she rounded the bend, she could see a guttering torch in a socket on the wall. Before a door halfway down the rank stood a water can and a mess tray.

She pounded up to the door. There was a metal rod slipped through loops, holding it closed. In addition, the inset lock looked formidable.

"Stand back!" she yelled.

There came a grunt from inside that she took for assent. She aimed her sidearm laser and melted the lock out of its metal housing. As she kicked the rod back with a booted foot, the door swung open.

Two bearded faces blinked at her in the brilliant light of her torch. She saw at once that their eyes weren't accustomed to light, and so she quickly killed the beam. The torchlight seemed terribly dim by contrast.

Hanse and Ardan looked terrible. She stepped back and looked down at the rations outside the door. Moldy food, slimy-looking water. Untouched.

"They were starving you?" she asked, her tone furious.

"Trying to soften us up. Do you have any clean water? That dirty stuff is all they gave us, and precious little of that," Ardan croaked.

Sep reached for her hip canteen. No pilot ever mounted his 'Mech without a supply of rations, no matter how tame the occasion. She had on her uniform, because of the special nature of the mission, and so its hip flask was ready to hand.

"Here. But drink slowly. First rule in the Survival Manual."

While they talked, a clatter sounded in the distance. Footsteps on stone...They'd better get out fast.

"This way," she said. "We made a new door into your dungeons, Your Highness. I hope you don't mind."

Hanse grinned, his lips cracking. "Lead on," he told her.

They came to the hole well ahead of their pursuers. Jarlik had his hatch open, listening for them. Reaching his armored limb down into the hole, he lifted up first Hanse, then the other two.

Sep mounted her 'Mech. Ardan climbed into the tight cockpit behind her. Hanse had already done the same in Jarlik's.

"Better run. There's armor coming," Jarlik said over the com.

The metal feet of their 'Mechs pounded across the paved terraces, the grassy spaces, the flower beds and borders. When they came to the wall, Sep blasted a portion of it down, and then she and Jarlik hammered through the debris without slowing their strides.

Through her scanners, Sep could see that the Summer Palace was abuzz with activity. Lights were on all over the residence, and red bursts of laser fire spat against the night. She suspected that the guard 'Mechs were mistakenly attacking each other. That was fine. Nobody had followed their rescue team, and their tracks wouldn't be immediately obvious until it got light.

She tore along beside Jarlik, heading for the port, where they were to rendezvous with Ref. If they were lucky, nobody would suspect it to be their destination until it was too late. Then she had a terrible thought.

"We haven't got our pilot!" she yelled into the com.

There was no answer for a moment, then she heard Jarlik's familiar gruff tone over the com.

"Never mind that," he said. "His Highness says he can pilot the thing. Just get him there in one piece!"

32

Katrina Steiner was no fool. As soon as her ambassador got word to her of his strange interview with Hanse Davion at the Summer Palace on Argyle, she put two and two together with computer-like speed. Then she called her daughter to her side.

"It looks as if you were right all along, Melissa. The Prince of the Federated Suns has just informed our ambassador that he is withdrawing from any treaties now in existence between our worlds, including the one signed on Sol several years ago. That man may have looked, talked, and walked like the real Hanse Davion, but he must have been the double Ardan saw all those months ago."

Melissa turned pale. "And Hanse? What of him?"

"All we know is that the Prince has left Argyle for New Avalon, which he has never done before at this time of year. That means that the real Prince is probably still on-planet."

"Mother, we *must* send help!" Melissa was regaining her color, and her chin was coming up into its fighting position.

"Not to Argyle. I have great faith in young Sortek. If he went to Argyle, he's smart enough to have the necessary back-up to do what he came for. By the time we got anyone into position there, it would be too late, given the many weeks of recharge it would require. But I do intend to send help…to New Avalon."

"New Avalon?" Melissa's tone was doubtful.

Her mother sat and drew her daughter beside her on the low couch. "If Ardan has found Hanse and freed him, they will follow the imposter back to the capital. I do not doubt that at all."

"But it's so chancy!" objected the girl.

"That is true," her mother agreed, "but Ardan and Hanse are two most ingenious and determined men. They have, as

237

well, devoted friends in positions to help them. I am going to move on faith alone. If they have failed, we will be in no worse position. If they have not, our ambassador will be in position to force the issue and to give the real Hanse the backing he must have to regain his throne. Ambassador Efflinger is now on New Avalon. I can get word to him via ComStar in a few weeks. We must hope that it will be in time."

"But what will you instruct him to do?" Melissa was looking impatient and confused, both at once.

"To keep a sharp watch through all his information networks for any hint of a 'Pretender' to the rulership of the Federated Suns. And if such a Pretender comes to light, to make certain he has the opportunity to confront the man now on the throne. To insist on exhaustive testing for both, using all the authority of House Steiner's position among the systems." Katrina wrinkled her forehead.

"We can only hope that it will be enough. In the meanwhile, I am fortifying those garrisons that might be vulnerable to attack from that direction. If all our efforts fail, we will soon be at war with our best ally."

Turning to her computer console at the small table beside her desk, Katrina tapped in the message for her assigned Adept to transmit.

Melissa stood at the window, watching the sun set over the ragged heights beyond the palace walls. Now the only snow was atop the tallest peaks in the distance. She wished for a moment that Ardan were still safely on Tharkad. He was her good friend, after all. Then she remembered Hanse...possibly a prisoner, or worse. Something between shyness and fierce protectiveness gripped her.

She turned to her mother, who had finished her message. "If things go totally wrong, I hope to meet that duplicate Hanse one day. Perhaps it can be managed. I do not intend for my betrothed to suffer the fate of that poor Esteren, his reputation destroyed by another man."

Katrina smiled. This young daughter of hers was growing up. All she said was, "We shall see ..." How often over the millennia had mothers taken refuge from their children's unanswerable questions with those three words?

* * * *

Maylor Efflinger tended to be lazy. So far from his home world and his demanding ruler, he was able to indulge his laziness without attracting too much notice. However, with a message as urgent as the one just come directly from House Steiner, he did, as the ancient saying went, get a move on.

Steiner had an enviable network of spies, both in friendly and unfriendly worlds. Those super-skilled agents were capable of finding out almost anything worth knowing about anyone at all. So when a ripple went through the rumor-mills beneath the surface of things on New Avalon, it came to Efflinger's attention with admirable speed.

"Four men and a woman have taken lodging at the House of Six Stars. They arrived in Avalon City on foot early last evening. They seem to have plenty of credits, though they look rather worn and seedy. One of them keeps the hood of his robe over his face most of the time. He is of the build of Davion, but no one has yet heard him speak."

Efflinger pricked up his ears at that report. He knew that there would be at least two men. If his informant were correct, there would be several more warriors, drawn from Sortek's friends in the Guard. And that big fellow with the hood…It sounded almost too much like Hanse Davion for comfort.

The ambassador had not really believed anything Katrina had said in that message. It seemed too far-fetched, though he knew she would never have involved her House unless firmly convinced she was correct. No matter what he thought, Efflinger knew which side his bread was buttered on. He went about finding the truth about those newcomers as quickly as he could manage.

239

He didn't use his spies. He knew that Davion's own spies were watching over him, just as he kept tabs on anyone of political interest to his superiors. His son, however, was another matter entirely.

Anyone trying to keep watch on a rake like Kolek Efflinger was in for a breathtaking time of it. Besides, it was unlikely that the Davion, Kurita, or Liao informants paid much attention to his frivolous son, who never did anything worthy of their interest anyway.

It was for that reason that occasionally Efflinger passed important messages to interested parties by way of his carousing son. Not a soul would suspect Kolek. Every sort of subtle investigation assured him of that. The House of Six Stars was a rather obscure inn, not exactly lower-class but edging in that direction. It did, however, have excellent beer.

As evening slid toward darkness, Maylor called his son into his study. "Ah, Kole," he began amiably, "I wonder if you would be so kind as to help me with a small matter..."

Kolek, as lazy as his father and therefore little inclined to earning his own living, was usually glad to do as his father asked. After all, the man supported him. "Of course," he said, dropping into a cushioned chair in a pose that should have disjointed both his hips and his backbone. "Just tell me what."

"Do you know the House of Six Stars?" asked his father.

Kole straightened a bit, his eyes growing brighter.

"Indeed, yes," he said. "Excellent beer they have there. I go there fairly often."

"So do others...some of whom I must contact in the most unobtrusive way possible." Maylor knew that his son was a subtle man, for all his seeming frivolity. He would be a fine diplomat, if ever he overcame his laziness.

Kole was now sitting straight. He enjoyed these commissions for his father, as they came rarely enough to seem more like adventures than scheduled tasks.

"Four men and a woman. Staying at Six Stars together, very quietly. One is a big fellow who wears a hooded robe. You should be able to pick them out by that. Few desert-worlders come here at this season. The rain drives them mad."

"And you want what?" asked Kolek. He was standing now, like a racer ready to take off down the track.

"To find out if the big man is Hanse Davion," his father replied.

Kole looked startled. "But what about..."

"May be an imposter. Steiner insists he is. It would seem to make sense, in light of the change of policy toward our systems. If this is the real item, take him and his friends to that little place where you used to keep your mistress. You recall it?"

A reminiscent smile lit Kole's face. "Of course. And then?"

Maylor grinned, looking for a moment no older than his son. "Get roaring drunk, as usual, and have someone carry you home, singing at the top of your voice. Then tell me if they are really who I suspect and go to bed. You will have done a fine job, either way."

Kole did exactly as he was instructed. In the early morning hours, the city Guard brought him home, together with a bystander, who turned out, to Maylor's amusement, to be one of the spies set to watch the Efflinger household.

Efflinger grumbled down the stair, opened the outer door, and helped to support his elevated son into the house. "My thanks," he said to the spy, handing him a credit he had brought for the purpose.

He turned to the Guard. "How much fine this time?" he asked wearily.

"The usual." The Guard was grinning broadly. Kolek was a young man who took his pleasures where he found them, but there wasn't a troublemaking bone in his body. Those entrusted with bringing him back home were always handsomely rewarded, and the doting father paid his fines without a word.

As soon as his attendants had gone, Kolek sat up in the chair where the Guard had deposited him. The dark eyes were filled with mirth.

"You do play a drunk quite well," Maylor observed.

Kole chuckled. "I should know how, by now. But you want my report. They are the ones you thought them to be. The big fellow is the real thing, too. Enough like the one in the palace to make you think you really *are* drunk!"

Efflinger sighed. "And they are safe in that quiet apartment above the tavern in Wine Street?"

"Safe as houses. Those are sound people. They didn't make any pretense, once they learned who I was and why I was there. They played along with me, getting drunker by the minute, until we all decided to take a keg upstairs to their quarters and make a night of it. And they had a scrambler that could break up the transmission if any sort of listening device was in their rooms."

"Good!" grunted his father. "It is really the Prince? You are sure?"

"I should say, yes. After I identified myself, they told me their story. It was quite a plot, once you put the pieces together, too. A double to break up the partnership between Steiner and Davion. A fast change, before NAIS gets their new security system into place. And removal of the one person close enough to the Prince to recognize an imposture, given time. Neat and quiet. But not quite successful."

"The city Guard and a detachment of the Royal Brigade have been scouring the city tonight," Maylor said. "I suspect that word has come through to the conspirators that the Prince has escaped from wherever they had him. They must be frightened that he is here, under their noses. Which he is. But where did he come from?"

"They made the switch on Argyle. Quite a nice tale... you should hear them tell it sometime. Dungeons and midnight escapes, and all sorts of bits you'd never expect to hear outside the ancient novels or operettas," said Kole.

Maylor was relaxing in his own deep chair now. "I was afraid, for a while, that we were about to go to war with

Davion. The broken treaties, the dismissal of so many of the old councillors that Hanse Davion trusted, not to mention that important announcement they have been touting for the past week. All those things were making me nervous. A war is no place for a man who likes his comfort."

"So what do we do now?" asked his son. He didn't look like the same young man who had been brought in, disheveled and flushed, a short while before.

"We take the opportunity they are giving us. We produce the real Prince and his friends at the palace when they have all the communications people there, all set up for their grand announcement. Then we demand, with all the weight our House can muster, that both be tested."

Kolek Efflinger nodded, his eyes even brighter than before. "And then...we shall see."

33

Avalon City was abuzz. Under the rulership of the Davions the people had become used to a smooth and peaceful life on this principal world. But now something seemed amiss. Ardan could feel it, even through the walls of the chambers he was sharing with the rest of his friends.

The snatches of conversation floating up from the street, the roars from the tavern below, even the whispers of chambermaids in the corridor outside their door all spoke of unease among the commoners. Sep, being the least recognizable of them, would don Ardan's hooded robe from time to time and slip out to gather news. It was uniformly bad.

"Some sort of announcement is in the offing," she said, as she doffed the robe and accepted a cup of soup from Ardan. "And war with Steiner is being rumored everywhere. Nobody is happy, Your Highness. Not at all. Your name is mentioned in tones I have never heard before. This imposter is going to ruin the Federated Suns in short order if we can't find some way to stop him."

"There is no time to foment a rebellion," said Hanse. He was staring down from the narrow window whose dirty glass hid his face from the street. "We have no one left in office to whom we can appeal. We can only trust Efflinger to pull this thing out of the fire for us. Who would have thought that Steiner would be the saving of our whole system?"

"You chose well when you signed the treaty with Steiner," said Ardan. "And even better when you contracted marriage with Melissa. You'll be pleasantly surprised when you see her again. She has grown into a woman of wit and strength. Much like her mother, though gentler-seeming."

Hanse smiled absently. Ardan knew that in his mind's eye Melissa was still the child he had known before.

"Just hope that the day will come when that marriage can come to pass," said the Prince. "We are in a predica-

244

ment. We cannot come forward, because the Guard would hustle us off to prison before we could attract any attention to our cause. I do hope Efflinger has something up his sleeve beside his lazy arm."

That evening, they learned that lazy as the ambassador's arm might be, it was effective when used to capacity. At mid-afternoon, Sep called the others to the window, pointing out Kolek Efflinger as he came into the inn with a pretty young woman much younger than he. The fugitives listened closely as a confusion of steps and running chambermaids came down the hall into the flat adjoining the one they occupied.

"I will need a personal attendant," the young woman was saying. "And I must go shopping at once. Will you see to that, my sweet?"

Kole's voice replied in a mumble, but his words must have been agreement, for she began to giggle. Doors opened and closed. The landlord's voice, too, sounded in the passage, conveying his willingness to assist with anything the distinguished couple wanted. They had only to ask.

Then the hubbub died down again. Heels tapped next door. Kole spoke quietly. The girl replied just as quietly. Everything became very still.

Jarlik grinned at Hanse and Ardan. Ref chuckled, and Sep tapped her fingernails on the table. What on or offworld was the young idiot playing at now?

There came a light tap at the door connecting their end room with the adjoining set. Jarlik stepped lightly as a cat to unlock it. Kole slid through and closed the panel behind him.

"Neat, eh?" he asked.

"She's a pretty one, yes," said Hanse. "But how will that help us?"

"Why, she's going out to shop this afternoon. She'll be bringing in parcels of all sizes and shapes. She will wear me completely out, paying for her purchases. And of course I shall buy some few matters for myself, too." He looked at their shabby uniforms, the noticeable robes.

"If you are to go to the palace tomorrow for the Great Revelation, you need to look a bit more sharp," he said.

The light dawned for them all. They would be outfitted with fresh clothing, even disguises, if necessary—all in a completely unsuspicious way. Even if Kolek were being kept under close surveillance, who would guess?

"The backstairs go down through the servants' quarters and end in an alley on Leather Street. You can go out after dark without seeing a soul. I know, because I've done it many a time. Prillie used to live in this set of rooms, instead of those next door." He looked sly.

"Don't ever tell my father, but I expect to marry the girl, when I'm ready to settle down and find work. Father will never consent, and will probably cut me off without a credit, so I'll have to be the one to make our living."

Hanse smiled broadly. "Come to me when you decide to take a job," he said. "I can always use sneaky people."

Kole nodded. "I thought you might," he said wryly. "Now I'd better go and help to buy out the town."

With a plan in progress, the five relaxed enough to nap the afternoon away. It was well done, too, because nobody could possibly have slept when the procession of parcels began to arrive next door. Sep, peering through a crack in the door, exclaimed at the variety of delivery people going and coming in the passage.

It took an hour and a half for all the bundles, packages, boxes, and bags to come to roost in the apartment next door. Then Prillie whispered at the connecting doorway, and the fugitives tiptoed into her bedroom, which was piled high with goods.

There was a gorgeous gown for Sep, but she was aghast at the idea of a MechWarrior wearing a cloth-of-gold overdress over full-legged pantaloons of white silk. Not to mention the jewels for hair and hands and bosom.

"You will never be recognized as Candent Septarian," said Hanse. "And it will get us into the grounds, I am sure. Besides, everyone will be staring so hard at you that nobody will notice any of the rest of us."

"Many thanks, Highness," growled Sep. "Once inside, we can get to barracks, where I can change. And then we'll be just another unit of the Guard, back on duty after leave. Denek has posted the orders."

For the men, there were formal uniforms. Kole had even managed to find the proper medals for Hanse and Ardan, while for Ref and Jarlik he had provided campaign clusters that put them into many places where neither had ever set foot. But they looked impressive.

Everyone tried on his splendid clothing, then took it all off again and fidgeted through the night. The announcement was to take place at midday. They must dress and be out of the house before the streets were busy. The desert robes would be used to good advantage again, covering Sep's grandeur and Hanse's distinctive figure. The formal uniforms were quiet enough to pass by day, though they were a bit fancy for most tastes.

"Kole says to enter the palace grounds with the throng, as soon as the gates open," said Prillie through the keyhole, as they got ready to depart. "And good luck to you all. This has been great fun!"

"Take care, Prillie," Sep replied for all of them, then they scurried down the dark stairway and into the streets of Avalon.

People were already moving about. Not only the early deliverymen in the thoroughfares, but crowds heading for the palace in order to get good places to wait out the morning. There would not be room for everyone who wanted to hear their ruler's announcement, and so people would be queuing up near the Palace walls to get into the grounds.

The five were lost in a throng so varied and colorful that Sep removed her robe. Even her cloth-of-gold wasn't noticeable, so gay were the garments of those about her. Only Hanse continued to conceal his face and figure.

They approached the palace grounds, working their way through the crowd until they reached the wall itself. Once there, Hanse motioned them to follow him along the ferrocrete expanse.

247

They rounded a corner. At a small door set deeply into the wall, Hanse paused for the retinal scan, then the door sighed open.

They shot through and closed the panel behind them, hidden now in a remote corner of the garden. Across its colorful expanse was the terrace from which Ardan had bitterly surveyed the scene so many months ago. The barracks were off to their left, behind a maze of walls and hedges.

They hurried through the plantings, around corners and through unexpected arbor-gates in the hedges. Once they saw a servant in the distance. He looked at them, startled, but they were gone before he could say a word.

The barracks buildings were abuzz. Sep hid in a hedge to strip off her finery. Beneath it was her old uniform, and she stepped out as herself, not as a painted Court lady. The others lined up behind her as she strode up the wide steps of the second building, where were her permanent quarters.

Sep's retinal scan at the door got them inside without question. She turned toward the office of the officer of the day and snapped to attention as Fram turned crossly from a pile of paperwork to glare at the newcomers.

His mouth opened. He sprang to his feet and rounded the desk, pounding Ardan's shoulder, greeting Ref and Jarlik, catching Sep into a bear hug. "You made it! By golly, you made it! And who's this?"

He was looking sharply at Hanse's hooded shape.

"The order should say Candent Septarian and group..." Sep's tone was a bit severe.

Fram looked at the posted notices. Then he nodded. "Exactly."

"This is part of the group. Now go back to work. And if Denek comes in, send him along to my quarters. We have a lot to talk about."

"And not much time to do it in. The big announcement happens in another two hours," Fram said. "We have to be on duty at the gates and in the grounds at eleven hundred hours.

"I'll see you then. Change the order, Fram, and put Ardan, Jarlik, Ref, and"—she glanced at Hanse—"Hannes behind the dais where the Prince is to speak. Can do?"

He looked curious, but nodded obediently. "Can do. What about you?"

"Check my *Warhammer* out of storage for me, will you?"

Fram glanced uncertainly at Ardan. "You agree, sir?" he asked.

Ardan was chuckling. When he had left Sep to learn to take command, he had wondered how she would deal with those under her. Now he knew. She had the knack and used it well.

"I don't know what she's planning, but I trust her judgment. Check her out, Fram. And tell Denek that he's relieved of command, if he wants to be. Or if he'd like to remain in place until after today, that will be fine, too."

Fram grunted, turning back to his paperwork. The sight of the feckless fellow chained to a desk amused Ardan mightily.

They followed Sep to her quarters, as Ardan felt it would be unlikely that his own were still available. Those in charge of this new government knew that he was supposed to be imprisoned and awaiting execution, or worse.

It was a relief to take turns in the Cleaner. Sep donned a fresh uniform and looked, once again, like the decisive officer she was. There now remained only a short time to wait before going to their assigned posts.

Jarlik had brought one of his uniforms for "Hannes". For a wonder, it fitted the Prince fairly well, and he now looked to be a veteran officer, as, indeed, he was.

At the appointed time, they moved out in orderly fashion, joining the ranks of MechWarriors assigned to duty for this important occasion. Only four were mounted on their 'Mechs. This was a formal occasion, not a battle, and the big machines took up space better assigned to officials and nobles from the city.

As Ardan took his place behind the dais, he stepped behind Jarlik. Standing near the podium, the false Hanse Davion never glanced at him. Nor did he bat an eye at the big fellow in the slightly tight uniform beyond him.

Ardan felt a rush of suppressed excitement. There would, indeed, be an unexpected announcement today in the gardens of the Palace on New Avalon.

34

The chronometer ticked forward, its dial nearing the midday hour. Seated beside the podium, the Prince nodded to the Maître of the Household on New Avalon. That worthy signalled, and the gates opened. A brilliantly clad throng surged into the space beside the gardens.

Ekkles, the aide, rose. His electronically enhanced voice quieted the buzz of conversation below, but Ardan was watching Hanse, who had moved forward to stand just in view of the imposter. As Ekkles was introducing Hanse Davion, the false Prince looked up. He turned pale.

Even as Ekkles gestured toward him, offering at the same time a sheaf of notes, the imposter pitched forward in a dead faint. A concerted gasp rose from the throats of the multitude. Ekkles bent over his fallen ruler, turning pale in his turn.

The court doctor stood. "Clear the courtyard! There will be no announcement at this time!" he shouted. The guard moved forward to obey him, and Ardan found the opportunity to beckon to Efflinger and two of his attendants.

He guided them around the outside of the palace and through a private door he had often used to visit Hanse. Then he heard voices from the Prince's chambers, which lay some distance down the corridor. Tense voices, straining to be quiet.

"You are a fake!" came Hanse's familiar tones. "I am Hanse Davion, and this is an imposter placed here by a conspiracy originating among our enemies."

"Arrest this man!" came another voice, in a near shout. "He is concerned in the plot I was about to expose...a plot against the Federated Suns. He is a danger to us all! Arrest him!"

Ardan drew his sidearm and went through the door in a rush. Ref and Jarlik had drawn their own weapons and were facing the four guards. It took only a moment to disarm them.

In the chamber were Ekkles, the doctor, the members of the Guard, and, to Ardan's surprise, three of the most eminent members of the New Avalon Institute of Science. When he moved, he saw that Efflinger, too, had joined the group, his usual languid manner touched with interest.

Ekkles was breathing hard, his gaze darting from the stymied Guards to the doctor, who was bending over the false Hanse, and then on to the ruddy-haired man in Guard uniform, who was regarding him with suspicion tinged with disgust.

There came a thunderous rap against the side of the building, and Ardan could see, through the glass doors, the legs of a *Warhammer* standing outside, trampling the shrubbery into shreds. Seeing that the thing could smash through the glass with the slightest tap of its massive toe, Ekkles moved to open the doors.

"There is, indeed, a conspiracy here," said Sep through her 'Mech's speakers. "I call for minute examination of both claimants."

The Maître, who had bustled into the room, gazed up at the huge machine standing before the doors, and he almost fainted. Before he could speak, another voice was heard.

"I quite agree." It was a cool voice, rather lazy, but precise. "I suggest that we compel both claimants to undergo all the standard physical tests, in order to determine which is the rightful Prince." Efflinger stepped from behind Ardan and stood beside the two identical Davions.

"You cannot interfere in the internal affairs of New Avalon," protested Ekkles. "You represent Steiner, our enemy…"

"Since when? And by whose representations?" the ambassador asked. "For years, House Steiner and House Davion have recognized many common interests and have worked toward mutual aid and prosperity. Then, without warning and certainly without any action on the part of Katrina Steiner, the Prince of Davion has declared us to be enemies. Has anyone noted any instance that might prove it to be true?" He looked at Ekkles, at the doctor, and at the Maître.

He pointed toward Ardan. "There stands Ardan Sortek, who has been the closest friend of the Prince since his childhood. He has suffered from suspicion and innuendo, after reporting seeing a double of his old friend in the Liao headquarters on Stein's Folly. Ask him which is the real Hanse Davion."

Ardan stepped to stand beside Hanse. Being so near the false one, he found him dizzyingly like the true one, yet there were differences. Perhaps only he could have detected them...the small scar above the left eyelid made by a stone gone astray in a game of slingshots, many years before ...the tiny white line where a furious bird had attacked the boys searching for birds' nests near her chicks.

He laid a hand on Hanse's shoulder. "This is the man I accompanied into the dungeons of the Summer Palace on Argyle not many weeks ago. Only the aid of friends in the Guard broke us free and allowed us to return home to expose this impersonation."

Ekkles was confused, angry. He spluttered, "Do you suppose that I, the Prince's own aide-de-camp, can possibly be misled? This man is our ruler. These two, for whatever treasonous purpose, are conspiring to unseat him in order to weaken the Federated Suns in a time of peril!"

Efflinger, his attendants now standing very close to him, stared arrogantly at the aide. "Make the tests. What can that damage? Who will be hurt by such an eminently sensible course of action? If the man who now rules is an imposter, it will mean that our Houses will NOT be at war. If he *is* the true ruler, then war will be the inevitable outcome of his policies.

"Not simply the rulership of a world is at stake here. There is war hanging in the balance. Do you truly want your House to be at odds with every major power in the Inner Sphere?"

253

The three doctors from NAIS moved forward together. "Test them," said Doctor Shali, the most eminent doctor of biological medicine in that group. "It will be easily done, and without arousing suspicion among the people. Bring them both to the private laboratories in the lower level of this palace. Send for technicians. They are vowed to secrecy in many matters, and this will be only one more. We will, ourselves, oversee this testing."

Ardan glanced at the faces of the Guard members who had not known what was happening. They looked puzzled. But one or two were staring at him, then at Ekkles, and their expressions were no longer those of men entirely convinced of the right way to go.

Ekkles could not refuse. To do so would be stupid, and he had never been that. He gave in with as much grace as he could summon.

"As this matter should not be bruited about—no matter what its outcome—we should, I believe, keep the entire question among those now involved, and those Techs who will conduct the testing. Will you Doctors of the Institute serve as observers? Will the Ambassador also consent to do that? And will the Guard who are now present swear never to reveal in any way what is happening here, on pain of death?"

Shali led the way to the labs, then took a place where she could oversee each step in the testing. When everyone was settled, and the people directly involved were in position, she signalled the work to begin.

Retinal scan was a common method of identification. It was the quick way to gain access to depositories of valuables, as well as to military installations. Thumbprints were too easy to recreate by way of plastic surgery. These were only the first of many tests, however, including blood samples and DNA testing.

As samples of tissue were taken, the scans and measurements done, Ardan was becoming increasingly nervous. Some instinct was telling him to beware—things were not exactly as they seemed. He found himself tense, his muscles aching with stress, as he held himself motionless on the bench next to Jarlik and Ref.

They were going to get away with the plot, that was the thing that kept hammering at his mind. Somehow, in some obscure way, they had managed to rig the testing. He felt it in his gut. The expressions of the Techs were deliberately blank, but he caught minute shifts of eyes, gestures immediately interrupted, that told him it was true.

Sep, down from the 'Mech in the garden, put her hand on his shoulder. He sighed. She felt it, too. It was the same instinct that told a MechWarrior when he was about to find himself in an untenable position.

What would they—could they—do if the most accurate tests known to mankind proved that the real Hanse was not himself?

When the announcement came, even Hanse, standing in his white smock below them, didn't seem surprised.

"This man is not Hanse Davion. The records on file find him incompatible in many areas with the tissue samples in storage. He is an imposter."

Doctor Shali stirred in her big chair. "You have done everything possible," she said, her tone strangely tentative. She turned in the chair to gaze at the assembled witnesses. "Yet I find myself dissatisfied. Something has been left undone...something crucial."

The aide-de-camp stood impatiently. "The testing is finished. It has been proven that this man and his accomplices are not what they claim to be. I demand that they be released to me for immediate execution under the Law of Emergency Procedures."

Shali frowned. She stood, and though she was diminutive, she exuded authority.

"That I will not do until I am completely satisfied. There have been...anomalies...of late. The Prince has withdrawn support of many items on the NAIS agenda that he had formerly been most anxious to pursue. And his policies have changed radically with regard to our allies. Men who have served long and well have been dismissed...or even arrested."

Her voice rose. "I will not relinquish control of this matter until I am fully satisfied. Has anyone any suggestion as to another test? Another procedure outside the limitations of science?"

The faces of those in the chamber seemed blank. Those most concerned were screening their reactions. The others seemed genuinely nonplussed.

Ardan was thinking furiously. There had to be something that the conspirators could not have known. Something so private that not even he would have the key to it. Something that only Hanse would know, of all people in the system...

Ardan rose to his feet as if pulled by strings."Madame Doctor," he said.

Shali inclined her head. "You may speak, Ardan Sortek."

"There is one thing that only the true Prince will be able to do. Not another warrior in all the systems could accomplish it. I suggest that each of these men be taken to the storage and repair area beneath Barracks A and asked to activate Prince Davion's *BattleMaster*."

There was a communal gasp from those in the room. It was true—none but its warrior knew the exact sequence of actions and words that would release a 'Mech from stasis.

Ardan looked toward the two Hanses. Neither seemed surprised or shaken at the suggestion. Now, having looked away, he found himself unsure as to which was which. But the Techs had put dye markers on their hands. It would be determined, when necessary.

Shali was smiling. Not her official, inscrutable smile, but a beam that touched her eyes as well as her lips.

"Well done, Ardan Sortek. A most useful suggestion. Lek, you will help these men to robe themselves properly. We will go ahead to await them in the 'Mech quarters."

There was a rustle of motion as the seated witnesses rose to follow Doctor Shali from the chamber. Ardan glanced back at the men, who were being led away into the robing room.

Even as he looked, one of the big, red-haired shapes turned his head slightly. A trace of a grin wrinkled the visible cheek. Ardan relaxed.

He knew, once more, which was his old friend. He found his step much more lively as he joined Sep and the others in the corridor. In only a short while more, the truth would become apparent to everyone.

35

The underground workshops and storage areas provided for the 'Mechs and their technicians were tremendous. To move the huge mechanisms in and out, as well as to hoist them for repair, required cavernous space. The bright metal of the walls reflected the brilliance of the work lights. The maintenance of a 'Mech was somewhere between mechanics and surgery, and the Techs were men of great skill.

The clang of metal on metal echoed through the vaulted chambers. Some of the witnesses winced at the noise until a runner sent by Ardan ordered the work to cease until this crucial testing was done.

The wait was a short one, however. The laboratory Techs arrived soon after, with the identical Hanse Davions in tow.

The compartment that held the Prince's *BattleMaster* was marked with both the Davion crest and the symbol of the Federated Suns. The monster machine stood there silently, its domelike upper body framed between tremendous arms. Lasers and machine guns bristled from its every port.

The Tech assigned to its care opened the sliding portal and moved the thing out on its tracked carrier. "It is always ready for use, though the Prince seldom has the time to drill in it any longer," the man said.

Looming into the space high above their heads, the machine was awesome. Even in another 'Mech—a *Warhammer* or a *Zeus*—it was a forbidding sight. Unprotected, unarmored human flesh instinctively cringed away when faced with such a potentially destructive behemoth.

"I shall go first," said one of the doubles.

Ardan could not tell which one it was. He found himself concentrating fiercely on the hope that his suggestion would lead to justice being done. If not...the destruction of the entire Federated Suns might well be a result.

The man climbed rather awkwardly into the cockpit of the *BattleMaster*. Within moments, the machine's great arms shifted position, and its legs relaxed from their rigid stance.

Ardan looked at the Hanse still standing on the floor. He looked astounded and ill. That had to be the real Hanse, then. In some way, the conspirators had decoded the unlocking sequence for the *'Master*.

Ardan felt sick, too. Beside him, Sep took his arm. Jarlik, on the other side, had read the situation at a glance. He was staring up at the triumphant face, crowned with red hair, that had emerged from the hatch.

"Arm it!" he shouted to the descending man. "A 'Mech is not operational until the weapons are armed and ready. Arm it, or come down and let its true master do so."

The man, dwarfed against the huge mechanism, halted. He looked questioningly at Shali.

She turned her delicate face up to speak to him. "Do as he says," she insisted. "An unarmed 'Mech is not operational. Arm the weapons and let us see them work."

The man hesitated, then crawled back inside and closed the hatch.

There came a long pause. The 'Mech's limbs shifted, as though restless. The turret swiveled slightly, though not to its full range of motion. The weapons, however, frozen into their inoperative position, did not budge. At last, the hatch opened again. The red-haired figure climbed down.

"I defy you to accomplish what I have failed to do," he said, rejoining his double on the floor at the feet of the monster. "The weaponry has frozen and cannot be activated. The 'Mech has sat idle for too long. That is the problem."

There was a murmur about them. Of course, such things happened. After all, a machine was a machine, subject to occasional breakdown.

But the other Hanse was now climbing up to the 'Mech, quickly, triumphantly. He slid into the cockpit with practiced ease, closing it behind him. After only a short pause, the 'Mech's arms lifted into a salute. The turret swiveled

259

smoothly through its full round of motions. And the weapons, those dark round mouths that could spit death in beams or bursts, moved and locked into position. The 'Mech turned on its heel and aimed them at the ferrocrete wall provided for testing weapons.

Red lances probed, leaving more dark scars on the pale stone. Machine guns chattered, their slugs bouncing harmlessly into the baffles set there to contain the ricochets. The *BattleMaster* went through its paces flawlessly.

Jarlik was grinning widely. Sep was clapping Ref on the back, and Ardan felt like dancing.

The 'Mech wheeled smartly and took up its position on the tracked carrier again. The hatch opened. Hanse Davion descended, amid greetings and subdued cheers from the witnesses. Doctor Shali was waiting when he jumped lightly to the floor.

"Although my discipline disapproves of hunches, Your Highness, I had a hunch that you were the real Prince of the Federated Suns. A human being is far more than the sum of his biological and chemical processes. There is another dimension. In another era, it might have been called spirit. Now we have no term for it, but it exists, nevertheless. Welcome home, Your Highness." She took his hand and turned to face the imposter.

"You will be questioned," she said. "I am sure that His Highness will concur in that. We have...facilities...in the NAIS for learning what we need from even the most reluctant informant."

Ardan, moving through the crowd, was joined by Jarlik, Ref, and Sep. He came up to the spot where Efflinger was standing, calm and cool. In his remote way, the Steiner ambassador was enjoying the results of his maneuvering.

"Well done, sir," said Ardan. "And please convey our thanks to your son."

Maylor smiled, his expression aloof. "Ah, yes. Kolek. He thinks that I'm unaware of his fondness for a certain young woman named Prillie. Never tell him differently, but I am hoping that he marries her soon. I shall make a tre-

260

mendous fuss and cut him off without a credit. That will force him to pull himself together and find work. And it will be the making of him, do you not agree?"

Ardan laughed. "I do, indeed. But he is not a bad boy, for all his youthful folly. He is shrewd. I suspect that he will go to work for the Prince...Will that make problems for you?"

"Not at all! Not at all! It will be one more link between the houses of Steiner and Davion. A most desirable state of affairs, wouldn't you say?"

They laughed quietly together. The Doctor and Hanse were leaving now, accompanied by the other witnesses. Soon the crowd would regather in the garden of the palace to hear the long-delayed statement...a far different one from that intended by the conspirators.

He sighed. "The people are going to be very happy, and never will they suspect how close we had come to a war with Steiner. The Lyran Commonwealth is not one to trifle with. We already have enough enemies to keep us busy."

Ran Felsner was standing at the head of the stair that led up into the warriors' quarters.

"Ardan! What in the name of the Seven Hells is going on here?" he asked.

Ardan came to attention. "Sir!" he snapped. Then he grinned. "Come with us to the garden. We're on duty there. We'll explain on the way."

As they hurried through the gardens, he talked furiously, knowing that Hanse himself would tell his commanding officer the truth later. By the time they reached the dais, Felsner knew just enough to be thoroughly confused. He took his place, just in time, at the end of a line of Guards.

Hanse, his dress uniform replaced with one exactly like that worn by the imposter, wore his own medals and ribbons. Beside him was a much-chastened and subdued Ekkles, and beyond were Doctor Shali and the Maître, who still looked puzzled.

The crowd had gathered again, on hearing the signal gong. In a short while, the space was filled with people.

261

They looked worried, as well they might after seeing their ruler taken ill so suddenly.

Ekkles stepped forward. "I am happy to say that the temporary indisposition...that overtook our Prince has passed without any danger to his life or health," he began. "Well do we know what terrible consequences might follow the loss of our leader, in these perilous times."

He looked down at the pile of notes on the podium left behind by that other Hanse. He shuffled them together and thrust them underneath the stand.

"Now it is my honor and privilege to give you our Prince, Hanse Davion." He bowed to Hanse, stepping back.

Hanse's color was high, his eyes alight with vigor and triumph. "I am happy to be able to speak to you today," he began.

The words were drowned in a sea of cheers. The people had thought, while waiting, of the effect his death might have upon the comfortable ways of New Avalon. They had reflected on the dangers lurking among the other rival Houses, not liking the picture they had conjured. The renewed health of their Prince meant that nothing (they hoped) would change.

"There have been rumors," said Hanse, once the cheering had died away, "of trouble with one of our most reliable neighbors. House Steiner has been the victim of vicious lies, spread among us by those who might benefit if we were at odds with our allies. To see us turn upon our friends would delight our enemies."

There was a murmur of agreement in the crowd. They had heard those rumors, had thought, indeed, that they emanated from officials of their own government. They knew very well that trade would suffer, the entire standard of living on their world might decline if such a breach occurred. Many of the assemblage turned to nod at Efflinger, who stood in his usual easy way, observing everything that went on with a cynical eye.

"Now we know, without any doubt, who our enemies *are not*!" said Hanse. "So let us return to our homes. Let us think of how easily we might lose much and gain nothing. Let us resolve to think deeply before believing such rumors, no matter from what source they seem to come." He raised his hands and smiled at his people.

This time the clamor was like an ocean in a storm. Hanse returned to his palace amid a roar of love and approval that died away only when he disappeared from sight.

Ardan, just behind his old friend, tapped Hanse on the shoulder. "You had a secret code, didn't you?" he whispered. "To activate the *Master*?"

Hanse turned to smile at him. "Yes, Dan, I did."

Ardan had a moment of comprehension. Something that Melissa had told him back in Tharkad came to him with sudden clarity.

"Starbird…" he murmured.

"Ah, my friend," said Hanse Davion with a smile, "that would be telling."

36

It took a week before the capital city and principal towns of New Avalon returned to normal. Hanse freed the imprisoned councillors and reinstated them with more pomp than usual. He hoped in this way to make some apology to them and also to reinforce the conviction, among the populace, that a great injustice had now been corrected.

In the meantime, the Prince's investigators discovered a network of informants throughout the Palace and even in the military. These were systematically weeded out and replaced with others known to be trustworthy. Ran Felsner took complete charge of the New Avalon contingent of the Royal Brigade again. His return from Stein's Folly at the tail end of the conspirator's plot had been convenient. He went right to work.

Hanse personally took charge of reorganizing the Court on New Avalon, and when the dust settled, there were some old faces missing and many new ones come in. Argyle, too, got its shakeup. Hanse had Cleery removed from his post with speed and neatness, then appointed Fani Littek as Maître in his place. Though many were dismayed by her promotion, most agreed she'd be perfect for the job.

Ardan, meanwhile, had been dispatched to Redfield to take part in the reconquest of that world. After a successful invasion, with only minimum Davion losses, he was soon back in Avalon City again. Seeing the many changes Hanse had been making, Ardan approved and was especially glad to see Maylor Efflinger still in place as Steiner ambassador. Without that man's help, Ardan believed that their desperate attempt to regain the throne would have failed.

One evening shortly after his return, Ardan stood looking down from the terrace as the pale sun vanished beyond the distant wall of the Palace garden. It was peaceful here, and Ardan was feeling the kind of pleasurable fatigue that often follows the successful resolution of a crisis.

Footsteps on the stone pavement caught his attention, and he turned. It was Hanse approaching, and for a moment, Ardan recalled that now-distant day when so much bitterness had existed between them. How glad he was to know that was all long past.

"Just the man I wanted to see," the Prince said. "I was hoping to personally hand you this invitation for tomorrow evening."

"Invitation to what?" Ardan asked, unable to keep a note of irritation from his voice. "I'm too bone-weary to attend some fancy affair, Hanse. Can't we have done with all this, and get on with other business? What in the world are you up to now?"

Hanse chuckled. "You will see what you will see, my friend. Now, don't be difficult just when everything is beginning to fall back into place." With that, he clapped the younger man on the shoulder and shoved him toward the door. "And don't be late!"

Back in his own chamber after a session in the Cleaner, Ardan stretched out on the bed in his soft robe. He picked up the invitation and slit it open, reading half-aloud: "...the Palace ballroom...eight o'clock...full dress..." Damn! he thought. Formal again.

He rose the next morning full of gloom. Ardan wanted to get back to his old work, without the confusing and distracting interruptions that seemed to crop up so often lately. This formal affair was not to his liking at all.

The day went quickly, for all that. He was working with Lal and Nym again, putting a new *Victor* into operational condition. The fine tuning of the neural helmet was a slow matter, and he spent hours in the 'Mech, testing the polymer muscles and weapons of the huge machine.

Dusk came before he knew the day was gone. Lal called up to him, "Sir, you have an engagement tonight. Remember...you asked me to remind you?"

Ardan sighed and climbed slowly down from his tremendous alter ego. "So I do. Remind me tomorrow that I have enjoyed it, will you? I'll never know, otherwise."

Lal chuckled, helping him on with his fatigue uniform. But Ardan didn't feel like chuckling as he made his way up the stair into the living quarters.

He found there a new dress uniform waiting for him. Hanse had evidently sent it during the day. It was even more elaborate than the one he had worn into the dungeons on Argyle. What a get-up for a soldier!

He went into the Cleaner and came out scrubbed but still unhappy. The thing fitted perfectly. He cursed Hanse's tailor. If it hadn't been a fit, Ardan could have worn a plainer outfit. Ready promptly at seven-thirty, he was waiting for his friends at the foot of the stair leading onto the walkway outside the barracks.

Hearing footsteps above, he glanced up. Then his jaw dropped. Sep was wearing the elaborate dress Prillie had chosen for her and that Efflinger had insisted she keep. Ardan now realized that he must have been so tense the last time she had worn the dress that he had not really looked at his second-in-command.

That had been a major error. Sep looked stunning. She was, after all, a handsome woman, even sweaty and dusty as she went about her work. Now, her hair done high, her skin glowing with artfully applied makeup and the jewels that were the gift of Steiner blazing at neck, ears, and fingers, she might have been one of the most sought-after women of Davion's court.

"Close your mouth!" she snapped, seeing his face. Her eyes were twinkling, however, and her tone was not angry.

Though Ardan managed to compose his expression, his heart was jumping about in his chest. He had always known that Sep was nice to look at. He hadn't known she was beautiful.

Jarlik thumped him on the shoulder. "Get a move on, Dan. We don't want to be late. I suspect that the Prince is about to explain some things. I'm told that he has been investigating everything he could possibly burrow into during these past weeks. What I want to know is how the conspirators rigged those tests. That boggles my mind."

Ardan stepped out to keep up with his long-legged friend, but he was very aware that Sep, in her gold and white splendor, was just behind him. A delicate scent of flowers kept teasing him, and he didn't know if it came from the gardens or from her.

They arrived just on time. Lackeys were opening the wide doors from the terrace into the ballroom. A small group of people could be seen inside, already holding filled glasses that glinted with shades of golden and ruby wine. The three friends mounted the broad, shallow steps onto the terrace and entered the room.

"Here they are now," Hanse said. "Come in. I want to introduce my rescuers...and those who helped them in their dangerous endeavor." The Prince clapped his hands, and the people in the room quieted.

Ardan, looking about, saw Kolek and Prillie. He recognized a few other officers of the Guard, as well as several of the staff members of the Palace, now in their best as guests instead of servitors.

He felt increasingly uncomfortable. Was this some sort of award ceremony? He didn't like those at all.

But Hanse was speaking again. "I would have preferred to publicly thank all of you who assisted me in regaining my throne, but this is a matter best kept among ourselves." He glanced about the room.

"I ask each of you to speak little, if at all, of any of the matters we have experienced together over the past months. We know the truth. We won the day. Now we must keep the enemy from profiting by so much as a rumor."

There was a murmur of agreement in the room. Ardan, looking from face to face, knew that these were people of the most solid sort, dependable to the ultimate.

"There are many matters that have been troublesome, and some seemed inexplicable as well. I know that you have wondered, as I did, what really happened. We have now ascertained, as well as will ever be done, just how this sequence of events came about." Hanse motioned to waiters with trays of glasses.

"Refresh yourselves again, my friends...it is a rather long story. I will make it as brief as possible, however." He waited while his subjects accepted glasses, found chairs about the tapestried walls, and settled themselves. Then the Prince sat on the footstool before his own great chair and stretched out his long legs companionably.

"All this began, we have learned, some years ago when the Capellan Confederation began looking acquisitively at our frontier worlds on their border. Maximilian Liao, being no man's fool, cast about for a method of weakening the power of the Federated Suns.

"He was unable to do this militarily, for obvious reasons. Therefore, he put his head together with advisors from...other Houses...and they decided to remove me from the rulership of the Federated Suns by replacing me with a false Hanse Davion, who would gradually alter my policies to further their own cause."

He clasped his hands about his knee and looked grim. "It demonstrates the wide differences between our systems when I tell you that they took a man—just an ordinary fellow who happened to be of my build and coloring—and wiped his mind clean of his own life's memories. I may have indulged in political maneuvering at times, but I have never allowed any basic interference in the personal rights of my people, and I hope that I never will."

There came a shocked murmur from the small crowd. He nodded. "They obtained, through methods that I have now blocked permanently, holographs of me in every possible place and activity. And they put that unfortunate man through extensive plastic surgery, copying every feature as far as science is now capable of doing. When they were done, he was, to any observing eye, Hanse Davion. Then through their agents in the Palace they replaced all my medical records, retinal scans, DNA, blood type, etc. with that of the imposter's."

Hanse turned toward Ardan. "Before bringing their duplicate back to consciousness, they allowed Ardan Sortek, my childhood friend, to see him. He had been captured, treated,

268

and held solely for that purpose. He, being the one person I know who could identify me without fail, would be the one accused of treachery, while I would be called an imposter. That would remove both of us at once. A quarrel between us, which was fomented by vicious rumors aimed at Ardan's ears alone, seemed to be a viable motive for his falseness.

"They had, however, a few strategically located people who were genuine traitors. Cleery, my Maître of the Household on Argyle, was one of them. There were even some in my own pet project, the New Avalon Institute of Science, and it was they who substituted the physical specifications of the double for my own, long before the testing that proved that I was not myself, but an imposter."

"Ah!" Jarlik sighed. "I wondered mightily about that. We thought it was impossible to fool the testing procedure."

"Within the year, it would have been. Our security system has been improved and upgraded to the point where my brainwaves would have identified me immediately and without doubt. Which is the reason for their haste to put the conspiracy into effect as soon as the duplicate was completed and trained."

Hanse now relaxed and stood before the group. "Jarlik, Septarian, Sortek, and Reflett came to my rescue in the nick of time. Officer Denek made arrangements that allowed us to travel here as soon as possible and to take our places near the false Davion on that important day of his great announcement.

"Maylor Efflinger, friend and ally, managed to get them into a position to follow through on Denek's arrangements. His son and daughter-in-law were of inestimable value in that affair, and my heartfelt thanks are due them. I might interject here the news that I am attaching Kolek Efflinger to my staff as personal liaison with the Steiner interests."

The newlyweds beamed, as did Maylor Efflinger, unable to hide his pleasure. Ardan felt a smile tugging at the corners of his own mouth to see the casual and effete facade fail the ambassador for once.

"The knowledge that such impersonations have taken place in the past, even into remote times when only chance caused physical similarities, should have warned us that this sort of thing might be attempted again. But we felt that our own culture was too civilized for that. We have learned differently." Hanse looked to Doctor Shali, who sat alone near the front of the room.

"I have been assured that the equipment and the technology for such transformations will be closely monitored from this time on. Not only because of its threat to any ruler, but also because of its utter devastation of the man chosen for modification into another. The person who was the imposter is innocent of any wrongdoing."

Jarlik muttered a protest, but Hanse quelled him with a glance. "This is quite true. He was chosen without his own consent. His mind was emptied of all he knew. He was reeducated with the most accelerated techniques to believe himself to be the true heir of Davion.

"I have granted a pension for his care. It may not be possible to wipe his mind again and return to him his past and his own personality. It may not even be advisable to try. But he has suffered enough. He will be cared for for the rest of his life...in comfort and quiet. In a remote place, where his peculiar attributes will make no problems for anyone."

Ardan was relieved, listening to his friend. This was Hanse Davion as he had always known him to be. A ruler, yes...one who must do whatever necessary to protect the interests of his sphere, but not a man who would be needlessly cruel.

Hanse was saying, "Maximilian Liao has made us much trouble in recent days, but our forces have proven their loyalty and their worth in battle once again. Stein's Folly and now Redfield are both ours again!" A smattering of spontaneous applause went around the room at those words, and the Prince smiled over at Ardan.

"Yes, Liao has been most troublesome of late," said Hanse Davion, "but if I were him, I'd watch my back."

270

37

Ardan Sortek was putting his unit through its nefarious paces, watching from the sidelines where he sat in his new *Victor*. The term 'new' was, he admitted, a misnomer. The 'Mech had been refashioned from parts of several wrecked ones, and some of its lasers were from totally dissimilar 'Mechs.

He yelled into his com, "Sep, get that monster moving! I don't know why you like that ground-hugging monstrosity when you might have had a jumper!"

"Stick to your knitting, Mother," came her drawl in return. "I manage to get there. Just you watch."

The *Warhammer* stalked between the jaws of the Gauntlet, dwarfed by its towering walls. Bursts of crimson light seared the armor, chatters of fire rattled from the turret and the limbs of the 'Mech she rode.

Her weapons cocked their wicked muzzles and bursts of fire raked the walls. The target areas went dark in quick succession, as she put the first segment of the Gauntlet out of commission. So that was how she did it...marksmanship. Unhurried, cool marksmanship.

Ardan resolved to begin intensive practice at once. Mobility was well and good, but that sort of quick and accurate fire would give a unit with jumping capacity even more of an edge.

He heard a heavy approach behind him. Another 'Mech. He swiveled to see who it might be...His own unit was out on the field at work.

"Good work," said the familiar voice of Hanse Davion approvingly.

"This is a surprise," said Ardan. "I thought you hadn't time for drill nowadays."

"I haven't. But this old baby was the saving of us all. I decided I'd better sharpen up my skills again. Never know when you're going to need them in this mad universe."

Ardan knew Hanse was right. If someone had forewarned him of all that had occurred within the past year, he wouldn't have believed it. And, to add to the confusion, Felsa had made him an uncle. Perhaps that Sortek would also become a MechWarrior one day.

"Hey!" he yelled as Hanse stalked past him toward the hell that was the Gauntlet. "Do you want to be a godfather? My sister asked if you would consider it. I've got a nephew!"

The *BattleMaster* turned in its tracks. Its arm, heavy with weaponry, came up in a salute. A laser, held high, shot red light into the sky in a celebratory burst.

"Of course," said Hanse Davion, Prince of the Federated Suns. "I can never have too many Sorteks in my entourage. Now come along. The Gauntlet needs a workout, don't you agree?"

Grinning, Ardan followed his friend and ruler into the mouth of hell.

GLOSSARY

Autocannon:

This is a rapid-firing, auto-loading weapon. Light vehicle autocannon range from 30 to 90 mm caliber, and heavy 'Mech autocannon may be 80 to 120 mm or more. The weapon fires high-speed streams of high-explosive, armor-piercing shells. Because of the limitations of 'Mech targeting technology, the autocannon's effective anti-'Mech range is limited to less than 600 meters.

BattleMechs:

BattleMechs are the most powerful war machines ever built. First developed by Terran scientists and engineers more than 500 years ago, these huge, man-shaped vehicles are faster, more mobile, better-armored, and more heavily armed than any 20th-century tank. Ten to twelve meters tall and equipped with particle projection cannons, lasers, rapid-fire autocannon, and missiles, they pack enough firepower to flatten anything but another BattleMech. A small fusion reactor provides virtually unlimited power, and BattleMechs can be adapted to fight in environments ranging from sun-baked deserts to subzero arctic icefields.

BattleMaster:

A formidable assault 'Mech, the *BattleMaster* weighs 85 tons and has a maximum speed of 64.8 kph. The firepower that the *BattleMaster* can generate in one volley is staggering and more than deadly at close range. Its main fire weapon is its right-arm PPC, and its three right-torso and three left-torso medium lasers provide close support fire. Of the six lasers, two are mounted on the 'Mech's right and left rear, making it one of the few models equipped with rear firing weapons. An SRM 6 and two machine guns complete the *BattleMaster*'s weaponry.

Command Circuit:

The Successor Lords maintain a series of charged JumpShips along important space routes so that the week-long wait for recharge is not necessary. Because it is expensive and JumpShips are so precious, the Command Circuit is reserved only for emergency or top-priority situations such as travel by the ruler himself or for sending a messenger across vast reaches of the Inner Sphere in less than a day.

Company:

A tactical military unit consisting of three BattleMech Lances, or for infantry, three platoons with a total of 50 to 100 men. Infantry companies are generally commanded by a Captain.

ComStar:

ComStar, the interstellar communications network, was the brain-child of Jerome Blake, formerly Minister of Communications during the latter years of the Star League. After the League's fall, Blake seized Terra and reorganized what was left of the League's communica-tions network into a private organization that sold its services to the five Houses for a profit. Since that time, ComStar has also developed into a powerful, secret society steeped in mysticism and ritual. Initiates to the ComStar Order commit themselves to lifelong service.

Corsair:

The *Corsair* is a 50-ton, medium-thrust AeroSpace Fighter armed with two medium lasers, four small lasers, and two large lasers. It is especially effective at close range, and its compact laser systems make it one of the better planetary atmospheric fighters.

Crusader:

A heavy BattleMech, weighing 65 tons, with a top speed of 64.8 kph. It is heavily armed even for a 'Mech, mounting a laser, heavy machine gun, and massed LRM batteries in each arm, and SRMs on each leg. The *Crusader* is capable of delivering a full spread of 42 missiles at optimum 160-180 meter range, with the potential of crippling or destroying even the mighty *BattleMaster*.

Dragon:

The *Dragon* is a well-armed 'Mech whose top speed of 86.4 kph makes it one of the fastest of the heavies. Armed with 24 rounds for its LRM and a whopping 40 rounds for its autocannon, the *Dragon* can carry on sustained battles without reloading. Even if ammo does run low, the 'Mech's left-arm and left-torso medium lasers ensure that it has other weapons to fire.

DropShips:

Because JumpShips must generally avoid entering the heart of a solar system and they lie at a considerable distance from the system's inhabited worlds, DropShips were developed for interplanetary travel. As the name implies, a DropShip is attached to hardpoints on the JumpShip's drive core, later to be dropped from the parent vessel after in-system entry. Though incapable of FTL travel, DropShips are highly maneuverable, well-armed, and sufficiently aerodynamic to take off from and land on a planetary surface. The journey from the jump point to the inner inhabited worlds of a system usually requires a normal-space journey of several days or even weeks, depending on the type of star.

The *Overlord* is the largest military DropShip in common use. It can carry a full-strength battalion of 36 'Mechs, 6 AeroSpace Fighters,

84 men (including Pilots, Techs, astechs, and medical personnel). The *Overlord* can also carry whatever infantry or vehicles the battalion owns, and sometimes even some family members.

HyperPulse Generator:

The ComStar communications net is composed of a large number of powerful HyperPulse Generators (HPGs) capable of transmitting and receiving an instantaneous signal across a distance of nearly 50 light years. About 50 of these "A" stations are scattered across the Inner Sphere. "B" stations are capable of communications over a 20- to 30-light-year span, and are located at most inhabited worlds of the Successor States. "A" stations transmit their accumulated messages every 12 to 24 hours; "B" stations much less frequently (two or three times per week).

JagerMech:

This 65-ton 'Mech mounts two light and two medium autocannon and two medium lasers. Its top speed is 64.8 kph.

JumpShips:

Interstellar travel is accomplished via JumpShips, first developed in the 22nd century. These somewhat ungainly vessels are made up of a long thin drive core and a sail resembling an enormous parasol, which can be up to a kilometer wide. The ship is named for its ability to 'jump' instantaneously from one point to another. After making its jump, the ship cannot travel until it has recharged by gathering up more solar energy again.

The JumpShip's enormous sail is constructed from a special metal that absorbs vast quantities of electromagnetic energy from the star it is near. When it has soaked up enough, the sail transfers the energy to the drive core, which converts it into a space-twisting field. An instant later, the ship arrives at the next jump point, across distances of up to 30 light years. This field is known as hyperspace, and its discovery opened to mankind the gateway to the stars.

JumpShips never land on planets, and only rarely travel into the inner parts of a star system. Interplanetary travel is carried out by DropShips, vessels that attach themselves to the JumpShip until arrival at the jump point. Most of the JumpShips currently in service are already centuries old, because the Successor Lords have been able to construct very few new ones. For this reason, there is an unspoken agreement among even these bitter enemies to leave one another's JumpShips alone.

The *Invader* Class JumpShips can carry three Drop-Ships. *StarLord* Class JumpShips can carry six DropShips.

Jump Points:

Jumps are made from either of a star system's two main jump points. These are located at the system's zenith and nadir, perpendicular to the plane of the system and passing through the gravitational center. These points do not change and are always at the same distance from any world in the plane of the system. Though other jump points do exist in every system, they are rarely used.

At the jump points for major worlds and along key trade routes are space stations where a DropShip can dock or orbit while making arrangements for the next jump if the owners do not possess their own JumpShip, or where they can stop over while their JumpShip recharges.

Lance:

A BattleMech tactical combat group, usually consisting of four 'Mechs.

Laser:

An acronym for "Light Amplification through Stimulated Emission of Radiation". As a weapon, it damages the target by concentrating extreme heat on a small area. BattleMech lasers are designated as small, medium, and large. Lasers are also available as shoulder-fired weapons operating from a portable backpack power unit. Certain range-finders and targeting equipment employ low-level lasers also.

LRM:

This is an abbreviation for "Long-Range Missile", an indirect-fire missile with a high-explosive warhead. LRMs have a maximum extreme range of several kilometers, but are accurate only between about 150 and 700 meters.

New Avalon Institute of Science (NAIS):

In 3015, Hanse Davion decreed the construction of a new university on New Avalon, capitol of the Federated Suns. Known as the New Avalon Institute of Science (NAIS), its purpose is to recover the lost technologies and knowledge of the past. The Institute functions more like a Terran military academy than a public university. Once accepted for admission, students become 'wards' of the ducal government and must commit to ten years' service to the Federated Suns after graduation. Though the course of study is arduous, there is a heavy backlog of candidates. Both House Kurita and House Marik have followed with their own universities, but neither is as well bankrolled or staffed as the NAIS.

The Periphery:
Beyond the borders of the Inner Sphere lies the Periphery, the vast domain of known and unknown worlds stretching endlessly into interstellar night. Once populated by colonies from Terra, these were devastated technologically, politically, and economically by the fall of Star League. At present, the Periphery is the refuge of piratical Bandit Kings, privateers, and outcasts.

PPC:
This is the abbreviation for "Particle Projection Cannon", a magnetic accelerator firing high-energy proton or ion bolts, causing damage both through impact and high temperature. PPCs are among the most effective weapons available to BattleMechs. Though they have a theoretical range limited only by line-of-sight considerations, the technology available for focusing and aiming the bolt limits effective range to less than 600 meters.

Regiment:
A military unit consisting of two to four battalions, each consisting of three or four companies. A regiment is commanded by a Colonel.

Security Checks:
The most common I.D. scanners are retinal scanners and thumbprint scanners.

Sparrowhawk:
The *Sparrowhawk* is a 30-ton AeroSpace Fighter whose ample armor often matches that of medium fighters. It is armed with two wing-mounted small lasers and two nose-mounted medium lasers. The small lasers are the least accurate, and wing damage can cause them to lose fire control. The *Sparrowhawk's* high rate of thrust makes it a perfect first-response craft. This speed factor often permits the craft to be the first fighter to engage an enemy attack.

SRM:
This is the abbreviation for "Short-Range Missiles", direct trajectory missiles with high-explosive or armor-piercing explosive warheads. They have a range of less than one kilometer, and are accurate only at ranges of less than 300 meters. They are more powerful, however, than LRMs.

Star League:
In 2571, the Star League was formed in an attempt to peacefully ally the major star systems inhabited by the human race after it had taken to the stars. The League continued and prospered for almost 200

years, until civil war broke out in 2751. The League was eventually destroyed when the ruling body known as the High Council disbanded in the midst of a struggle for power. Each of the royal House rulers then declared himself First Lord of the Star League, and within months, war had engulfed the Inner Sphere. This conflict continues to the present day, more than two centuries later. These centuries of continuous war are now known simply as the Succession Wars.

Stuka:

The *Stuka* is a well-armored, low-thrust 100-ton AeroSpace Fighter. It mounts two large lasers on each wing, and one nose-mounted and two rear-mounted medium lasers. It is also equipped with one nose-mounted LRM 20 and one SRM 4. With its 30 heat sinks, the *Stuka* is capable of maximum use of its firepower for prolonged periods in battle. Its Monitor 200 guidance system also makes it a graceful vessel that can perform like a medium-weight craft in many situations.

Successor Lords:

Each of the five Successor States is ruled by a family descended from one of the original Council Lords of the old Star League. All five royal House Lords claim the title of First Lord, and they have been at each other's throats since the beginning of the Succession Wars in 2786. Their battleground is the vast Inner Sphere, which is composed of all the star systems once occupied by Star League's member-states.

Thrush:

The 25-ton *Thrush* is one of the fastest and most agile AeroSpace Fighters of the present day. Its Mujika Type 12 frame can withstand the gravitational forces and stress of most of the combat maneuvers it must perform. Its Rawlings 250 fusion engine also provides all the energy it needs for movement and to fire its single nose-mounted medium laser and its two wing-mounted lasers. These must be fired sparingly, however, to avoid unnecessary heat buildup.

Thunderbolt:

The *Thunderbolt* is a 65-ton heavy 'Mech, and is one of the best-armed 'Mechs in existence. Its arm-mounted large laser packs a powerful punch. Combined with its three left-torso-mounted medium lasers and the SRM 2 mounted on its right torso, the 'Mech has ample firepower at long and medium ranges. For close combat, it mounts a torso-mounted SRM 2 and two left-arm machine guns.

Valkyrie:

A 'Mech design seen only among the forces of House Davion, the *Valkyrie* is a highly regarded light 'Mech. Its six tons of armor, top speed of 86.4 kph, and 150-meter jump capacity allow it to outmaneuver heavier units in battle and to absorb a fair amount of damage. Its left-torso LRM is unusual in a light 'Mech, making it a potentially tough opponent at long range. At close range, its right-arm medium laser and super jump capacity can be a potent mix. Though no match for a medium or heavy 'Mech in one-to-one combat, the *Valkyrie* is effective when part of a lance.

Victor:

This 80-ton assault 'Mech moves at a maximum speed of about 64.8 kph, and is the only one of its class with jump capability (120 meters maximum). The *Victor* mounts an autocannon in its right arm, two medium lasers in the left arm, and an SRM 4 in its center torso. In battle, the *Victor* is often able to throw its opponents off guard, as they do not expect to find a heavy 'Mech with jump capability.

Vindicator:

The *Vindicator* is a 45-ton medium 'Mech that is not particularly fast (top speed 64.8 kph) for its size. One of the most common 'Mechs among the House Liao forces, the 'Mech mounts an LRM in the left torso, a PPC in its right arm, a small laser in its left arm, and a medium laser that bulges from the left side of the 'Mech's head.

Warhammer:

Because of its size and weaponry, the 70-ton heavy 'Mech *Warhammer* is one of the most dangerous and powerful on the battlefield. It mounts PPCs on both right and left arms, an SRM on the right torso, and a medium and small laser and a machine gun on each side of its torso. These give it the sheer firepower needed by a first-line fighter. The special searchlight mounted on the 'Mech's left torso ties in with its tracking system. Able to function either as a light or as part of the targeting system, this feature makes the *Warhammer* a formidable night-fighter. The Mech's top speed is 64.8 kph.

Zeus:

The 80-ton *Zeus* is the pride of House Steiner, whose designers created it as a heavy 'Mech capable of performing hit-and-run tactics. It mounts an LRM in the right arm, a large laser and medium laser in the left torso, a medium laser in the center torso, and an autocannon in the left arm. The 'Mech's top speed is 64.8 kph. Its excellent armor, especially around the chest and legs, allow it to withstand all but the heaviest fire. Its strong, heavily armored legs make the *Zeus* a feared kicker, and a bludgeon feature on its left arm gives it a mighty punch.

Thunderbolt

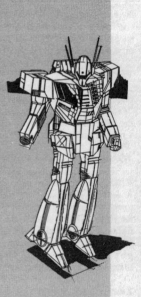

Valkyrie

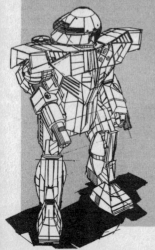

Victor

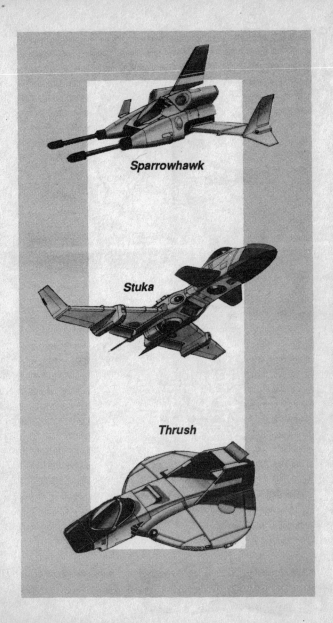

Sparrowhawk

Stuka

Thrush

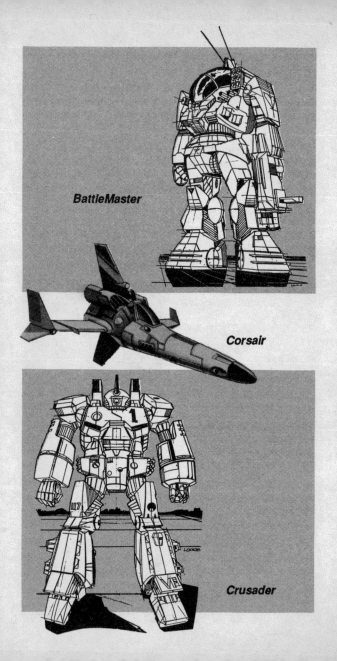

BattleMaster

Corsair

Crusader

Dragon

DropShips

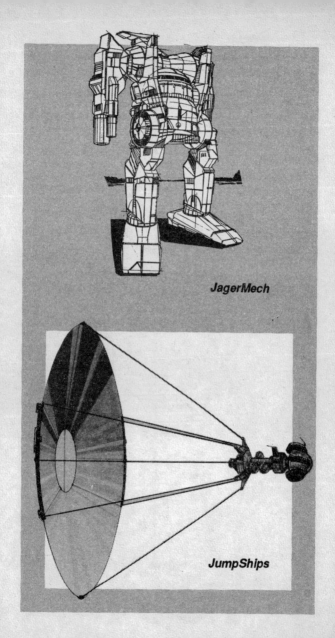

JagerMech

JumpShips

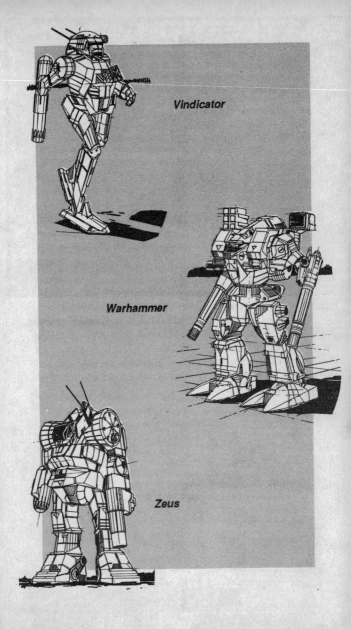

Vindicator

Warhammer

Zeus

BATTLETECH NOVELS
"Die MechWarrior! Die"

Grayson Death Carlye had been training to be a MechWarrior since he was 10, but his graduation came sooner than he expected. With his friends and family dead, his regiment vanished, young Grayson finds himself stranded on a world turned hostile. And now he will have to learn the heardest lesson of all: it takes more than armored weaponry to make a MechWarrior.

To claim his title, he will have to build a BattleMech regiment from the ground up. All he has to do is capture one of those giant killing machines by himself.

If it doesn't kill him first.

DECISION AT THUNDER RIFT $3.95
Stock #: 8601   ISBN#: 0-931787-69-6

BATTLETECH
A GAME OF ARMORED COMBAT

fasa

The battlefields of the Succession Wars are dominated by the most awesome war-machines in man's history, the **BattleMechs**. These huge man-shaped vehicles are faster, more mobile, better armored, and more destructive than a battalion of 20th-Century tanks. Now, you can control the **BattleMechs** in this exciting game of warfare in the 30th-century Successor States.

This game includes 48 full-color 1" x 2" counters showing 14 different types of 'Mechs, 2 22"x17" full-color terrain mapsheets, 4 sheets of full-color playing markers, 1 48-page rulebook and 2 dice.

BATTLETECH $20.00
Stock#: 1604 ISBN#: 0-931787-64-5